HOSTAGE to FORTUNE

Praise for *Hostage to Fortune*

"...ingenious and thrilling... an admirable piece of writing."
Robert G. Morris, Retired Senior Foreign
Service Officer, author of *Diplomatic Circles*

"...convincingly authentic..."
Barrett McGurn, journalist, author of *America's
Court: The Supreme Court and the People*
and *YANK: The Voice of the Greatest Generation*

"...characters are believable, some even heroic..."
Ronald Frazee, Colonel, AUS, retired

"The women are beautifully drawn..."
James R. Morrison, author of *Treehouse*

"A whacking good yarn about the Foreign Service."
William E. Knight, Senior FSO-retired, author of
The Bamboo Game

"How clever of you to weave all the characters together so well."
James Page-Roberts, author, illustrator, RAF pilot,
and member of the (British) Society of Authors

"...captures the exotica of a third world island awash in
political intrigue."
John H. Waller, author of *Beyond the Khyber Pass*,
Gordon of Khartoum, and *The Devil's Doctor*

"Your insight into the inner workings (of our embassies) is
thoughtful and revealing."
Gen. Richard H. Thompson, USA (retired)

HOSTAGE
to
FORTUNE

TED MASON

Bartleby Press
Silver Spring, Maryland

Like the Island of Sharqiya and its government, the characters and events in this novel are entirely fictional and no reference to any person, living or dead, is intended.

Cover photo by the author

ISBN-13: 978-0-910155-38-0
ISBN-10: 0-910155-38-0
Library of Congress Catalog Card Number: 99-72859

Published and distributed by:
Bartleby Press
8600 Foundry Street
Savage Mill Box 2043
Savage, Maryland 20763
800-953-9929
www.BartlebythePublisher.com

Printed in the United States of America

10 9 8 7 6 5 4 3

To my dear wife Geneviève, for her love and support over the years at hardship posts at home and abroad.

Glossary of Abbreviations

AEP	Ambassador Extraordinary & Plenipotentiary
AID	Agency for International Development
Am.cit	American citizen
AWOL	Absent Without Leave
C & R	Communications and Records
CMD	Chef de Mission Diplomatique
CRO	Communications and Records Officer
DCM	Deputy Chief of Mission (the Ambassador's ranking assistant, running routine operations; Chargé d'Affaires in his absence.
E & E	Escape and Evacuation
Eyes Only	Document to be seen by the addressee only
FSO	Foreign Service Officer
GDRS	Government of the Democratic Republic of Sharqiya (cablese for a government)
IGN	Institut Geographique National
LIMDIS	Limited Distribution
Memcon	Memorandum of Conversation
NCOIC	Non-Commissioned Officer In Charge
NIACT	Night Action (requiring action on receipt)
OCS	Officer Candidate School
PAO	Public Affairs Officer, responsible for press and cultural relations
PNG	Persona Non Grata (unwelcome, told to leave)
R & R	Rest & Relaxation (leave to USA from a hardship post; travel paid by Govt.)
RSO	Regional Security Officer
Sciences-Po	Ecole des Sciences Politiques

Prologue
Wednesday, May 2

Tonight they were early. It was just ten-forty when the two Marines reached the gate of the American Cultural Center for their nightly security check. This was fine with Corporal Ronald Corker. He had a date with his girl at twelve.

Vary your time, vary your route, they were told. It was hard to vary the route with the Center on a one-way street, but you could vary the time. Security's idea was to keep them guessing, and Drew was trying to catch the guard asleep.

"I find that guy under the stairs tonight, I'll bust his ass," he growled. Drew was tall and skinny, with straight black hair and narrow, sharp features.

"I thought we wasn't supposed to lay a hand on 'em," said Corker. Small and blond, with a brush cut and less than a year in the Corps, Corker was only nineteen. But he was cocky.

"I know that, stupid. What I'm sayin' is, I'll damn sure call Cross and get him fired."

Drew was five years older and a sergeant; so Corker had to do things Drew's way. It wasn't always easy.

"Last time we called Cross at night he chewed us out."

"That's why we write it up so he can find it in the morning. Blow your horn and we'll see if the guy's awake."

Corker sounded the horn, and Drew looked at his watch.

"If it takes him over ten seconds to open that gate, it means he's asleep. Four, five, six..."

The gate clicked. The front door onto the veranda opened.

1

An old man in a jellaba and tarboosh was silhouetted against the light.

"That's a security violation right there." Drew watched the man run up to swing the gate open for them. "He clicked it open before he even seen who it was. And where he was standing, anyone coulda picked him off and walked right in."

They drove into the yard and up to the house. It was a big, comfortable villa in the French colonial style, with thick walls and high ceilings. Bougainvillea climbed one of the white walls, and a broad veranda reached around to a garden in the rear. Corker parked the van.

"Sleeping again, Mohamed?" Drew asked.

"No, sir. No sleep. All night wake up."

"You better believe it. Next time Mohamed sleep, Mohamed no job. Got that?"

"Yes, sir!" The guard grinned, snapped to attention and saluted the French way. Black snags showed under the unkempt gray mustache. "Me good soldier, sir."

Drew snorted. "Shit, if this guy'd ever been in any army, he'd know not to salute a sergeant. You looking to join the Marine Corps, Mohamed?"

The old man grinned again, not understanding.

"I guess a little duty in the Corps wouldn't hurt any of 'em," Corker said. "C'mon, Drew. Let's get this over with."

Drew shook his head. "Take it easy, kid. You'll make your date."

"Man, I better. I need it the worst way."

Corker felt good tonight. In fifteen minutes they'd be through, and then back to the Marine House to change clothes and check out for the Magic Carpet and his date with Fatima.

They entered and stopped at the reception desk.

"Who's been here tonight, Mohamed?" Drew asked.

"Nobody, sir. No movie tonight. No talk. Library close six o'clock. English class finish eight o'clock. Everybody go home."

"Let's see your sign-in book."

Corker laughed. "Two months since the inspectors told

Pascal to use a sign-in book, and he ain't done it yet. 'Course, they don't need security," he sneered. "They got culture!"

"Well, there's no classified anyhow. Nothing to steal here but books. Let's go into the library."

They opened the French doors and turned on the lights. Dog-eared volumes in English, French and Arabic lined the shelves: American classics, standard periodicals, and new works on the United States. Nothing political, with the Sharkies playing footsies with their friends up in the Gulf. Just keep your mouth shut and stay out of trouble.

Corker wondered why we even stayed around if they didn't like us. Why not just walk out and let them rot? But Drew'd said it was so they could keep an eye on the Sharkies. Besides, it was U. S. property and we didn't want to see it left empty and mildewed like the other houses where the French had all left in a hurry—the ones that didn't get their throats cut, that is.

"You made your rounds tonight, Mohamed?" Drew asked.

"Oh, yes, sir. Always make rounds."

"Then how come that window's open?"

The guard scurried across the room and closed the window, returning with a sheepish grin.

"This has got to be the sloppiest Center I've ever seen," Drew muttered, pulling out a book at random. "They leave the windows open and then wonder why half the books are missing." He glanced at the volume—*Les Aventures de Tom Sawyer*.

"C'mon, Drew, let's get upstairs and finish the job," Corker whined, walking toward the staircase.

"What's the matter, Ron?" Drew grinned. "Afraid your Fatima's gonna run off with some Sharky?"

"She won't do that," Corker said. "Fatima's a good kid. She'll wait for me. She'd better."

They crossed the hall and climbed the marble staircase. On the second floor a broad landing opened into four or five offices. Drew went from door to door with his ring of keys while Corker looked inside each office, flipping through papers in the in-baskets. At the last door he said, "Now for Pascal's office and we're through."

Corker whistled through his teeth every time he went into that office. They'd made it over along with everything else at the Center so Pascal could meet Sharqiya's top cultural people there. Real fancy. Easy chairs and a couch around a coffee table, bookcases, a big mahogany desk and paintings on the walls— some by Sharky artists too! All that and a door opening onto a balcony. Man, if it didn't have that metal file cabinet in a corner with a bar and padlock, you wouldn't even know it was an office.

He noticed the desk piled high with papers. "Just look at that crap! The guy doesn't even clean off his desk at night!"

"Well, start in on it. I'll check the cabinet."

Drew went to the file cabinet, jiggled the bar and pulled the padlock. He wrote his initials and the time in the space reserved for them on the form taped to the top of the cabinet. He went to the French door and windows, opening each to test the closed shutters on the outside. "OK," he said when he'd finished. "Now let's go see Fatima."

There was no answer. Corker was reading a sheet of paper he had extracted from an envelope on the desk.

" Come on, Ron. I thought you was in a hurry to get laid."

Corker didn't look up. "Hey, how about this?" he murmured.

"How about what?"

"This. It's not only Secret, it's Limdis too."

"You're kidding."

"No shit. Look at it."

Drew found himself looking at a photocopy of a typed Memorandum of Conversation between the Ambassador and some Frenchman. It was marked "Secret" across the top of the page and "Limited Distribution" farther down. "Jesus!" he murmured. "Where the hell did you find this?"

"In the pile."

"Where in the pile, stupid?"

"I dunno. Right about here, I guess."

"Then we better go through every goddamn paper on that desk. Here, gimme half."

Corker pushed part of the pile across the desk. They went through the papers one by one.

"Now the desk drawers."

When they had scoured the room, Drew shook his head.

"Security violations this guy has had, but never worse than Limited Official Use. This time it's gonna be his ass."

"Let's write it up and get outa here. Gimme a pink slip."

"Easy, kid. You'll make your date. This thing is hot. We gotta do it right."

He sat at the desk and filled out a Report of Security Violation. When he'd finished, he slipped a copy under one corner of the desk blotter.

"Now gimme that Secret document. We're taking it back to the Embassy to secure it. Then we write it up for Cross. Everything by the book."

"You ain't gonna call him at home, are you?" asked Corker.

"Nothing says we gotta call him as long as we secure it. I don't want my ass reamed out again for that."

At the reception desk Drew stared into the old man's eyes.

"Mohamed, you sure nobody came in here tonight?"

"Nobody, sir."

"How about Mr. Pascal?"

"Mr. Pascal he go home six-thirty."

"And nobody else came in?"

" No, sir. School finish eight o'clock. Everybody go home."

Drew shrugged his shoulders. "If that's his story, he'd better stick to it."

They went outside and waited while Mohamed opened the gate. The van was old, and Corker had trouble starting the engine. When finally it caught, they lurched into the street.

"No accidents tonight," said Drew. "This document's gotta get into a safe, and we gotta write a report. After that you can think about seeing Fatima. And I wouldn't wanta be in Pascal's shoes for all you could pay me."

Day One
Thursday, May 3

1

Admin Officer Lou Cross sat down at his desk precisely at seven-thirty each morning to concentrate for twenty uninterrupted minutes on the night's cable traffic. He had never yet been caught short at a Country Team meeting. Others could suffer embarrassment when the Ambassador asked their opinion of some cable they hadn't read. Pascal, for instance, could miss half the meetings and be unprepared for the rest. But not Lou Cross. With fifteen years in the Foreign Service, he had more pride than that. Punctiliousness, a former rating officer had called it, and it had sounded like a compliment to him.

He started reading the cables. They were stacked neatly in his in-basket, in precise chronological order. As he finished reading each one a second stack rose just as neatly in the out-basket at the opposite corner of his desk. The contents varied little from day to day: instructions from the Department, administrative and personnel queries or answers, info copies of messages from nearby posts and the usual traffic on some jazz artist's itinerary through Africa or the Middle East.

Cross was a smallish precise man in his forties, with thinning hair. He had a low opinion of cultural activities in general and of their local advocate, Pierre Pascal, in particular. Nevertheless, he was glad his own wife Marilyn was teaching at the Center's English Language School.

It had been smart of him to get her that job. He'd married her after his divorce five years ago, determined to make a success of it this time. But unfortunately she'd married him dreaming of Paris or Rome, and all they'd had so far were hardship posts, so it was important for him to keep her occupied.

A few hardship posts along the way didn't bother Lou Cross. Some of the housing was better than in the so-called good posts in the West, the pay was higher and there were plenty of servants available. Sure, he missed the ball games, but he got some of them on tape. Even a revolutionary socialist island in the Indian Ocean like Sharqiya, with nothing in the stores and no commissary within hundreds of miles, had its good points. There was tennis and golf and even some safe beaches. At his grade he'd rather be the honcho at a small post than somebody's flunky in Paris or London. If he could convince Marilyn, he was even thinking of extending for an extra year.

As he took the last telegram from the In-basket, he noticed a pink sheet underneath and jumped to his feet.

Goddamned stupid Marines! A security violation, and they put it underneath the cable traffic instead of in the middle of my desk where I told them always to put it! And with only— he looked at his new quartz wristwatch—five and a half minutes before the Country Team meeting!

Cross always had the right time. He checked it each morning by the Voice of America newscast, and when he had nothing urgent to do he went around the Embassy checking the battery-operated clocks.

"Where are those Marines?" he shouted at his empty office.

He started for the Marine office, then, remembering the classified cables on his desk, ran back, scooped them up and took them too.

"Where's Drew and Corker?" he asked Sgt. Hernandez, noting with approval that the NCOIC's desk was spotlessly clean.

" Off duty, sir. They were on last night."

"Get them in here fast. And get me that Secret Limdis."

The sergeant passed the order by phone to the Marine House and went to the safe. He missed the combination and began again. By the time Cross had the document there remained exactly three minutes before the Country Team meeting. He glanced at the paper only long enough to see that it was indeed a memcon marked Secret, Limited Distribution, and drafted by the Ambassador. He bounded up the stairs to a steel door which clicked open for him as another Marine recognized him from behind a mylared window, then up a second flight of stairs to the acoustically secure room where the Country Team meetings were held. He unlocked the door and took the seat just inside, where he could control access. He read the document as the others filed in.

Country Team was an extravagant term for the handful of remaining section heads at the American Embassy at Al-Bida in the Democratic Republic of Sharqiya. The AID mission and the Peace Corps had been phased out after the coup against the pro-French government; the Commercial/Economic Section had been reduced to the Counselor and one junior officer who also handled what little consular work there was; the Press and Cultural section was down to one Public Affairs Officer; and the Defense Attaché's office was left with a single naval officer.

Nevertheless, Cross insisted, Sharqiya was a critical listening post on the oil tanker routes outside the Persian Gulf. It occupied the spot where the north-south and east-west shipping lanes in the Arabian Sea crossed. And because Sy Levin, the Deputy Chief of Mission, was on his annual month-long R and R leave in California, Cross's job took on that much more significance. In fact, it gave him an opportunity to act as DCM himself and keep his inexperienced ambassador out of trouble. He intended to ask Levin to mention this in his next efficiency report.

Rereading the document now, however, he failed to notice the absence of the Public Affairs Officer. In fact, he almost neglected to stand when, two minutes late but well within the five-minute leeway he gave himself, Ambassador Harold A. Potter, tall and spare in an open shirt and lacking only a pipe to look like the professor he was, walked into the room.

Cross respected Potter as an expert on French colonial history but distrusted him as a political appointee. He'd heard Potter was admired at the State Department for his astute and accurate assessments of the delicate new relationship between France and her former subjects. After all, he'd been tapped by the new administration for this ambassadorship, and it was not expected to be his last. With a wife like Catherine Brent, the daughter of one of the principal fashioners of the Marshall Plan in Europe, they already had extensive contacts, both in the government and in the diplomatic community. And with fluent French they were well equipped to try to counter the serious threat of Islamic fundamentalism.

But as for running an embassy on a day-to-day basis, Cross was frustrated by Potter's lack of concern. He wished the man would explode, just once, and crack the whip. It would make for a tidier embassy in general and keep unruly elements like Pascal in line.

"I don't have much this morning," Potter said to open the meeting. "A call on the Minister of Economy to nudge them toward a new commercial treaty, a few words with the head of the National Bank on his trip to Washington next week, and then back to the Residence for a luncheon my wife has been planning. What do you fellows have?"

Cross cleared his throat.

"Mr. Ambassador, about that rental agreement on the Residence..."

A blue light flashed in the ceiling, indicating someone at the door. Cross stopped in mid-sentence, his jaw hardening, and rose to admit a youthful, bearded man of forty in a wrinkled safari suit.

"Sorry. I had a phone call," mumbled the newcomer.

Public Affairs Officer Pierre Pascal called himself a Creole from Louisiana and was seen among the locals as a living example of the decline of racism in the United States. With fluent French and a smattering of Arabic, he felt perfectly at ease in Sharqiya. But for Cross, whose French was not that good yet who discounted the lack of it, a necktie and greater punctuality would have been an improvement. "Stick around," he murmured when he had finished his interrupted report. "I want to see you afterward."

Commander Jack Warnecke, the Defense Attaché, was commenting on military items he expected to see at the Academy graduation exercises later that day, and Phil Finley, the junior Economic Officer, was waiting to report on the latest export figures.

Finally, it was Pascal's turn.

"Not much here, except that I've got an exhibit lined up, I think. A Sharqiyan painter who is really good. I'll let you know more as it develops."

Is that all he's got? Cross asked himself. He's telling us nothing. It's worthless.

The meeting had taken just over twenty-two minutes, by his wristwatch. Potter rose to go.

Cross spoke softly to him.

"Mr. Ambassador, something important. Can I see you alone?"

"Sure, Lou. Come on downstairs."

Pascal stopped him.

"What's up? I've got somebody waiting at the Center."

"Have you been to your office yet?"

"I just came from there. Why?"

"Didn't you see the security violation on your desk?"

"Sure, but I didn't read it. What did I leave out this time, the phone book?"

"No, wise guy. This time it was a Secret Limdis."

"Bullshit. Let's see it."

Cross handed him the Marines' report.

"Let's see the document."

Cross held it up without offering it to him. "This document you don't even see in the reading file. Nobody sees it but Millie Novak, who types it, and Charlie Agar, who sends it. So what was it doing in your in-basket?"

"How should I know?"

"Then you'd better stick around. The Ambassador's going to want to talk to you about it."

"I told you I've got somebody waiting for me. If the Amby wants me, I'll come back. But right now I'm in a hurry."

He was gone before the intercom buzzed to summon Cross.

The sonofabitch doesn't even care, Cross said to himself. Meticulously he placed the document in a folder marked Secret and headed for the office of the Ambassador.

Millie Novak worshipped Harold Potter. True, she was lonely in a Muslim country where a Western woman couldn't walk alone except in a few downtown streets, where her schoolgirl French limited her contacts to a few English speakers and where as a secretary she was not invited to most diplomatic functions. But her feelings for Potter were real, and that made up for it. She needed to care for someone.

For companionship she had only the Marines, but at thirty she was older than most of them, or Pascal, who was forty and divorced. Or Finley, who was her age but immature. He at least played tennis. So tennis it was, whenever she found time.

On the job she doted on her boss, anticipated his every wish, protected him savagely against intrusion and lived in fear of incurring his displeasure. When a Marine had once found a Confidential document in her desk, she had been on the brink of despair because it was a memo dictated by the Ambassador. He had laughed it off, and the others had forgotten the incident. Millie hadn't forgotten.

When Lou Cross entered the Ambassador's outer office with a classified folder in his hand and a grim look on his face, a vague suspicion crossed Millie's mind. She reviewed each message she had handled in the last two days, and she remembered her check of the Ambassador's office—desk top, safe, waste basket, everything. There had been no slip-up, she was sure. What could Cross have found?

Ten minutes later, Cross emerged grimmer than ever, the classified folder still under his arm. Millie sat up straight, waiting for the blow to fall. Cross didn't even glance in her direction. This was worse than she imagined. The Ambassador would reprimand her himself.

Nothing happened. No sound came from inside the office. Her phone rang, and she went through the motions of making an appointment for him. Then it was time for his coffee. She always brought him a perfect cup; she found nothing demeaning in it. Now she had her excuse to confront him.

She knocked, but there was no answer. So she opened the door a crack. He was just staring into space with his long legs up on his desk, his chin on his fingertips and his permanently furrowed brow giving no hint as to his thoughts.

"Thanks, Millie," he said absently. He brought his legs down and swung in his chair to take the cup. She held her ground. He looked up. "What's the matter?"

She took a deep breath and stiffened her slim body to receive the reprimand. "I've got a security violation, haven't I?"

A smile came to his lips. "What makes you say that?"

"Mr. Cross came in with a classified folder. He never does that unless it's a matter of security."

The furrowed brow almost cleared. "Millie, you're wonderful. I'm going to make you my private investigator. Yes, there's a security violation. But no, it's got nothing to do with you. So stop worrying."

She wanted to kiss him. Still, something clearly was bothering him. A few minutes later she called the Residence for him. She sensed his hand over the mouthpiece but overheard him say the words "back room" and "typewriter". Then, louder, he said, "Don't touch it. Leave everything as it is. I'll be there at twelve."

His voice had frightened her. Even if it wasn't her fault, she knew one thing: she adored this man, and somehow he needed her. Whatever the problem, she would never fail him.

Harold Potter was sitting at his desk with eyes fixed on the wall map opposite. He focused on a tiny spot in the center of the Arabian Sea, midway between India and the Horn of Africa: the crescent-shaped island of Sharqiya—or la Charquie on French maps or Al-Jabel al Sharqiya ("The Mountain in the East") in Arabic transcription. Not more than a hundred miles from east to west and half that at its widest point, it consisted of a high dorsal ridge with a broad sloping plain in the south and an abrupt drop to a rocky coast in the north. The southern slopes were relatively green from the monsoons, but the north coast was as bare and inhospitable as most of the Arabian peninsula beyond. A third of its million-odd inhabitants were crowded into the old Arab walled city of Al-Bida, where the industrial and commercial activity was concentrated and where twenty-odd embassies and consulates paid court to a fledgling state liberated from French post-colonial influence in a bloody coup.

Potter knew the story well. He knew how France felt about her former colony and client state—like a possessive mother resigned to her daughter's departure from the nest, resigned to her defiant new life style and rejection of her careful nurturing at the fountain of civilization, resigned first to a liaison with the Russian bear in confidence it would never last. But not to the new suitor courting her Islamic masses now in the form of fundamentalism, bringing with it a rejection of all things Western, from unveiled women to representative art.

Interior Minister Qasim led this group, and it constituted a threat which France feared. For if the extremists came to power, it could mean another bloodbath in the streets of Al-Bida. And this time the throats which would be cut would be those not only of the remaining French colonials but of all Europeans, Americans and even those of Sharqiyan moderates like President Abderrahman and Defense Minister Rashidi, who were trying to bring their country into the modern world.

Potter had learned all this before reaching his post. He took infinite pains to support the Sharqiyan moderates without trying to displace the French. He assured them the United States had no designs on Sharqiya. There was no oil, no mineral wealth, nothing but tropical products readily available elsewhere. All we wanted was to keep it out of radical anti-Western hands, for what it did have was a strategic position near the Gulf and astride the oil tanker routes. And so the possibility of another fundamentalist state with a knife at the world's jugular vein was, quite simply, unthinkable.

This was American policy in Sharqiya, and this was why a single sheet of paper just shown to him by an administrative officer who had no notion of its significance beyond its classification had sent a chill down his spine.

What the hell is going on here? he asked himself. The Marines find a photocopy of a Secret Limdis memo in the PAO's in-basket? A memo that looks to be written on my portable that never leaves the Residence? And they find it in the PAO's in-basket!?

Not only that; it bears today's date, with Gaston Girardot as the source. I won't even see the old guy until lunchtime! So how could I report what he told me before I hear it from him?

He pulled his legs off the desk and swiveled around to examine the memo. It was addressed to Clayton Ridgeway, the Country Director at the Department, reporting a plot to land mercenaries on May 13 to overthrow the government and reestablish French control—and recommending we back the plot!

May 13! A sacred date to the old colonialists, he mused, when they rose up in 1958 and brought de Gaulle back to power. And even after he gave Algeria its independence, some of them were still dreaming of the old days.

The old colonialist pipe dream. Sure, there had been rogue attempts on other islands. But they'd embarrassed the French, they were a nuisance to the civilized world, and not one of them had succeeded. There had even been rumors about Sharqiya, and they'd all been false alarms. So why would he, Hal Potter, cable Washington about this one?

Maybe he wouldn't. And he damn sure wouldn't recommend we back the invaders, as it had him doing. That would be the fastest way to get his tail booted out of here.

But if someone was trying to trap him, they'd put him in one hell of a spot, because they'd demonstrated that his Embassy leaks like a sieve. For what he held in his hand was only a photocopy. The original must be in the hands of whoever wrote it.

Potter grimaced as the implications of the forgery began to occur to him.

Gaston Girardot! The old guy had survived every shift in policy since colonial days, and now he was stuck here with all his holdings because he couldn't liquidate them and take his money out. But he could if a bunch of mercenaries overthrew the government. He'd love that. He ought to know, however, that it couldn't happen once the government heard about it, because they'd come together long enough to stop it from happening.

So why would he tell me? Potter asked himself. Is he just a pawn, or does he really think—or know—there's to be an invasion?

He looked at the memo again and winced. He would have to report it to Washington—not so much the invasion rumor, which he'd heard often enough, but the fact that security had been compromised by the forgery, and on his typewriter!

He rose from his desk and began to pace his office, his hands shoved into his hip pockets as more aspects of the plot occurred to him. He'd have to tell the Sharqiyans too, if only to cover himself because they might have the original to use against him if he didn't. But tell them what? Not that an invasion was coming; he didn't know that. Just that a memo had been found, maybe.

He sat down again at his desk, put his feet up and locked

his fingers behind his head, his brow more deeply furrowed than ever.

So someone knows all he needs to know about my reporting habits, my style and the inner workings of the Embassy, and he was able to use my own typewriter to plant a memo exactly where it would be found by the Marines: in the PAO's in-basket.

He wished Sy Levin were here. But he was on leave in the States, and Potter was stuck with Lou Cross.

Maybe he never should never have let Cat talk him into accepting the high-sounding title of "Ambassador Extraordinary and Plenipotentiary," where even if he did make history it could just as well be as a loser. Ah, vanity! He'd been happier analyzing the past than maneuvering in the present.

But it was too late now. He had a hot potato in his hands. His future would depend on what he did with it.

2

Pete Pascal was ten minutes late for his appointment. But he wasn't worried; his visitor would wait. Like the others, this one wanted something only Pascal could give.

Brahim Zerkaoui was an art dealer and head of the local artists' society. He wanted Pascal to exhibit the works of an unknown Sharqiyan at the American Cultural Center. Larbi, he explained, was an illiterate goatherd without so much as a day's instruction in painting. Yet somewhere he found pieces of cardboard, plywood—whatever the back alleys and garbage dumps might offer—and using paints he mixed himself he painted what he saw while his goats grazed on the rocky heights. He painted literally, photographically, with a fine sense of composition and detail even though the colors remained flat. Until he was discovered by Zerkaoui, he'd been unaware that paintings could be sold for money. It simply pleased him to represent what he saw.

Pascal was interested, and said so.

Zerkaoui smiled. "Such talent is a gift from God. Here in the city we form our little clubs. We imitate the masters and display our imitations to one another. But when such a man as Larbi comes along, we can only stand aside. You know, of course, that Madame l'Ambassadrice has already purchased one from me. I advised her on where to hang it in her salon."

"That is very impressive," said Pascal, "and of course I'd like to have an exhibit at the Center. But I have two speakers and a film program next week. It would have to be afterward."

"Why not before?" Zerkaoui said. "I have dozens of his works at my gallery. You can see them this morning and have the vernissage next week. Then the people who come for your other programs will see the paintings while they're here."

He was right. "I'll need time to have posters printed and to send out invitations and put ads in the paper," Pascal said. "How about Tuesday for the vernissage?"

"Perfect. Now you must come to see the other paintings.

I warn you, some have no frames. But you won't mind that when you see them."

This was how Pascal liked to do things. Spur of the moment. A sudden inspiration. He was no bureaucrat, nor was he a political activist. He'd served his time in Nam, and for years afterward he'd shunned government service. It was only when he'd realized that in cultural work overseas he could further understanding between peoples that he'd changed his mind. Now he'd found work he loved, and he gave it all he had.

When Zerkaoui was gone, he asked for his invitation lists.

"The Ambassador's office called," his secretary told him. "He wants to see you now."

Pascal groaned. "Call him back, Leila. And tell me something. Did you put anything on my desk last night after I left?"

"You stayed late, sir. I left before you did. Don't you remember?"

She was a Sharqiyan educated in local French schools, with three children. He assumed reports of his activities went from her to her husband, a local policeman, and on to the Ministry of the Interior. But he didn't care. He ran an open shop.

"Then let me ask you another question. Did you look at everything you put on my desk yesterday?"

"Sir, I always do. Is something missing?"

"No. At least, I don't think so. Anyway, call the Embassy."

Yes, the Ambassador did want him, and right away. He sighed and took the pink violation slip with him. Outside the Ambassador's office he was disconcerted to find not only Millie but Cross and two Marines.

"That must have been some document," he wisecracked. "I'd like to have a copy to frame." He laughed at Cross's solemn expression. "What's the matter, Lou? You didn't put it on my desk, did you?"

"You'd better worry about your own problems," said Cross.

"Oh, I always do," he said airily.

Millie interrupted. "The Ambassador will see you now, Mr. Pascal. Alone."

He whistled. "Why didn't you tell me, Lou? If I'd known it was going to be that formal, I'd have worn a necktie."

Cross stiffened but made no answer. Pascal went in and closed the door behind him. Potter rose from behind his desk. He motioned Pascal to one of the big leather chairs.

"First of all, I want you to take a quick look at this and tell me if you've seen it before."

Pascal scanned the photocopy. "Maître Gaston Girardot (protect source) told me privately this evening that he expected an attempt to overthrow the government on May 13..."

He read no further. He couldn't care less about coups. You picked up rumors in every café, and half of the time he didn't even bother to listen, much less report them.

"Sir, I can swear I've never seen it before—unless it was in the reading file, which I admit I've neglected."

"And I can swear you didn't see it in the reading file. Secret, yes. Limited Distribution, never."

"Then I've never seen it."

"Any idea how it got into your in-basket?"

"I'm not sure it did. All I have is the Marines' word."

Potter called Cross and the two Marines in. "Now tell Mr. Pascal where you found this document."

Drew cleared his throat and recited the tale.

"Where was it exactly, Corker?" Pascal asked the other Marine. "In the in-basket or on top of the desk?"

" It was in the in-basket, sir," said Corker, snapping to attention. "Yes sir, that's where it was."

"Where in the in-basket? On top or on the bottom?"

"Well, not on top, or I woulda seen it right off. I was goin' through the stack, and I come across this unsealed envelope..."

"Was anything written on the envelope?"

"No, sir. That's why I opened it to see what was inside."

Pascal sat back. "Well, that proves I didn't know anything about it, doesn't it, Lou?"

Cross stiffened and cleared his throat. "Does it?" he replied carefully.

"It's very simple. I go through my in-basket from the top, just like you. Then I put the items somewhere else. If I find a Secret Limdis, I don't put it back in the envelope and then back into my in-basket, any more than you would."

Cross glanced at the Ambassador, saw his lips twitch and shot back, "The document was in your office, wasn't it?"

Pascal grinned. "Hey, you've really got it in for me."

Cross answered calmly. He'd succeeded in irritating Pascal. "Not at all. I'm just trying to place the responsibility."

"All right," Pascal began, like a teacher explaining an equation to an eighth grader. "Let's say the purpose of putting the document on my desk was not to frame me, since I'd have no access to Secret Limdis anyway. It was to embarrass you, Mr. Ambassador, and let you know it had been compromised. It was put in my office because it's a lot easier to get in there than into the Embassy. All kinds of people come into my office every day, and even if they don't know about the Marine inspection, they know I go through my basket and that I'd pass it on to you."

Potter stared at Pascal for a minute, then dismissed the two Marines. He was alone with Cross and Pascal.

"All right, Pete, so you say you haven't read this memo."

"No, sir. Absolutely not."

"Good. Then, you don't know what's in it. But you're going to cooperate with Lou in finding out how it got there. Openness is one thing, but using it to plant forged documents is something entirely different. Have you got that?"

"Yes, sir. Absolutely."

Pascal walked out feeling ruffled but vindicated. It should be Cross's job to find out how it got there, he told himself. He's the Security Officer, and I've got a painting exhibit to set up.

"What do you think, Lou?" Potter turned to Cross.

"I think he said a mouthful when he told you it would be easy to plant something at the Center. Security there is lousy."

"Lousy there, yes. But lousy at the Residence too if someone can forge a memo on my typewriter. And lousy even here in the Embassy."

Cross flushed. The Embassy was his personal domain as Admin Officer, and the accusation hurt. "How's that, sir?"

"The forger had to know my style, didn't he? So you

might try to find out who inside or outside the Embassy can gain access to any of the private memcons I write at home and bring to the office to rework as cables."

Cross smiled grimly. "I'll find the answer, sir. It'll be my first priority."

"I hope so, because otherwise I'm going to have to call in the Regional Security Officer."

Cross was alarmed. "Don't do that, Mr. Ambassador. Dan Boyle was here only two months ago. They know who he is, and they'd be suspicious. Besides, I know my way around this Embassy better than he does."

"You ought to," said Potter mildly. "OK, today is Thursday. Can I have your report tomorrow afternoon?"

"Yes, sir. Tomorrow afternoon, I promise you."

"Good. Because I'm going to have to tell the Foreign Ministry I've got this forged memo and offer our help."

Cross shifted nervously. "I don't quite see that, sir."

Potter took a deep breath. Sy Levin would understand. Nevertheless, he had to bring Cross in on the big picture.

"Lou, you read the memo. It could be a case of entrapment. If I say nothing, whoever set the trap could tell the world I recommended backing an invasion. That would give them an excuse to break diplomatic relations."

"I thought they wanted us here," Cross ventured.

"Some do, but not Qasim and his fundamentalists, and they control the police. I have to assume they know about it."

"But if the invasion succeeds, the fundamentalists will be out of the government, won't they?" he asked more confidently.

"Sure, but if the word is out, it probably won't succeed. An operation like that requires the element of surprise, and they'd have lost it. In fact, no one would want it to succeed but the mercenaries themselves and a few of the old colonials."

Cross's pride at being brought into the Ambassador's confidence was tempered now by nervousness at being taken in over his depth. "But you don't want too many people to know about it, do you?"

"Well, I'll certainly tell the French there are rumors. And

I'll ask if they've heard them. They may deny it to me, but at least they'll be warned. And a mercenary coup would hurt French interests throughout the Third World."

Cross was filled with doubt. "Sir, I wish you luck."

"Thanks, Lou," said Potter gently. "I may need it."

Cross thought he detected irony in the Ambassador's smile. Was Potter toying with him, or was he serious?

He returned to his office shaken not so much by the Ambassador's arcane political calculations as by the fact that he himself was now under the gun. He hated to confront Pascal. But what Pascal ran over there was a kindergarten and an art gallery, and when someone planted a Secret Limdis in his in-basket, the blame fell on Cross.

He buzzed his secretary to send in Drew and Corker.

"I'm sorry, Mr. Cross," the voice came back, "but Madame Cross is here to see you."

Oh God, what now? "All right, send her in."

But the door was already open, and Marilyn Cross was standing there, blond and full-bodied in the blue pant suit he didn't like her to wear. The pants were too tight and displayed her ample rear. Worse, there was already a tiny flush in her cheeks which only he could recognize.

He hurried to the door and closed it behind her.

"Honey, I thought you were teaching this morning."

"The schedule was changed. I've still got my afternoon class. Your cashier is out, and I need money for shopping."

He kissed her and noticed it wasn't on her breath, but that was because she was chewing gum.

"Then why don't you and the other girls go for a drive? Have a picnic or something?"

She sniffed at the suggestion.

"Because I've seen this island from end to end, top to bottom, inside and out so many times I could make a map of it for the National Geographic. It's the same day after month after year. The only thing that changes—when the government feels like it—is when something new comes into the stores. So maybe today is my lucky day."

Her hand was out. Cross began to plead.

"You know I don't like having you hang around down-town where all those Sharqiyans can look at you. Why don't you go to the Club and have a swim and read a book?"

"Because there's nobody there in the morning, darling, and I haven't been in the stores for a week. What's wrong with shopping? Come on, give me some money."

"Then go to the Cultural Center and read a book there. You'll see people you know."

"I'm there this afternoon. This morning I want to shop."

Her hand was still out, and she wasn't smiling any more. Cross counted out some bills. They smelled of fish from the market. The government hadn't issued new currency in a year. But at least he knew how much she'd be spending. Credit cards and personal checks were no good here.

"But please don't walk in the streets, honey. I'm an Ameri-can diplomat, and we do have to keep up appearances."

She threw back her head and laughed. "Jesus! What do I do, cheer? Over a year in a place where nobody speaks En-glish, where there isn't a movie or a decent TV program to watch or anything happening from one day to the next except maybe a new dress or two in the stores, and I'm supposed to get goose bumps because you're a diplomat! Oh, brother!"

He felt the blood rising in his cheeks.

"We've been all over this before, baby. I've got my career, and you've got a house full of servants, a tennis club, and pres-tige. We meet important people. We see the world. What more do you want?"

Her laughter rose above his voice.

"Not a thing, darling. Not a thing. I'm just as proud as I can be to have a diplomat for a husband. What more could any girl ask for? And he gives me shopping money too!"

She tossed him a kiss and was out the door.

3

Toward mid-morning each day Ambassador Harold Potter summoned Millie Novak to the acoustically secure conference room and dictated outgoing classified cables and letters. Millie went there alone with him and remained closeted behind a locked door, responsible for his honor, his integrity and his career in a room not even his wife could enter. The first time, she'd felt her heart beating as if this were an assignation. Here at least she would be the mistress of his secret thoughts. As she took it all down, each word of each telegram was like a whispered endearment, meant for her ears alone.

"Just one today, Millie," he said. "But it's a beaut."

She felt elated. Not only was she innocent of any security violation, but she was to be one of the few to know the secret behind the secret.

"This is for the Country Director personally. It's not Immediate, but it's Secret Limdis, for Country Director Ridgeway. Are you ready?"

"All ready," she breathed.

"OK, here goes: 'A major security breach at this Embassy came to light this morning when a photocopy of a forged Secret Limdis memcon ostensibly from me to you was discovered at the Cultural Center by the Marine Security detail and passed to me. How such a document was written (on my personal typewriter at the Residence) and planted at the Center is now under active investigation, but the implications are serious. Barring an unlikely hoax, I feel I may have been trapped by persons unknown.

"Paragraph. 'Subject of memcon was warning of invasion of this island by unidentified mercenary forces in effort to overthrow present GDRS or eliminate anti-Western elements, with my recommendation it have US backing. Source, usually reliable, was French resident Gaston Girardot (protect), at a luncheon not to take place until today, indicating memcon was planted, intentionally or accidentally, one day early.

"Paragraph. Accordingly, if Girardot approaches me with same information at luncheon today, I shall report to you immediately. Should he say nothing, I shall regard invasion plot as another hoax, but not the fact of my entrapment, since forger apparently has original of memo for future use. I therefore urge Department to track this lead down and have planned invasion, if any, called off. Request concurrence, guidance and action. Potter."

Millie's fingers chased the sounds across the pages of her pad. When she had finished, she looked up wide-eyed.

"Then you didn't write the memo they found?"

"No, Millie. But it was written by someone who knows my style and the symbols we use and who somehow had access to my typewriter. That means anything else I may have written at home may have been compromised in the same way."

"But they can't hold you responsible for that."

"Yes, they can. I shouldn't generate classified material at home. Period."

Millie was shaken. She took her notes and returned to her desk, transformed the symbols into a legible message, read it over for mistakes and carried it to him for his signature. He looked at it, changed a word or two and initialed it.

"Now pass it to Agar, but tell him not to send it before he hears from me, probably after lunch. Then we'll see what Clayton Ridgeway does with it. He'd better act fast."

She looked at him in anguish, wringing her hands. "Do you have to admit it was forged on your typewriter?"

"Unfortunately, that's the truth of it, and they'll need all the information I can give them to head this thing off."

She sighed, unconvinced, and left him.

Upstairs, at the metal door to the Communications Room, she buzzed. A bald and bespectacled young man appeared.

"Whatcha got, sister?"

"Something important," she snapped. "But not to be sent until the Ambassador calls you to confirm, probably after lunch."

The young man grabbed the telegram, fumbled it deliberately and caught it in mid-air while his feet danced and his eyes rolled in mock terror. "Ohmygawd," he wailed. "What'll I do? Should I burn it now or after I send it?"

"Don't be so silly, Charlie. It's important."

"Am I holding it up?" he asked, and closed the door in her face.

She descended the staircase uncertainly. Damn Charlie Agar. Always some wise remark. She supposed sitting up there in C & R all day with nothing but his radio equipment and his messages to stare at was an excuse, but he didn't have to be quite so childish.

She settled behind her desk. The excitement was over. The boss was leaving for home and his luncheon. The telegram would be on its way, and with Washington nine hours behind Al-Bida there wouldn't be an answer before mid-afternoon. But she had a sense of foreboding. She felt something was going to happen. Unable to calm herself, she picked up the phone and dialed the Economic/Commercial Section.

"Is Mr. Finley there?...Phil? How about tennis before lunch?...Good. Meet you downstairs at quarter to twelve."

That would help her work off some of the tension. She considered Finley a lightweight but fun to be with at times. He had the virtue of often being available when she needed an escort. She wouldn't mention the telegram to him. She never talked about her Ambassador's business outside his office. So she took a deep breath and promised herself she wouldn't even think about the "major security breach" at the Embassy until the end of the afternoon.

There were days when Pierre Pascal wished he'd never accepted the job of Public Affairs Officer in Sharqiya. As Cultural Affairs Officer at a large embassy in West Africa he'd dealt with artists and intellectuals in complete freedom. He did everything he was doing here without any of the administrative chores, and enjoyed his first tour out of the throes of matrimony in a country bad enough to cause a divorce but not so bad as to prevent him from enjoying his new bachelorhood.

And now he had let them talk him into a hardship post where most of the government was unfriendly and where the entire burden was on his shoulders. It was a step up, they'd told him. His career would really move forward now. Only one thing was overlooked: the fact that when things went wrong the fault would be his. This included Secret documents in his in-basket.

He suspected his secretary. Leila and a dozen others were part of his inheritance. Most had been there since the days when the Center had been one of the most sought-after places of employment in the city. But working for the imperialists had become suspect. He was sure some of them had been ordered to report on his activities, and if so why spoil their fun? Spying was what socialist governments did best anyway, perhaps the only thing they did well. So let them spy; he had nothing to hide. But why forge a document and plant it in his office when she knew he would suspect her first?

He called her in.

"Leila, who besides yourself puts papers in my in-basket?"

"No one, sir. I open everything except your personal mail and stamp it with the date and the time. There is no one else."

"After you've stamped them, how do you prevent someone from putting a letter in the stack while you're not looking?"

"It's not possible, sir. I watch everything."

" Tell me about yesterday. How many times did you bring in the mail?"

The secretary counted on her fingers. "Three times. I remember because the basket was empty each time. You read everything yesterday."

"Except the last batch, right?"

She bit her lip. "I can't say. You were still here when I left at six. I hope nothing is missing, sir."

"Nothing is missing, Leila. I was just curious."

Her eyes almost filled with tears. "I try hard, sir."

"I know you do. And I trust you, Leila."

Like hell, he thought as she ran out. Now the whole office would know about it.

Filled with doubt, he returned to his plans and made ready to go to the gallery to see the rest of Larbi's paintings. But before he could leave, his door opened. It was Lou Cross.

"Don't mind me bursting in. Just having a look around."

"I guess it would have to be something serious to bring you to a Cultural Center."

"Don't worry, I get my share of culture at home."

"Then I'd say, 'Be my guest,' except that you seem to be already. What can I do for you?"

"Just checking the access, that's all." He walked around the room trying the windows and doors. "The Marines say your office door was locked."

"It usually is, at night after I leave. Isn't yours?"

Cross made no answer, but opened the bathroom door. "I remember we remodeled this old john before you got here and put another one in the closet opening out the other way. Who uses the other john?"

"Anybody outside my office. Staff, teachers, students."

"Then I wonder why we left the old door between the two johns instead of putting in a partition. Do you keep it locked?"

"I never touch it. It must be locked on both sides."

Cross tried the door. "It's locked on this side. But even so, we should've walled it up. From now on I'll have the Marines check the lock on both sides every night."

"I told you I never touch it."

"Sure, sure. Well, I've got to get back. Take care now."

When he had left, Pascal went into the bathroom and tried the lock himself. What a nosy son of a bitch, he muttered.

Youssef had polished the ambassadorial limousine with its CMD plate and had unfurled the flag on the fender. In his blue uniform and peaked cap he stood with the rear right hand door open as Potter bounded past the Marine and out the main entrance of the Embassy. The opportunity any ambassador would welcome was here, yet already he was in potential trouble over a simple security violation. The telegram he had just dictated would focus the attention of the entire bureau on Sharqiya. If the landings took place, the NSC would get into the act, and it would land on the President's desk. He heaved a long sigh. The next ten days would make him or break him.

The limousine eased slowly into the street and turned left, though a right turn would have been shorter. Youssef knew his business. He varied the route often enough to earn top marks from the security people. No ambush was likely when Youssef was at the wheel.

They drove swiftly through the rundown center of the city, where neat French sidewalks had caved in with the rains and parking meters long out of use leaned at odd angles like a fence on a prairie. Department stores once bright with the latest Paris fashions were shuttered or displayed only the drab utilitarian offerings of a socialist state.

Potter's eyes were drawn to a figure in a blue pant suit, immediately identifiable as an American. He recognized Marilyn Cross and sighed. An accident waiting to happen. But how could he impress the point on Lou? Catherine wants to send her home. But what about Lou? He needed Lou, especially now. Ah, well...

In another instant the car was past and the figure was out of sight. Now through the market area, with its perpetual stink of fish in the sun, and onto the corniche leading to the villas of the few remaining rich and the principal ambassadors.

The American Embassy Residence was two kilometers out of town, on a point of land leading down to a rocky shore. At the sound of the horn, the gate swung open now and the limo pulled smoothly into a graveled parking area large enough for two dozen vehicles. Potter got out and went into the house.

Catherine Potter was dressed and putting out place cards on the table. A childhood in the Foreign Service had made the details of dinner parties and receptions second nature to her. As the daughter of Ambassador Alexander Brent she was utterly at ease in the diplomatic life in a way he never would be. Modeling herself after the old school wives she had known as a girl and smoothly yet ferociously rejecting the claims of a younger generation who resented taking orders from the boss's wife, she asked herself what greater sense of fulfill-ment a wife could have than to advance her husband's ca-reer? She had done so in Academia, seeing her children safely through school and college and into their own homes; and now at last she'd been given an opportunity to make a model ambassador out of the awkward student she had met in Paris in the fifties.

The limousine drew up to the door, and Potter greeted his wife. Looking at this handsome and formidable woman, with her gray hair and strong features, he readily admitted that it was she who had taught him the diplomatic skills he needed. Born in a factory town in Connecticut, he'd worked his way through Yale, earned his commission at Fort Benning and led an infantry platoon in Korea. From there he'd gone to Paris on the GI Bill to attend the prestigious *Sciences-Po* and prepare for a career as an historian. Taking the Foreign Service exam was never considered, even after meeting Catherine and attending Embassy functions where he had met her father and others he had never dreamed of encoun-tering. He was no cookie-pusher, he'd told her, and he couldn't stand the superficiality of cocktail parties and small talk. Her father had thought him uncouth, but twenty years later Catherine had had the satisfaction of hearing old Brent, on his deathbed, admit he'd been wrong. "You weren't wrong, Dad," she'd told him. "You saw him as he was. I saw him as I could make him."

Potter by that time had gained self-confidence and could handle the social chores of the head of a History Department, and now a chance to observe French colonial policy on the spot was something he couldn't resist. He'd listened to her advice as if the voice of Alex Brent were lecturing him from beyond the grave, but he felt he was long past needing it. It was only rarely now that she could talk him into or out of some action he had decided to take.

Today she recognized the look of concern on his furrowed brow.

"What's wrong, dear? What was all that about your typewriter?"

He led her into his den, where there was a desk, an ancient portable, a bookcase and a cot, all as spartan as a monk's cell. He had always written his drafts here after a conversation worth reporting, and carried them himself later to the Embassy, knowing full well this was against the rules but taking care to leave no trace at home.

"Who comes in here besides you?" he asked.

"Only Hanifa, to clean up."

"When did we send out the invitations for this noon?"

"About a week ago."

"Then whoever it was had plenty of time to brief Girardot on what to tell me, if he didn't plan it himself."

"But you can't write anything until after the luncheon is over."

"Sure, I can. They planted it too soon. But if they can get at my typewriter and forge a memo on it, they must know a lot more about us than I thought they did."

"But you don't know how much. This was just one violation. Don't leave yourself open to criticism."

"I signed off on a cable just before I left the office."

"You didn't mention the forged memo, did you?"

"Of course I did. That's the whole point of the cable."

"I mean, you reported what Girardot supposedly told you about the landings, but you didn't say they'd used your typewriter, or planted it at the Cultural Center, for heaven's sake."

"Certainly I did. What else is there?"

"Harold, that's an admission you've violated the rules on security and been compromised. You can't tell them that!"

He raised his arms as if to tear his hair. "I have to, for

God's sake. Don't you understand? I've got to make them appreciate the seriousness of this thing."

"But the invasion threat is serious enough. You shouldn't mention a security violation in the same cable, especially if it involves you. Levin would tell you that. And believe me, if landings do take place and the government is overthrown, the violation will be forgotten."

"Yes, and if the government isn't overthrown, I'll be in worse trouble for not mentioning it."

Her eyes flashed. "Now listen to me, will you? You can wait until after the invasion scare is over. By that time we may be able to get to the bottom of the security violation. Just mention the report of an invasion, that's all."

"Look, Cat, I've told you invasion rumors are a dime a dozen here. They'd laugh at me for sending a Limdis on one report."

"Then don't send anything until after the luncheon. Do another cable when you get back—if Girardot tells you what the forgery said he did. And limit it to that."

He knew she was right, dammit. "All right, what do you suggest?"

"Agar hasn't sent it already, has he?"

"No, I said I'd confirm after lunch."

"Then call him now and tell him you're doing another."

"Oh, for Christ's sake! How would I look rewriting a cable after I've signed off on it?"

"Do you care what Agar thinks? My Daddy used to rewrite his cables over and over again."

"Yes, dear, but your Daddy was a stylist. He wrote for posterity. I'm just trying to get information to the Department."

She flushed. "That's not fair. Daddy was doing the same thing you're doing."

"Where I come from," he said, "you admit your mistakes and go on from there."

"Not in a bureaucracy, dear. In a bureaucracy you never leave yourself open to criticism."

"You mean you cover your ass. Is that what Daddy told you?"

"Don't be vulgar, dear," she said. "Just do it."

He called Agar and stopped the cable. "Now are you satisfied?"

She kissed him. "Don't worry, dear. You've done the right thing. After all, I don't want my Ambassador in trouble over a minor violation."

Then, after a pause, she said, "And while we're talking shop, I've had more complaints about Marilyn Cross."

His guard went up. "What has she done this time?"

"One of the English teachers complained to me this morning about her drinking. This has got to stop, Harold. If her husband can't control her, she will have to go."

"What makes you think I can tell Lou how to control his wife? He has trouble enough keeping her as sober as she is."

"Then sending her home should solve the problem."

"Or make it worse. Look, Cat, with Sy gone, I need Lou now more than ever. He may not see the big picture, but he does play an essential role, and I can't risk destroying his morale."

This was called asserting your independence in small matters. It assuaged his bruised feelings, especially as he recognized Catherine's tactical error in mentioning it immediately after his defeat on the cable. But Catherine just shook her head.

"You have a New England conscience, dear. It takes more than a shining example to make an embassy run smoothly."

"Spoken like a true daughter of Alexander Brent. Maybe you should write my evaluation and sign your father's name."

"Oh, shut up. Now let's get ready for the luncheon."

4

Pascal bounded down the elegant marble staircase of the American Cultural Center and out into the garden. The place was visibly alive. Businessmen and professors were getting answers to their most arcane questions either on the spot or via a new computer hook-up. Grantees were visiting the States to contact experts in their fields. And events at the Center itself—films, lectures, exhibits and a library—were showing Sharqiyans with open minds what their country was missing. Now the exhibits would include the works of a local artist to demonstrate American interest in Sharqiyan talent. In West Africa, a sculptor discovered by Pascal had had an exhibit in a New York gallery thanks to his efforts. If all went well, the same would be true of the paintings of the goatherd Larbi.

The guard opened the wrought-iron gate, and Pascal swung easily into the palm-lined avenue at the end of the street. Along the Boulevard de la Révolution (formerly de la Libération) the once-white office buildings and glass-front shops were mostly closed and shuttered as private businesses followed the flight of the French colonials. Even the cafés were ill-frequented now, and the grimy movie houses offered, instead of the Parisian fare of the past, Middle Eastern films in Arabic and without subtitles.

Pascal parked in front of one of the cafés, tossed a coin to a shoeless gamin who had run up shouting, "Garder voiture?" and walked around the corner to a plate glass-fronted shop with a sign bearing the words *Les Amis de l'art.* Inside there was a hodgepodge of the cheap, the flashy and the mildly interesting. Renoir reproductions hung beside daubs of the Pont Neuf and the Sacré-Coeur. Miniature Eiffel Towers shared space in display cases with polished egg-shaped examples of Sharqiyan marble. Gilt and black samples of available frames leaned against a pair of forlorn wooden cherubim. Behind the counter was Brahim Zerkaoui.

"Mon ami, you're just in time. I've found Larbi and have

brought him here along with some paintings he was holding back. He didn't want to give them up, but I convinced him they would be worth lots of money."

Most of which would go to Zerkaoui, Pascal thought. He had known Zerkaoui for some time, but this would be their first joint venture. Zerkaoui was a well-dressed, sharp-featured son of a North African father and a French mother and had studied at the Ecole des Beaux-Arts. He had come to Sharqiya to work as a middle man between local artists and the French community. Now that most of the latter were gone, he had turned to the export trade and had persuaded the revolutionary authorities that an influx of francs from French buyers justified continuance of such bourgeois pursuits as dealing in art. He was one of a handful of Sharqiya's foreign community who could still visit France whenever they pleased. Pascal considered him a valuable contact.

Zerkaoui lifted the hinged counter and opened the half-door under it.

"Come into the back room and see for yourself."

Pascal followed him past the dusty stacks of easels to a large storeroom with a door opening onto a back alley.

"This is where I bring only my best customers," he said. "Back here I can show them anything they want to see. Rugs?" He waved his hand toward a hundred carpets stacked like pancakes against the wall. "Precious stones?" He winked and touched his forehead. "You name it. I have it."

What he had now, leaning against every upright object in the room, was a collection several times as large as the few paintings Pascal had seen earlier. And in front of them, carefully placing one of them, was Larbi the faithful goatherd.

"Here he is," Zerkaoui beamed proudly, "Sharqiya's finest painter: Larbi." He continued in Arabic, apparently telling the artist that Pascal was the man who would make him rich and famous.

Larbi was a small man with kinky black hair and shy but penetrating black eyes. He spoke almost no French. Presented by his benefactor to this distinguished visitor from the other side of the earth, he bowed and touched his chest and his forehead in the Arab manner. He smiled shyly as his works were praised. Prices were not Larbi's business, Zerkaoui confided. He would leave that to Si Brahim, who was an honest man and would see that he had enough to feed his family and continue painting. That was all he really cared about, and now both of these worries were to be taken out of his hands.

They began to choose paintings for the exhibit. Pascal half recognized many of the sites: bays and inlets and points of rock crowned with ancient watch towers, some seen from far above almost as if in an aerial photo and others head on at eye level from across a bay. In most, a figure or two could be seen in the foreground, a farmer on a donkey with his wife behind and carrying a load of faggots, or a pair of fishermen repairing a sisal net in the shadow of the prow of a boat painted with an eye or other magic symbol. The human figures lacked spontaneity; they had not learned to move with ease. Even man-made objects were rendered amateurishly. But the land, in contrast, in all its barren splendor and its unending duel with the sea, was vibrantly alive, more so than any living figure except the goats. Larbi loved his goats and even when rendering them as tiny blobs on a distant hillside seemed to give each one life and individuality.

"You know what I'd like to know?" Pascal said suddenly. "The exact spot where each one of these was painted. I'll bet people would buy the sites they've visited, just like buying picture postcards. It's crass, but that's what sells paintings."

"Then why don't you photograph the sites and display the photo next to the painting?" suggested Zerkaoui, infected by Pascal's enthusiasm.

"Brilliant!" Pascal cried. "What an exhibit that would make! Every European who's ever picnicked or weekended on the north coast would buy a painting of his favorite spot!"

But then Zerkaoui sighed and shook his head. "I'm afraid you won't have time, not if the vernissage is Tuesday."

"Sure I will," Pascal said, carried away. "If Larbi is free, we can go tomorrow."

"Yes, but you couldn't take all the photos in a day."

Pascal's eyes shone. He thrived on overcoming obstacles. "We can spend the night somewhere on the north coast and come back Saturday. We'll set up the exhibit over the weekend, and I'll have prints ready by Monday. Why don't you come with us?"

"I'm afraid not," Zerkaoui demurred quickly. "Saturday is my busiest day here."

A flat female voice interrupted them.

"Anybody home?"

Pascal recognized the voice even before the blue pant suit emerged from the shadows.

"Oh," said Marilyn, seeing Pascal. "Am I interrupting something?"

"Of course not, Madame," Zerkaoui cried. "Do come in."

The art dealer, to Pascal's surprise, seemed highly nervous. He dashed about busily and with bursts of attentiveness seemed to be trying to transform the storeroom into a palace worthy to receive a wealthy American customer.

Drinking again, Pascal noticed. Before noon, with a whole afternoon of gin-and-tonics before she starts teaching at six-thirty. A great advertisement for the school.

"Pierre! What are you doing, looking at pictures?"

Pascal felt a fleeting pity for Lou Cross.

"We're having an exhibit at the Center next week, Marilyn."

"Can I show some of mine too?"

"Well, some other time, maybe. This one is for our friend Larbi, the greatest primitive painter in Sharqiya."

Pascal noted that Larbi, not understanding, still bowed low before the foreign princess, while Marilyn smiled back the smile she saved for ambassadors. She inspected the paintings, occasionally holding one up to the light.

"He really is good, isn't he? I'm furious with envy. When is the vernissage?"

"This coming Tuesday, the eighth."

"I'll be there. But promise me the next one will have some of my paintings in it."

"Oh, absolutely," Pascal purred.

She turned to Zerkaoui. "Mine *are* good enough, aren't they?"

"Of course, Madame. They are excellent."

Again Pascal noticed Zerkaoui's embarrassment.

"Well, I guess I'd better be going," she said hastily. "Sorry to be in such a hurry, but you know how it is."

Marilyn's smile generalized itself to take in all three of them. She withdrew with a little wave into the dark hole from which she had emerged, like a film in reverse.

"She drops in rather often," Zerkaoui explained unnecessarily. "She's a good customer but not a very good painter."

Pascal returned to the matter at hand. "Ask Larbi if he wants to spend the next day or two spotting these sites with me."

Listening as Zerkaoui asked the question in Arabic, he tried to repeat the words. "I'm sure we'll be able to communicate with bits of both languages," he said confidently.

"He says he would be proud and will look after your safety," Zerkaoui translated.

"Tell him thank you, but he may be safer with me than in the city."

They all laughed at that. Pascal waited until he was fairly sure Marilyn Cross was far away, and then he left.

Marilyn left the shop and walked into the blazing sun. Now what? It was too early to go to the club and too hot to shop in the main streets. If she went into a *souq*, where the alleys were shaded by bamboo awnings, some gamin might steal her purse for the third time. The first time they'd simply snatched it from her hand, but luckily Lou had an orderly mind and had kept photocopies of her ID and other cards on file. The second time she'd been carrying a thick leather bag with a heavy shoulder strap over her head, and they'd cut the strap with a razor and pushed her into the gutter. Lou was furious. They'd had to put off their first R&R, and now she wore a pant suit with pockets and a purse small enough to fit inside. Lou hadn't even reported the second theft to the Ambassador, since she already had enough problems with Her Highness Mrs. Potter. But at home Lou had raised hell.

"What are you trying to do, ruin my career?"

"Some career, a tour of the world's slums. Can't you get a good post just once?"

"This is a good post. The job is one grade above mine."

"Yeah, and a woman can't even walk in the street."

"So stay home. You've got servants and a garden, and the house is twice as big as anything we ever had before."

"And so are the cockroaches, and all my best clothes are mildewed. Did you ever think of that?"

"Then get busy doing something useful."

"Like Her Ladyship's weekly teas? No, thanks."

"It wouldn't hurt my career one bit if you'd volunteer just once."

"What for? You said yourself Levin can't even mention me when he rates you, no matter what I do."

"There are other ways, Marilyn. There are plenty of ways to build a guy up or tear him down without mentioning his wife. You're making me vulnerable, I tell you."

"You mean I'm ruining your career all by myself, is that it?"

"I didn't say that. I just said..."

And so on and on and on. He always took it out on her when he had a problem, and yet he seemed to get promoted with the others.

Of course, she had her piano. And she'd been good at it, once. She'd even given recitals back home. But what was the point in a dump like this? Besides, her fingers didn't seem to respond any more. There was a kind of numbness in them, as if she were hitting the keys with gloves on. So instead she got up late and went out and walked around and taught a few English courses at the Center. And counted the days until R&R.

She crossed the street to the shady side, killing time, and saw the limo with the flag on the fender and the CMD plates glide by. There he goes now, the Ivy League's gift to the Third World, no doubt on his way to feed his face at some reception. Thank God she and Lou didn't get invited to many of those.

She reached her car and withdrew the key from the pocket of her pants, looking around before she did so. At least she'd learned that lesson. They wouldn't rob her so easily next time.

She drove slowly to the club, parked in a shady spot and sauntered past the pool to the terrace, where tables with white tablecloths were already set. It was the sort of facility the French had built for themselves from Saigon to Tananarive to Rabat. No natives, of course, and even French membership had been from the top down. Independence had opened the doors a crack, but now with the departure of most of the French, the club found itself in financial straits. So dues were up, and the members were mostly from the diplomatic community. Lou never came here, but he paid his dues without a whimper, no doubt hoping she would do less drinking here than alone at home.

She chose a table facing the tennis courts and ordered her usual Beefeater-and-tonic. People were beginning to drift in for lunch. Among them was Maître Girardot, a lawyer and a nice man. He was a widower and a real old world gentleman. He always kissed her hand. He approached now, his face lighting up as if he had been looking forward to seeing her.

"Chère Madame, what a nice surprise!"

His round body rolled rather than bent to grasp her upraised hand as he performed the kissing ritual. "I haven't seen you in a very long time, I think."

"You're the one who's been hiding, Maître," she scolded him. "I'm here almost every day. Where have you been?"

"It's true. I have been neglecting this lovely place. And your company. Forgive me."

"Only if you'll sit down and tell me everything that's new."

He drew up a chair which protested loudly beneath his

massive form. "I have heard from a very reliable person that the works of a new painter are to be exhibited next week at the American Cultural Center. Did you know?"

"I just heard about it this morning. How did you find out?"

"I am an admirer of the arts. I go to all the galleries."

"There's only one good one that I know of—Mr. Zerkaoui's."

"Which I visited earlier this morning, and where I saw a collection which astonished me. Your Center is very alert to recognize the works of the goatherd Larbi. I must compliment Monsieur Pascal. And since the prices will surely go up after the vernissage, you really should take advantage of the situation and buy now. Go this afternoon."

She felt an involuntary resistance to the idea. She had just gone there and been badly received. So if Brahim Zerkaoui was embarrassed to have her there, he could just wait for her next visit.

"This afternoon I'm busy. I'm teaching at the Center."

"You teach every afternoon?"

"I teach on Mondays, Thursdays and Fridays at six-thirty. Last night I was there too, but that's because I had an extra class."

"But evening classes shouldn't prevent you from going if you really love painting."

"I do love painting," she said a bit stiffly. "You see, I paint too. I buy all my materials there."

His eyes lighted up in surprise." I should have known. I should have seen from the first that you have an artistic temperament."

She felt her cheeks flush. "I play the piano too," she confided. "I've given recitals. Not here, of course. No one would appreciate them. But in other parts of the world where we have lived."

"Then you must play here too. I insist. And you must show me some of your paintings. They are hanging in your home, no doubt?"

"A few. Most are just stacked in a closet."

"Why don't you let Zerkaoui sell them for you? Or have an exhibit at the Cultural Center yourself?"

She fidgeted. "They're sort of special. I'm not sure people would like them."

"How can you tell if you don't try? Seriously, you must let me see them and tell Zerkaoui and Pascal what I think of them. Who knows? We may have a second genius in Sharqiya."

Her face reddened at the sacred word, and she frowned. "Maître, you're making fun of me."

"Never! Did I say you were a genius? How can I tell until I have seen your work? What I do know is that you are an extraordinarily sensitive woman and that you need encouragement."

This was flattery too, but she liked it. "I don't know what I need. Whatever it is, it's probably too late." Self-denigration helped. It excused many things and laid the blame on time.

"Nonsense. If you will permit, and if your husband does not object, I should like to pay a call on you at home to see your paintings and hear you play. What day would be convenient?"

Now she panicked. Did she really have canvases stacked away? She was afraid, but the joy of being cared about overcame everything.

"Let me see now, " she said carefully. "Tomorrow I teach. How about Saturday afternoon at three?"

"Perfect. I'll be there. Now I must leave you. I have a luncheon engagement."

When he was gone, she sat basking in this new attention, going over each word, knowing in her heart that some of it was merely French gallantry, yet loving it even as she feared it.

Then she ordered another Beefeater-and-tonic.

Philip Finley, junior Foreign Service Officer, had been at Amembassy Al-Bida for four months as an Economic/Commercial Officer. It was his first overseas assignment after two years in the Department, and it was considered a good post for a junior officer. There were practically no commercial relations any more, but the economic reporting would be interesting as the GDRS drew farther and farther away from the West and toward the radical states. And there would be limited consular duties involving the few Americans in Sharqiya and the few Sharqiyans traveling to the United States, mainly to the UN and to the World Bank.

Finley was happy in his assignment. He worked directly under Sy Levin, the Ambassador's deputy and his Economic Counselor, and thus was able to observe an old Middle East hand in action. Besides, there was a two-bedroom house which Uncle Sam had purchased in palmier days with a more senior officer and his family in mind.

So he hosted dinners for young businessmen and members of the diplomatic corps of his rank. It was all part of his training. Besides, he was astute enough to see that only he could backstop the Levins and the Potters properly. The Crosses were not able to do it, first by virtue of his purely administrative functions and second because of his wife's uncertain health, as it was euphemistically labeled. Pascal was too much of a bohemian, and Warnecke, the Defense Attache, limited himself to military contacts. So Finley had no competition. He was free to cut a figure as an eligible young bachelor and diplomat.

For this reason a tennis date with Millie Novak had advantages even though she was only a secretary. It let him be seen in public and also put him in contact with the person who knew most about what the Ambassador was doing. So far Millie had been very discreet in her references to her boss, but sooner or later she would open up if he persisted.

"I met an amusing fellow at a dinner last night," he began as they drove toward the club. "A French lawyer named Girardot. He's been here forever."

Millie was noncommittal. "I remember his name, but I don't think I've ever seen him. What did he have to say?"

"One tale after another about the good old days. He may not remember all the way back to 1908, but he does remember seeing Maynardier, the general who conquered the place, on his final visit here in the thirties. The Sharqiyans were bug-eyed listening to him."

"I should think they would have resented him."

"They did. He's an unabashed colonialist. But it's part of their history, after all. Whether they like it or not, the French brought them into the modern world."

"And now the revolution is taking them out of it."

"Oh, the French will be back as soon as the Sharqiyans realize the radical states aren't capable of helping them develop."

"I wish I were as sure of that as you are."

Finley smiled placidly. "The Department has been looking at the situation rather closely. We're pretty much agreed the thing to do is simply to wait for the French to be asked back."

Finley had learned to associate himself with current policy thinking. He had that combination of self-assurance and deference to his superiors' opinions which reassured them concerning his reliability and would help guarantee him regular promotion.

They parked at the club and went to their locker rooms to change. Millie had reserved a court by phone and was out ahead of him, in white tennis shoes and ballet skirt, to claim it. He watched her with amusement, thinking to himself that there were not many Washington secretaries who could play tennis on their lunch hour.

It was only after they had played a couple of sets that he noticed, seated alone at a table on the terrace above them, a blond woman with huge sunglasses and a blue pant suit. Millie had noticed her too. "Isn't that our Admin Officer's wife up there behind the glasses?" she asked as they exchanged courts.

"Now let's not be catty," he scolded mockingly. "You know Marilyn never has more than one glass in front of her at a time."

"I didn't mean it that way, Phil. And you're the one who's being catty. Shame on you."

They separated, and Finley served. The most important thing to avoid, he thought, is a wife who can't adjust, who won't do her share. He felt sorry for Cross. He admired his efforts to make up for his wife's deficiencies and wondered how Catherine Potter managed to put up with her. She must be a pretty sight by the end of the day. And if there's one thing Muslims abhor, it's a drunken woman. He made a mental note to drop in at the Center some evening after work and have a look at Pascal's highly-touted English language teaching program.

A moment later, looking up at the terrace again, he saw that Marilyn Cross had been joined by a large, round figure whom he had no difficulty at all in recognizing. He winked at Millie as they changed courts again.

"Who is that with her?" Millie asked.

"You mean you don't know the famous Maître Girardot?"

She stopped in her tracks. "*That* is Maître Girardot?"

"In the flesh, if I may use the expression. What did you expect?"

"I don't know," she laughed. "Somehow not that ... I had no idea. It's just that..."

She ran to her position. But her game was off, and he took the next set as if from a beginner.

"Had enough?"

"I guess so. It's back to the showers for me."

And he could not prevail on her to have a snack on the terrace afterward. Instead, she insisted on going to a café downtown which hadn't served good food since the French had left. It made him wonder what it was about the sight of Gaston Girardot that had thrown Millie off her game.

5

It was a small luncheon, with eight guests. Harold would have preferred six, but you can't do that when you're having the wives too. Everyone knows eight at a table is impossible. With the guests of honor on their right and the next couple in importance on their left, you'd be left with two men together on one side and two women on the other. It just wouldn't work.

They had agreed to add two of the island's oldest residents, the Frenchman Gaston Girardot and the American Ida Gant Richard, both of them certain to be past the age of involvement in GDRS controversies, they thought. Girardot had accepted immediately, but Ida had felt obliged to decline. She was almost 90, she'd had a hip replaced and she rarely left her mountainside aerie, The Watch Tower, except for her weekly visit to the orphanage. The orphanage had been her favorite charity for a half century, and tomorrow was her day for that visit. Two trips into town on successive days were too much for her. Instead she had invited the Potters to The Watch Tower for drinks at six, when they could view the renowned Sharqiyan sunset from the best observation point on the island.

Catherine was delighted. She admired Ida as the country's oldest living American and the widow of a Frenchman long prominent under the colonial regime. Malika Hariri, one of Sharqiya's few woman attorneys, was available to replace her. And so it was settled.

Potter's mind, however, was not on protocol. "I want you to keep the others busy while I try to maneuver Girardot off to one side."

"But I can't do that, Harold. I can handle the women, but you can't just leave the Secretary General of the Ministry of Tourism. You have to say something to him, and to Mukherjee too. After all, you wanted to hear their points of view."

"Originally, yes. But Girardot is the important one now.

I can discuss tourism and business with the others when we're seated at the table. But I want to be alone with Girardot."

"Then this is your chance," said Catherine. "Here he comes now."

They watched the old Citroën lumber up the driveway, its owner's twin in heavy metal, and saw Girardot lumber toward the door.

"I'll try to get to him right now," said Potter, forgetting protocol and going to greet him before the servant could reach the door.

"Le voilà!" he cried, giving Girardot a hearty handshake and a slap on the back. "The world's leading expert on Sharqiya, the only man who knows the place inside and out. Comment ça va, mon vieux?"

"Expert only because I am a prisoner here," said the fat man, his round body shaking like jelly. "Naturally, I'd rather be on the Côte d'Azur, but destiny seems to will otherwise."

"Come now," chided Potter. "Sharqiya has its own Côte d'Azur. Let me show you the painting Catherine bought the other day. She hung it in a prominent spot so that our hosts can see what a beautiful country they have."

But as he was leading the Frenchman across the room to the painting, he heard another vehicle outside, and the Mukherjees, Sharqiya's leading Indian merchants, appeared at the door.

"Excuse me, old fellow. Have a close look at it, and I'll be right back," said Potter, muttering "Damn!" under his breath as he rushed away to perform his duties.

The Mukherjees were Indians by birth, long time residents of the island and leaders of the small Hindu community. Potter had wanted to hear Mukherjee's views on local sisal production, but that was secondary now. He was about to return to Girardot's side when the other guests arrived, and his opportunity was gone. Now it's chitchat, he said to himself, at least until lunch is over. He did, however, manage to alert Girardot by saying, "I do want to show you that painting. Do you recognize the scene?"

"Perhaps, perhaps," murmured Girardot without turning away from the stark blue-and-white coastline depicted.

But Potter was already greeting the Mukherjees as an official sedan drew up bearing the Ibrahims, number two at the Ministry of Tourism and an ally of Interior Minister Qasim. Then came Madame Hariri, driving her own small Peugeot, to be greeted by Catherine, who was already in conversation with the two wives. And finally the Samaras from the Ministry of Commercial and Economic Affairs, neutral both in his appearance and in his record as a fence-sitter ready to jump in either direction as the occasion arose. An interesting mix, Potter had thought, if he could have a frank exchange of views with them on commerce and tourism.

But such an exchange was now far from his thoughts. As they were served drinks (non-alcoholic in deference to Ibrahim's strict Muslim rules), and at the luncheon table too, Potter used all his diplomatic skills, chattering away on one subject while focusing on another.

He kept an eye on Girardot. Did he note a certain lack of the Frenchman's usual ebullience? A touch of hesitancy on the old man's part seemed to indicate that. His mouth spoke the obligatory words to his other guests, but his mind wondered why Girardot remained silent. Maybe he had nothing to say simply because he knew nothing. But if so, why is he mentioned as the source?

At one point during dessert Catherine mentioned the painting, saying she had bought it from Brahim Zerkaoui.

"You're an art lover, Maître," she said, smiling brightly at Girardot. "You must know Mr. Zerkaoui."

"Yes, I know him... slightly," Girardot allowed. " A good businessman, I understand. But what real value the paintings he handles may have I can't tell. However, your painting does seem interesting, Madame, and with your permission I'll have a closer look at it later."

"By all means, Maître," Catherine said. "I'm anxious to have your opinion of it."

That's the way, Cat, thought Potter. You've flushed him out. He may have something to say, after all.

An opportunity arose after the meal. Potter regretted there was no fumoir in the old French tradition, where men could discuss business over cognac and cigars. But in the large salon there was ample room for two men to have a conversation apart from the others. So, professing delight in his wife's acquisition, he took the Frenchman aside to admire it.

"You haven't told me yet whether you recognize the spot," he said for openers.

"Yes," murmured the other. "Of course I recognize Ras el-Qasr and Madame Richard's beach house. I even spent a few days there once upon a time."

"Oh? Then you know her well?"

"On an island this size, all of us in what is left of the European community know each other well."

"Just between us," Potter confided, "we did invite her to this luncheon. But she begged off."

Potter noticed that the Frenchman's eyes revealed not so much polite regret as sad resignation.

"It's her age, no doubt. We're all growing older."

"But she is remarkable for a woman nearing ninety."

"No doubt. I haven't seen her in years," he shrugged. "As for the painting itself, it's excellent even if it does violate Islamic law by representing a part of God's creation."

"Do you really think that matters here?"

"Oh, not in a Western home, of course. And not for the majority of *les indigènes*. But in the eyes of *les fanatiques*," Girardot continued, using a colonialist terminology, "no Muslim should paint such a scene."

"That's a good point," Potter said, hoping to bring the conversation around to the subject on his mind.

But now they were interrupted by the smiling approach of Qasim's man. "I recognize that spot," said Ibrahim. "It is called Ras el-Qasr."

"You're absolutely right," said Potter. "We spent a weekend there a few months ago and fell in love with it. When Catherine saw the painting, she couldn't resist it."

He cursed the man under his breath for the interruption.

"No doubt you stayed at the home of your compatriot Madame Richard?" Ibrahim went on.

"How did you guess?"

"Ida Gant Richard," Girardot said, intervening. "Her husband, Noël Richard, built the place before the war. It was thanks to him that tourism began to develop on the north coast."

Potter watched the Sharqiyan stiffen. Tourism was a sore subject to him, and Girardot had drawn blood. Potter wondered if the old man was burning his bridges, or was all this for Potter's benefit.

"Richard has been dead a long time," Ibrahim said finally, as if the name were synonymous with colonialism.

"Yes, and his family, except for his American widow, are back in France," Girardot went on. "They sold everything and moved out, and Sharqiya lost their talents."

"While they took with them the wealth earned from the sweat of the Sharqiyan workers."

"But they left behind a tourist industry which unfortunately has been allowed to deteriorate."

Girardot wants the last word, Potter mused. This may not be a charade, after all.

But it was the Sharqiyan who would have it.

"At least we learned our lesson," he smiled. "The remaining French won't walk away so easily with our wealth. And now, Monsieur l'Ambassadeur, I'm afraid I must be getting back to my office."

Touché! Potter and Catherine went through the motions dictated by protocol on a guest's departure. So Ibrahim and Girardot are like oil and water—unless it's part of the act.

"Back to our painting, cher Maître," he resumed, taking his French guest back to the blue-and-white piece of representational art, "What else can you tell me about it? I'm really interested, you know."

The old lawyer looked around at the guests still present and seeing them in conversation drew closer to Potter. He began to speak.

"I wonder, mon ami," he murmured, "if you are aware of what is being planned for May 13?"

At last! Potter wanted to clap him on the shoulder and shake his hand. But knowing better than even to turn in surprise, he merely replied by asking, "Is something being planned?"

"I've heard so." The pudgy finger went to the canvas, where a rocky, barren coast rose from a deep blue sea. "Just about here, in fact, as well as at other points farther down the coast, in rubber boats by night, there being no moon, and with certain strategic points in mind--the radio transmitters, the headquarters of the Gendarmerie, the power station, the Presidential Palace. I'm told there will also be support locally. It could all be over by dawn."

Potter's finger went to a part of the canvas where the sea melted into the sky.

"But out here, even without the moon, the tropic nights are so clear in the starlight that you can see for miles."

"Perhaps. But nights in the tropics have lulling effects. Vigilance is often forgotten. After all, it is almost a century since French warships first appeared on this horizon, and they came by day."

Potter's finger withdrew from the painting. He cocked his eyebrow skeptically. "And this time, coming by night, they count on surprise?"

"Not quite. First, they will not all be French."

"What will they be?"

"Who knows exactly? A ragtag group of mercenaries, no doubt including Frenchmen and no doubt financed by private interests. There are many unwilling to see Sharqiya become an outpost of extremism."

"But why tell me?" asked Potter, pressing his informant.

"Why should I take it more seriously than any of the other invasion rumors we've had? And where did you hear it?"

"I cannot answer your questions, mon ami, except to assure you that this time I would take it very seriously."

"So you think I should report it to Washington?"

Girardot shrugged and smiled. "You know better than I as to that. I merely pass on the information."

"Who told you to pass it on to me? Come on, Gaston, you can tell me."

"Then let us just say I overheard it and thought of you."

"In any case, I still want Maître Girardot's informed opinion of the painting's value. So I hope you will linger on and give it to me later, Maître."

"Ah, I wish I could. Unfortunately, however, I too must get back to my office. An important client is waiting for me."

The house was empty again. "So now we have our informant's message exactly as it was reported in their memcon," said Potter. "And I imagine our opponents think I'm writing my version now to send tonight."

"Do you think Girardot suspected we had the memcon already?"

"If he did, he put on a good act. He seemed to be leading up to it until Ibrahim broke in. Then after Ibrahim left, he let it all come out. But did they know he would?"

"Perhaps they told him about the invasion but nothing else," she said, "knowing he'd be here this noon and would tell you."

"Then you don't think he's part of the plot?"

"Not as your typical French colonial, although they might have held out the possibility of a reward for his cooperation."

"That's too Byzantine for me," said Potter. "They had to be absolutely sure he'd tell me in order to implicate me with their memcon--and then plant it to let me know I was hooked. By the way, what about that painting? How did you come to buy it?"

"I'd been to Zerkaoui's, for frames and supplies. Last

Saturday, I saw the painting and liked it. He almost begged me to buy it, and he insisted on delivering it personally. I thought that strange at the time, but I agreed."

Potter's ears pricked up. "You brought him here?"

"I told him when to come. He appeared on time, walked around the salon and the dining room, held it up against the wall and selected the spot where you see it."

"That shows a lot of curiosity on his part, if you ask me. Were you with him all the time, or was he alone?"

"He may have been alone at first. I don't think I kept him waiting over five or ten minutes."

"Giving him that much time to snoop around."

"You don't think... ?

"I don't think anything. But it's curious. Now I'd better get back to the Embassy and rewrite that cable."

"Without mentioning the forgery. Don't forget."

"Yes, yes," he replied. "I told you I'd take that part out. "

"By the way, there's the Japanese reception tomorrow noon," she reminded him. "You'll have a chance to warn Thierry," she added, referring to the French Ambassador.

"Yes, dear, I'm aware of that," he said testily. "And I have every intention of bringing the subject up with him."

6

"**B**etter shape up, Corporal."
Corporal? Corker knew he was in trouble.

"I seen you sleeping behind that window," Sergeant Hernandez barked. "What if some Sharkie comes in here after the Ambassador with a grenade and you buzz that door open for him? Ever think of that?"

"I wasn't sleepin', Sarge. I knew it was you comin' up the stairs."

"Then how come you kept your head down on that desk while I walked right up to your window?"

"Aw, Sarge, I thought you went through the door into Admin. Besides, I was lookin' for somethin'."

"You never even looked up to see who it was. You're here to protect this Embassy, Corporal, and you better shape up."

Corker squirmed, then relaxed when the sergeant finally left. *Shit, I know what I'm here for. And I wasn't asleep, neither. And even if I was, I was still awake enough not to let no Sharkie get at the Ambassador.*

From where he sat, Corker looked out through a mylared safety-glass window down the stairs to the front entrance of the Embassy. At the top of the stairs on his right was a heavy metal door which he could open with a buzzer on his desk. He was to open it only when he clearly recognized the visitor as one with access to the upper floors where the Ambassador had his office and the Communications Room was located. But hell, there wasn't never no trouble here. This town was dead. If it wasn't for Fatima, he'd go nuts.

The night before, when he and Drew had made their report and went off duty, there she was at the Magic Carpet waiting for him. Plenty of opportunities, but no screwing around for Fatima. She was Corker's woman, and she knew it.

He'd really lucked out with her. Not only was she a good lay, but she was educated too. The main thing about her was she was faithful. He'd only caught the clap from her that one time, and that was because that other prick of a Marine had shipped out and left her flat. After he'd promised to marry her too. So you couldn't blame her for sort of going nuts.

But as soon as she saw what a good man she had in Corker she straightened out fast. He'd had no trouble with her since. Took her to the flicks at the Marine House, bought her booze and perfume and even a dress through the mail order catalog. She really liked that even though she had to wear it under her jellaba when she was outside. She lived in the medina with her mother and her kid brother and sisters, and they didn't want people thinking she was a whore. That's why she put on her veil too when she went out.

Corker knew she had some funny ideas. But he wasn't worried. She'd adjust fine as soon as he got her back to the States and married. And wouldn't she get a kick out of the snow! Where he come from they had it up to their ass, and she'd never even seen a snowflake.

These nights were beginning to get to him. He'd got back to the Marine House at six a.m., and then at seven forty-five they'd shagged him out of bed to see old man Cross about that violation at the Center. And then it was the Ambassador, so that by the time he hit the sack again he had only a couple hours before he had to go back on duty. No wonder he was groggy. Now at eleven-thirty tonight he'd be off to see Fatima again like last night. He wondered what shape he'd be in. He kind of hoped she wouldn't want to screw just this once. But he didn't want her to think he was losing his potency either.

He looked at the tiny TV screens in front of him. One camera was trained on the front entrance of the Embassy from the outside so he could see anyone coming in the door. He could move it from where he sat and look up and down the street, and sometimes when he was bored he'd just sit there moving that camera like you'd wiggle your toes. It must look real weird to the Sharkies in the street, he thought, to see that camera trailing them all by itself. Then there was another one on the side of the building over the garage and a third one at the back entrance. He had all three of the screens right in front of him, and he could move them any way he wanted. There'd be no Sharkies coming in here behind old Corker's back.

It seemed he was wiggling the cameras two at a time just for fun, and then he blinked and next thing he knew there was Cross standing there looking at him through the glass.

"Is this the way the U. S. Marines guard our embassies?"

He sprang to attention automatically. Cross would say it like that, like Corker wasn't a good Marine or something.

"Yes, sir," he managed. "I mean I was guarding it."

"Corker, your camera isn't even pointed at the front entrance."

"I was looking at something suspicious down the street, sir," he said, putting real sincerity into his voice.

"The street was empty. The receptionist let me in, and you didn't even look up. I think you were asleep, Corker."

"No, I wasn't, sir. Honest."

But Cross didn't believe him. He just gave him that cold stare. "We can't have Marines sleeping on duty, Corker. Not the way things are right now."

He walked away, and Corker knew he'd put him on report if Sgt. Hernandez didn't. Old Cross didn't fool around. He was tough.

But it wasn't Corker's fault he'd found a security violation. He did what he was supposed to do, and then they went and woke him up, and now they blamed him for sleeping on duty. Next time he had half a mind not to report it. That'd show em. Screw 'em if that's the way they're gonna act. He blinked.

The door from upstairs opened, and Charlie Agar came out with a piece of paper in his hand.

"You seen the Ambassador? He ain't in his office."

Corker winced. They were putting him on the spot again.

"He came back from lunch, but then he went out again, I think."

"Well, tell him I got an answer back on his cable."

Cross appeared from the Admin Office. "I'll take it."

"Can't let you have it," Agar told him. "It's Eyes Only."

"If the Ambassador isn't here, I've got to see it. It may be important."

"Sorry, Mr. Cross. You know the regs."

Corker saw something on one of his screens.

"There he is, sir. Just coming in."

That showed them he was on the ball. Not only that, it kept Cross from seeing the message, and that helped make them even. He looked at his watch. Four-fifteen! Was he asleep all that time? He'd seen Millie and Finley pull in at two, but that was all he remembered.

The Ambassador appeared, and Agar handed him the message. He read it, folded it double and said, "Lou, come on upstairs with me." Corker buzzed the door open for them, and Cross climbed the stairs behind the Ambassador, just like a little dog, thought Corker.

He was alone again. Something was going on, and he hoped it would be important enough to take Cross's mind off him. Boy, what an ass-kisser! Didja see him hop up them stairs? He just hoped it didn't mean an alert. He had a date with Fatima right after eleven-thirty, and he didn't want to be late this time. Last night was bad enough, but if he was late tonight, she'd really be sore.

Cross followed the Ambassador into his office. Millie was busy at her desk. She'd been late again this afternoon, but Potter would never mention it to her. He left it to the Admin Officer to ride herd on his staff. Admin Officer! With Levin on R&R Cross really was the unofficial DCM now, responsible for holding the Embassy together while the Ambassador kept the high-level contacts going. He wondered if the Department realized that. Maybe he could get Potter to add something to that effect when he endorsed Levin's rating on him. He made a mental note as he closed the Ambassador's door behind him, leaving himself alone with Potter and the Secret Eyes Only from Washington.

Potter handed it to him. "Your eyes too, Lou. They can't expect me to handle this alone."

Cross liked hearing that. He frowned and read the text:

"SUGGEST YOU HOLD OFF ON ANY INITIATIVES WITH GDRS UNTIL WE'VE CHECKED YOUR REPORT. YOU MIGHT WISH TO INFORM FRENCH WE ARE QUERYING QUAI. THIS WILL PUT THEIR FEET TO FIRE IF THEY KNOW OF PLOT. ALSO, THIS MAY BE GOOD TIME TO TIGHTEN SECURITY. RSO BOYLE, WHO IS TRAVELING IN AREA, WILL THEREFORE ALTER SCHEDULE TO BE WITH YOU MONDAY MAY SEVEN. YOU SHOULD AVOID GIVING GDRS ANY HINT OF INCREASED ALERT."

Cross felt his cheeks flush. "I'm sorry you asked them to send Boyle in, sir."

"I didn't, in fact, and I didn't mention the forgery either. Nor do I want you to mention it. But I can't hide the fact of a security violation from him. It's on the record."

"Mr. Ambassador," said Cross, trying not to beg, "they'll know something is up if Boyle comes here, no matter what the Department says. They'll recognize him from last time."

But Potter's thoughts were elsewhere. "They'll know anyway when I tell them, which is what I've got to do in spite of the Department. I just wish Ridgeway could understand that."

Cross pressed on. "I don't need Dan Boyle, sir. If they'd only give me a little more time, I could find out how that violation happened. We've got ten days before the landings."

Potter looked up absently. "Well, do what you can. But don't create an atmosphere of crisis. No one is to change his habits or cancel any appointments just yet. On the surface, we go on as before. It's up to you and me."

Cross squared his shoulders. He knew what he had to work with: six Marines, eight vehicles and three drivers. The Marine House was next door to the Embassy, but the other Americans were scattered all over town. The phones worked erratically, but at least there was an emergency radio net. Once a week each person picked up his walkie-talkie and called in for a radio check. In fact, tomorrow was the day, and he was duty officer this weekend. He smiled grimly. He'd tighten this place up like a real DCM.

Pascal had gone to the printer about posters for the exhibit and to the office of the one newspaper editor who would give it good coverage despite the fundamentalist stance of the GDRS. By the time he got back to his office it was late afternoon. A pouch had come in that morning, and his in-basket was stacked high with circulars, pamphlets and official letters. The security violation had already eaten up two hours of his day, and so from now until closing time at six he would have plenty to do if he was driving up to the north coast tomorrow.

An hour later his in-basket was empty. Leila appeared with glossies of Larbi's paintings to help him spot the sites. He put them in his attache case and went to the bathroom to throw cold water on his face. He examined the incipient bags under his eyes. You're getting that dissipated look, old boy, he told himself. Gotta take it easy. At least tonight he could go home at six; he was one ahead.

There was a tapping on the door connecting with the other bathroom. Oh, no, he thought, not tonight.

"What is it?" he asked, knowing perfectly well.

"Let me in." It was a woman's voice.

"You were here yesterday," he whispered back.

The voice was more insistent. "Open the door."

There was an edge of hysteria now, and the tone was louder. He turned the key in the lock, and the door opened from the other side. Suddenly there she was, in her blue pant suit with a smile of relief on her faded doll's face as her fingers worked behind her back to lock the door behind her.

"Aren't you glad to see me?"

He forced a smile. "Baby, this place is full of people, my office door is wide open, and Leila is coming in any minute for a signature."

"She giggled. "I'll wait here."

He tried to explain. "Look, we had an agreement. It was

to be Monday, Thursday and Friday, after six o'clock and before your six-thirty class so I could say I was working late and
lock my office door."

"And today is Thursday."

"But you came yesterday instead."

"Not instead. I had an extra class. That doesn't mean we
have to miss our regular day, does it?"

"Honey, you can't just come in any time without warning. Someone will catch on."

"But this isn't any time, darling. This is our regular date,
and I'm keeping it."

"I'm leaving at six."

"Another girl?"

"No, I've got work to do at home, in my dark room."

"Then let's do it now."

"Before six o'clock? And with my office door open? Are
you crazy?"

She was between him and the door to his office. Her fingers were unbuttoning her jacket. "About you, yes."

He began to panic. "OK then. But don't talk so loud," he
whispered. "Someone will hear us. First let me sign a telegram."

But when he tried to move past her, she put her arms over
his shoulders and pressed against him. He had a sudden whiff
of her breath.

"Baby, you're in no shape to teach tonight. Why don't you
go home and get some sleep?"

"What's the matter? Are you tired of me?"

Careful, he thought. She'll make trouble. "Just let me sign
that telegram. I'll come right back, I promise."

"Give me a kiss."

Her kiss was like a dishrag soaked in gin. Gently he
pushed her away and slipped back into his office, thinking,
Oh Jesus, this is getting too complicated for me.

He found the telegram, signed it and took it to his secretary, noting with relief that there were no visitors.

"Send this off right away, Leila. I'm going to do some
more work before I go, and I'm locking my door."

She shook her head sadly. "Sir, you work too hard. You look tired."

If you only knew, he thought. Back in his office, he locked the door, closed the shutters, squared his shoulders and walked to the bathroom. The robin's egg blue pant suit, like a lifeless puppet, hung loosely from a hook on the wall, and Marilyn Cross stood facing him. She was laughing softly, and she was naked.

"OK, come on out," he said. "No one will bother us now."

But she only stood there giggling. "I like it here."

Again he sensed hysteria. "Will you promise to be quiet?"

"Cross my heart and hope to die."

The hell you will, he thought. As she embraced him, he turned on the faucet to drown out the sounds and wondered how he could bring this thing to an end.

Catherine Potter had spent the afternoon at the Overseas Women's Club sorting garments for Ida Gant's orphanage. Until the revolution it had been called the American Women's Club, there having been enough American residents. But now, with the Americans down to Ruth Levin, Gladys Warnecke and herself and of course Ida (you couldn't count Marilyn Cross, whose husband paid her dues but who had never attended a meeting after the first one), "overseas" was the only word which could describe its membership. But whatever the name, Catherine intended that the club should remain American in spirit.

She accomplished this in various ways. American holidays were observed. The American Cultural Center was raided for books, magazines and films. In exchange, she rounded up the membership for American cultural events and used the premises for occasional meetings. And she organized balls, raffles and rummage sales, all for charity.

It was second nature to Catherine. As Alexander Brent's daughter she had learned to make up guest lists, gather second-hand clothing and toys and books for resale, fill out invitation cards, place people at dinner and direct servants and chauffeurs. By the time she met Hal Potter her father was Ambassador in Rome and she was standing in frequently for her mother, who suffered from migraine. So she had accustomed herself to being ready in advance. She said she was merely doing her duty. Those who were unable or unwilling to do so should stay out of the Foreign Service.

In the years since then, such wifely duties had been codified--negatively, in Catherine's view. No longer could she suggest to a young wife that she really ought to belong to the Women's Club and have her take the hint and join immediately. No longer, in fact, could a wife even be mentioned in her husband's annual efficiency report, regardless of how much discredit she brought on the Service.

Catherine found this outrageous. In her father's day a

woman like Marilyn Cross would have been sent home long before her drinking had become an embarrassment. Why, simply refusing to take part in Women's Club activities would have blighted her husband's career.

Very well then, she said to herself as she arranged flowers and straightened cushions in her living room. She would just have to do Marilyn's share as well as her own. And she would know how to let the Department know about it, so that this interlude in a Third World backwater most Americans had never heard of might lead to an ambassadorship for Harold in a country that counted. Then her years of waiting would be over. Then old Alexander Brent, white-maned and full of dignity somewhere beyond the sunset, would smile down and pat his own little girl on the cheek and say again, as he had before: "Stout fella!"

They were leaving for cocktails at Ida's, where she would discuss with the old lady the decisions made at the club that afternoon. But even without guests it was simply a matter of pride that her home should always represent the United States at its best. Her performance as a hostess was intended as much as a course of instruction for visitors from the Revolutionary Council and their hopeless wives as training for the dinners she would be giving before long in some world capital where the guests would recognize her skill. And perhaps some evening a distinguished elderly gentleman would approach her and say: "You're Alex Brent's daughter, aren't you? I knew your father."

Now she was in Harold's den, noticing the desk with his notebooks piled high and his maps and the small portable typewriter on the table next to it. But honestly, she would have to get rid of that Hanifa. Look at the dust! Granted, it blew in from the mountainside even when the windows were closed. But Hanifa had strict instructions to dust every day.

Catherine ran her finger along the desk top, then went to the linen closet and ran a dustrag over the surface. Then she began on the typewriter table. Funny! Why should there be so much less dust here? It was as if the table had been dusted more recently than the desk. Was the girl really that forgetful? Or else...What was it Harold had asked? Whether the typewriter had been moved? If so, there might be traces on the dusty surface—unless someone had dusted it afterward to efface them.

Catherine stood looking at the table in puzzlement. Was it possible someone had taken the typewriter to forge a document and returned it later? Perhaps she'd been reading too many whodunits gathered for the Embassy rummage sale. And yet it was Harold's idea, not hers. And no one had ever accused Harold of being an alarmist. Should she mention it? Or would this just add to his worries?

She heard his car on the gravel of the driveway. He was late, and they would just have time to get ready for drinks at Ida's. Quickly, she made her decision. She would handle it herself and say nothing until she'd gotten to the bottom of this mystery for him.

Ida Gant Richard had something to tell Harold Potter. Which surprised her since she thought her active life on this little island was over. She would be 90 in September, and she was increasingly frail and unsteady on her feet, though her eyesight and her hearing remained good.

But she had seen all she wanted to see of the world. She'd watched French rule give way to independence, with a new flag, a UN seat and a list of ministerial titles twice as long as the French had ever needed. Just to spread the graft, she'd decided; she hadn't grown up near Kansas City for nothing. There were a million mouths to feed, and half of them belonged to cabinet ministers' families and so were entitled to graft, of course. But she didn't care. From now on she was just an observer. Let them run their own country, or try. She'd believe it when she saw it. "I'm from Missouri," she'd always say when a Sharqiyan official exposed some grandiose development plan. And then, seeing a puzzled expression, she would add, "And if you don't know what that means, you don't know a thing about America."

She sat rocking now on her front piazza as she had for a half century or more, watching the sun sink toward the sea to her right, counting the ships in the harbor below, scanning the horizon to see how many others were passing her by without making port. It wasn't east and west any more, with Sharqiya a coaling station on the route to the Orient. Now it was all tankers heading north into the Gulf high in the water and then back again past Sharqiya on the other side loaded down with their polluted grease. They'd better not spill any of it here. The sea was her front lawn, and she intended to keep it clean and pretty. It was a blue lawn instead of a green one, and instead of chipmunks she watched ships that were the same size from where she sat. But it was her lawn as long as she sat here.

Back home she'd grown up with people who'd never even seen the sea, and on her trips home they'd regarded her as if she'd arrived straight from the moon. School children who cared (and there weren't many) asked if Sharqiya had real sharks, and she'd answer, "Of course. Where do you think the name comes from?"

For most of the old-timers she was just that strange, headstrong girl who'd wanted to be different and had gone off in the first World War in the Red Cross and married a Frenchman and followed him to some French colony somewhere, abandoning comforts America valued for something out of the Arabian Nights. They didn't realize that she'd brought America with her. When Noël Richard had shown her the magnificent villa built onto a crumbling qasr on the mountainside overlooking the city, with its cool fountains and tropical plants and slippered servants, she'd simply refused to live in it until it had a piazza where she could look out over her blue lawn and watch the chipmunks.

And so it had been for over a half century, through wars and revolutions as the chipmunks gave way to silver hawks swooping down and bringing America within hours of her instead of weeks. Her husband's family wanted her in France, and her own family—grand-nieces and grand-nephews— begged her to return "home" to America, fearful for her safety as the world turned ugly. But they didn't understand either that it wasn't Missouri at all but "Sharky," la Charquie, Sharqiya as it was now called, which for her had become, simply, home.

She was watching the sunset now as the Potters drew up in the Embassy limousine, first the orange ball breaking against the far edge of her lawn like an egg yoke, staining the blue with its long outpouring of shimmering lava, then disappearing into it, pulling the light like a cloak after it and leaving a darkened surface behind until, magically, the chipmunks became fireflies down below and danced like stars in the harbor until the real stars made ready to appear above them. It was the same spectacle night after night, year after year, the one thing that didn't change. She had never tired of watching it, nor ever would.

But when she invited guests to watch it with her over drinks and they arrived late, she scolded them unmercifully. "You've missed it again," she called down to the Potters. "I've a good mind not to ask you back."

It was Catherine who answered. "We're sorry, Ida. Harold was held up."

She snorted at that. "That's what my husband used to say when all the time I knew he was with one of his mistresses."

"Ida, please," Potter protested. "You promised not to tell."

"Oh, I have no doubt you're behaving as a diplomat should. It must make life dull, though, when work keeps you from women and a Sharqiyan sunset too."

"Dull isn't the word, Ida," Catherine answered. "It's just hell."

Yes, Ida thought, she'd met women like that before. And this one is driving her husband into an early grave with her ambition. "Well, come have your drinks in the dark then."

She smiled to herself as they joined her. She enjoyed shocking Harold Potter. He was too serious about his work, too driven. Maybe it wasn't his wife. Maybe it was just the contrast with colonial days when the American colony had been headed by placid consuls general and their wives planning a well-earned retirement. Now it was all bustle, and she didn't like it at all.

"What's the problem today, young man?" she broke into Potter's somber thoughts. "Don't tell me we're about to be invaded."

She realized she had touched a nerve.

"Nothing like that, Ida," he said hurriedly. "You know this place isn't worth invading. No oil, no minerals, no wealth of any kind."

"Don't softsoap me," she said as the houseboy brought out a tray and drinks onto the darkening terrace and turned on the outside lights. "I know what it's worth to the French. I've got a pretty good idea what it's worth to us, and I've got strong suspicions of what it's worth to some of its neighbors in the Gulf."

She watched him counterattack, as he always did. "Then you tell me."

"All right, I will. I watch the tankers pass. I know where they're headed, and I know how far we are from the Gulf. So if that doesn't make this a pretty attractive spot for somebody to land an army, then I don't know what does."

"What makes you think anyone is going to land here?"

"I didn't say they would. You're fencing and trying to confuse the issue, just like a diplomat. I ask a simple question and end up answering yours."

"I'm not fencing, Ida. I'd just like to know what you may have heard. Besides, I know you're dying to tell me."

He had her this time. It was the reason she'd asked them to come alone, and he had guessed it. But still, it irritated her to be caught.

"Sometimes you exasperate me so I'm ready to break off diplomatic relations."

"Never do that," Catherine interjected. "Where would civilization be without diplomacy?"

"Bosh. This place was never so well off as when the French were running it. Now look at it—diplomats everywhere, talks, negotiations, trips to Washington and Paris and the UN. And what have we got? MiGs, parades and anti-American propaganda. Why, you can't even find bread or oil at the market any more. They grow sugar cane, and there's no sugar. We're surrounded by the ocean, and there's no salt. The only way to get enough to eat these days is to be a government official—or a diplomat."

"So there!" said Potter, laughing at her tirade.

"Yes, so there. Now ask me again, politely. And maybe you'll learn something you didn't know."

Potter threw up his hands. "All right, I am interested. Now be a good citizen and tell me what you know."

"Please."

"Please."

"That's better. Now," her eyes narrowed. "What would you say if I told you the stars and the planets had moved out of their orbits and had begun chasing all over the sky?"

"I'd say the world was coming to an end."

"Don't be funny. Look down at the stars and the planets I see every night. Not the ones in the sky; the ones right down there on my front lawn."

As Potter looked, the lights twinkled as if from the touch of Ida's wand.

"I see them, and I envy you your view."

"And don't think I don't know what each light is. Down there to the left, that's the corniche, looking like a pearl necklace. And this side of it is the port area. You can tell how many ships are in port by counting the lights. And over here on the right is the Caserne Maynardier, which is usually dark at night. And way over on the right is the airport. Before a plane even shows up in the sky I can tell from the lights on the runway that they're expecting one."

"And lately you've noticed changes?"

Potter had stopped his bantering. He was interested, as she had known he would be.

"I have. In the port, for instance. Some of the lights are from small gunboats, or whatever you call them. Last night two of them moved out of the harbor and up the coast, one to the right and one to the left. A half hour later two more did the same thing. And today all four are back in port. I'll bet the same will happen tonight."

"Coastal patrol, probably. Interesting."

"I said the caserne is usually dark at night. Well, it's all lighted up now. And last night about a dozen trucks moved out and up onto the mountain. They're not back yet."

"To defend the north coast, maybe. Anything else ?"

"The runway lights at the airport. They were on just before you came, and I know there's no scheduled flight due in. It turned out it was for two of their fighters. They landed, and then the lights went off again."

"Recon flights, I suppose. Well, Ida, I had no idea you were a military observer."

"I was in the first World War before you were born, and the second one after it. I've got medals to prove it."

"Touché. What should we do then, put you on the payroll?"

"Better not. Uncle Sam couldn't afford to pay me what I'm worth."

"Then how about donating your services out of pure patriotism?"

He was bantering again, but the proposition was a real one. Ida tried to hide her satisfaction.

"You don't really think it means anything, do you?"

"It's hard to say. But it's the kind of thing we report so others can decide. You know Jack Warnecke, don't you?"

She nodded, her small eyes aglow.

"Then why don't you invite him up for drinks some evening—tomorrow, for instance?"

"Why don't I? Because everyone knows who Warnecke is and what he does."

Potter reflected. "You're right, I suppose. Then how about Millie Novak? She could report what she sees."

"Suits me fine. I like Millie."

The conversation drifted off to other subjects. Catherine, trained to remain silent when substantive matters were under discussion, was ready with her report on the Women's Club. Potter and Ida joined in, but their thoughts were elsewhere.

Harold Potter and Catherine lay awake in silence on opposite sides of their king-size bed back at the Residence. Catherine tried to piece together what she had seen that day: the worry on Harold's face that morning, the disappearing typewriter, the forged report, the need to speak to the Frenchman Girardot and now Ida's report on military movements. She had held her tongue in the car because of the chauffeur, but coming into the house she had asked if Ida might really be on to something.

"You never know. We have to act as if she were."

Catherine sighed. "It must be sad to watch your world disappear, to be without children and see your friends depart or die and all your works disintegrate before your eyes. Why on earth doesn't she give up and go back home to be with her own people?"

His answer had drawn back a curtain on himself. "Perhaps she feels she made her choice long ago. What would she look like to them, assuming any of them are still alive? They'd say she was admitting she'd made a mistake."

Catherine was reminded that her own life and Harold's were fundamentally different. Hers had been charted from birth; his a series of steps into unknown territory which it would take a lifetime to justify. At his words, she had wanted to squeeze his hand, but something told her her dependence now would serve him better than her comforting warmth. The decisions would have to be his. Any help from her would have to be given secretly.

Potter knew she was awake but made no effort to speak. He felt satisfaction that he had been able to act without listening to her advice. It hadn't always been that way. It had taken time, even at the university, to overcome the good counsel of Ambassador Alexander Brent as transmitted through his daughter. The cable that morning was an example. He'd given in to her and eliminated anything which might have brought criticism on himself, but he had also removed some of the sense of urgency he wanted to convey. Now Boyle was coming in on Monday, and he'd have to keep their talk off the typewriter and on the physical security of the Center.

At least he'd turned her down on Marilyn Cross. He hoped it was a problem he could solve at post. Marilyn was no credit to the Service, but Sharqiya was a tough enough post without getting flak from the Ambassador's wife. He needed all the back-up he could get from Lou Cross.

He'd made Catherine an Ambassador's wife after all. That had paid off a debt of sorts. Naturally she wasn't satisfied with Sharqiya, but he'd have to see this job through before worrying about a prestige embassy. For a specialist on French colonialism this was an ideal post, just the thing to check his accumulated theories against reality.

So pull up your socks, son, he told himself, and get your ducks lined up. You know what you've got to work with, and if you don't know the strengths and weaknesses of your own people by now, you'd better find out fast. Because you'll be needing every one of them.

The pep talk reassured him. By the time he felt sleep coming on he thought he heard Catherine's regular breathing, and this reassured him too because, in a sense, it left him in possession of the field.

At that moment, however, Corporal Ron Corker was running at full speed down the empty starlit street toward the labyrinth of the medina. He was soaked in sweat, his jacket was gone and his pink sport shirt was torn down the back even as his broad cream-colored necktie remained neatly knotted under his collar, giving him a well-groomed look from the front except for the trickle of blood from his cut lip which was dripping onto his necktie and shirt. He was heading for the arched gate opening onto the main street of the medina where the tarbooshed merchants sold their brass trinkets and rugs by day. Now the stands were shuttered and dark in the starlight.

Corker knew what the stands looked like, and he knew there were alleys behind. But he knew nothing of where they might lead or exit, which was all right too because at least this way he could duck anyone who might be following, especially his fellow Marines. Beyond that, he didn't have much idea where he was going, and anyhow he never had thought very far ahead and yet he'd always managed to get out of any spot he was in.

He guessed he really was in a spot this time, though. Damn that Fatima, anyhow. If he'd told her once, he'd told her a thousand times to stay away from other guys, especially Sharkies. And yet there she was, after he'd pulled duty all afternoon and evening when he should've been in the sack getting the sleep he'd lost the night before, finally getting to the Magic Carpet for a little fun and relaxation and out of a sense of duty to her, his fiancee—there she was, in one of them dark booths in back with some Sharkie feeling her up with one hand and the other hand inside her dress where it was unzipped down the back—the dress he'd bought for her.

And then he remembered pulling the table back from the bench and seeing this guy with his fly open. Now what kind of an impression did she think she was going to make on the folks back home if she acted like that after he married her? Drew had seen it too, and he would bet Drew didn't blame him one bit for what he'd done.

Sure, you weren't supposed to get into brawls, but what else could he do? Naturally, he dragged the guy out of the booth and let him have it. As for Fatima, he probably wouldn't even have hit her except that when she stood up he could see she didn't even have her pants on under her dress. That's what did it. They was getting ready to go at it right there in the booth, the girl he was going to marry and take back to the States with a guy she'd never even introduced him to. Man, that did it. He was sorry if she'd lost a couple of front teeth, but that Fatima had to learn a lesson if she was expecting to marry Ron Corker.

Anyhow, he'd managed to get out of there in spite of Drew and the others. He'd been running ever since, and not a single car had come after him so far. So he figured if he could just lay low for a few days, things would quiet down and he'd be able to report back to the Marine House. Maybe Fatima would be up and around by then. At least he hoped she'd be up. She was laying there awful quiet the last he'd seen her. Well, she wouldn't be screwing around on him for a couple of days at least. He was sure of that.

Yes, he was sure of that, he said to himself.

And kept on running.

Day Two
Friday, May 4

1

Pascal knew dawn would be early enough to start out. At this time of year the sun rose just before six a.m. and set just after six p.m., giving him time to take at least half of the pictures he would need. If he could find a place to sleep, he could finish the job and be back tomorrow.

He maneuvered his jeep into the empty street. In his attaché case he carried four-by-six glossies of at least two dozen paintings of the mountain and coastal areas. With Larbi's help he would locate the exact spot where each had been painted and record it on film. Then at the vernissage each work would have displayed beside it a small photo identical in every way except for the foreground features, to demonstrate how faithfully Larbi had reproduced the reality of his everyday life. His was the work of a primitive, but seen with the eye of a hawk.

Larbi had left his eldest son on the mountain with the goats and was waiting for him at the Center. His face was scrubbed and his ragged jellaba newly washed as if he were about to pay a call at the Presidential Palace.

"Ready to go, Larbi?" he asked in French. "Not afraid of hairpin turns, I hope?" He grinned and drew sharp curves in the air.

Larbi laughed and nodded his head vigorously. It didn't matter. He'd get the turns whether he liked them or not. Conversation wouldn't be easy, and Pascal asked Allah to make Larbi's answers short. They climbed into the jeep and set out.

Pascal had brought with him a large-scale IGN map of the road net as it had been before the revolution. He knew that once in the general vicinity of his objectives he would have to depend on earth roads, marked tracks and finally, guided by Larbi, his own feet. But this didn't bother him. The air promised to be cooler along the naked spine of the mountain, and the view down into the blue but shark-filled waters would be spectacular. He had two 35-mm. cameras, color and black-and-white. The color film could not be developed on the island, but he could do the black-and-whites in his own darkroom in his apartment and print large glossies for display.

They circled the walled medina and cut onto the road leading over the mountain. After a fifteen-minute climb they rounded a curve, and the Watch Tower home of Ida Gant Richard, perched over the void, suddenly came into view.

Why hadn't he thought of Ida? Her beach house would be a perfect place to spend the night. Would she be up so early? And if she were, would she let him have the key?

The guard recognized the jeep with its bearded driver and swung the gate open with a smile.

"Is Madame up?"

The guard's hand extended grandly toward the garden beyond and beneath the piazza, and before he could speak again the old lady, with a dressing gown over her frail body, a sprinkling can in one hand and her cane in the other, came into sight.

"What are you doing up so early, young man?"

"I was just passing and dropped in to see if you were up, Mrs. Richard."

"Ida to you. I'm up before six every morning to see the sunrise. Can't sleep, and it's the best time of day anyhow."

She took him into the garden.

"See where the lawn dips down to the wall?" she asked, pointing with her cane. "The rain washed it out, and there's a hole under the wall big enough for a man to crawl through and come right up onto my property."

"With a sheer cliff on the other side?"

"Don't worry, some of these people climb like goats. I've put chicken wire over the hole, but that won't keep a burglar out. They're coming to fix it next week--maybe--and I won't feel comfortable until they do. That's just to show you having property isn't all fun. Now come in and have a cup of coffee."

Pascal introduced Larbi and told her of his plans.

"Sounds logical," she said in a strangely conspiratorial voice. "Harold Potter told me he'd get back to me, but I didn't think he'd act this fast. I'll bet he gave you some pretty serious instructions."

Pascal laughed uncertainly. "Matter of fact, I didn't have time to tell him what I was doing. I should have, I guess."

She nodded knowingly. "And you're driving all over the island just to take pictures of pretty scenes. Well, if that's your story, I'll accept it. But be careful all the same. These people can be pretty ugly if they think you're photographing their precious military installations. But I suppose Harold Potter has briefed you on all that."

Pascal grimaced. "Ida, I'm no spy," he said softly. "I wouldn't photograph anything military if they paid me."

She only nodded. Then she went into the house and returned with a key. "I think the beds are made up, but there's probably not much in the kitchen. The main switch is behind the kitchen door. It'll start the fridge and turn on the lights. But if you want hot water, you'll have to turn the knob on the gas bottle. Don't forget to turn it off when you leave. I don't want my house burnt down.

"You're a sweetheart, Ida. I'll take good care of your place and leave it just the way I found it."

But then Ida made another strange comment. "I'm not worried about that," she said in the same conspiratorial tone. "After all, it's in a good cause. It's about time we Americans learned to stick together."

"Sure, I understand," he said.

But he didn't. And left puzzled but not caring.

Lou Cross rose with one top-priority project—to prepare for Dan Boyle's inspection on Monday and head off any criticism in connection with the forged memcon.

He had taken the Ambassador's words as a go-ahead for the plan he had in mind. Rummaging through his classified file, he'd found Boyle's recommendations from his previous visit, and he was ready to implement them at the Cultural Center whatever Pascal might say. Pascal was on the spot. Cross would provide labor and materials, and Pascal could spend the next four days putting them into effect. It wouldn't solve the mystery of the forged documents but at least it would deflect some of Boyle's criticism.

Arriving at the villa, however, he noticed that Pascal's jeep was gone.

"What time do you expect Mr. Pascal back?" he asked the secretary.

"Not until tomorrow night, sir," said Leila, anxious to please. "Is there something I can do for you?"

"Tomorrow night?" Cross exploded. "Where the hell has he gone?"

She stiffened. "He went to the north coast to photograph the sites of Larbi's paintings for the vernissage on Tuesday. Didn't he tell you?"

"No, and I'll bet he didn't tell the Ambassador either. What sites? What vernissage?"

"Didn't you know, sir?" she stammered. "We're having a big vernissage Tuesday. There will be over thirty paintings. I'm sending out the invitations today, and the posters will be all over town tomorrow. We expect many important people. It will be an honor for our Center to have such a great artist's works on display."

Cross was speechless. Shaking his head, he watched dozens of visitors enter and leave the building--students, professors, businessmen and simple members of the public here to borrow a book, consult a source, attend an English language class or whatever--all innocently learning something about the United States and the American people.

Innocently, my eye! How many of them were here to spy? How many to drop another forged memcon while Pascal is off touring the north coast, no doubt with his snorkling equipment? What kind of an embassy is this where officers take off without telling the Ambassador, where Marines can't stay out of trouble, where classified documents float around in people's in-baskets? Anything to make him look good with Security!

Well, maybe it was better this way. At least he could go over Boyle's check-list and start the clean-up without having Pascal on his neck.

He called his office to have workmen cover the inside of every pane of glass with transparent mylar to prevent shattering. He removed books at random from the library shelves and felt behind them, then pushed the books back to leave no space for a bomb. He ordered the potted plants inside and out removed as so many more likely places for an explosive charge. He'd send Pascal a memo citing the discrepancies and the steps he was taking. Get it on the record, he said to himself.

Now to go upstairs and take another look at that Mickey Mouse john with the connecting door to the other john.

He used a pass key to enter Pascal's office and went over the Marines' instructions for their inspections. He walked into the bathroom and with another key into the adjoining bathroom and out into the language school hallway, then retraced his steps until he was back in Pascal's office. Only the door between the bathrooms required a key not available at the Center.

Finally, he called in the Director of Courses. Marge Henry was an American who had married a Frenchman while he was studying in the States. With three children she was wedded to Sharqiya as long as her husband's contract with the French aid program lasted. She ran the school with eight or ten teachers giving courses five days and evenings each week.

"Hello, Mr. Cross. Something valuable has been stolen, I hear."

"Nothing like that, Marge. I just want to know who

comes over here to use the hall bathroom from your side of the building."

"I do, and so do the teachers, including Marilyn. There's no other bathroom for us on this floor."

"But most of my wife's classes don't start till six-thirty."

"That's true, but she comes in regularly at six to use the bathroom. We've all seen her."

"Well, I guess there's nothing wrong with that, if everyone else uses it too."

Marge Henry hesitated. "That's just it. I'm sorry to have to tell you this, Mr. Cross, but she stays there usually a half hour. The other teachers have complained to me, and I've spoken to her about it. But there doesn't seem to be much more I can do."

Cross stared at her. Finally he said, "I think that's all for now, Marge. Thank you."

He watched her leave and when the door closed behind her fell into one of the easy chairs and buried his face in his hands. Oh my God, she's at it again, and I'd been praying it was all over! What a fool I was!

Pacing, he grasped at straws to find another explanation. Maybe she was only hitting the bottle. That could be it, couldn't it? But no. Why would she wait to get to the Center before having a drink when she's got all day at home? No, it was to get into this office—Pascal's office! Three times a week she's been meeting that sonofabitch in this office! Good God, he whispered to himself, and all this time I thought she was cured!

He went into the bathroom, opened the connecting door with his pass key, closed it and reenacted his wife's entrance into her latest lover's office. Each step was agony for him.

But planting a forged memcon? No, she wouldn't know how to write it even if she knew what to say. No, it's impossible.

Then, in spite of his denial, his mind took the next logical step. Yes, he told himself, but she could have planted it for someone else!

Oh Christ! he almost cried out, pressing his head between his hands. Then there'd be two of them, two men at least, Pascal and the one who gave her the letter!

He wanted to pound on the walls but only shook his fists in the air. What am I going to do now? he wailed silently. What am I going to tell the Ambassador?

Potter had already heard Jack Warnecke's account of his visit to the Military Academy, and now he wanted to talk to him about the latest developments.

"It's going to be a busy day, Jack. I hope you don't have any firm commitments."

"None that I can't break, sir."

Potter liked Warnecke. He was a professional. His French wasn't very good, and he had no Arabic. But he knew his weaponry, and he could count. He did so at parades or from the window of his car at the passing of a chance convoy. He could estimate the size of a crowd or the length of a column or even memorize at a glance the names on a roster. He made sparing use of his camera, since photographing even most public buildings was forbidden. But his mind remembered what his eyes saw. He stretched the rules where he could, but he tried not to be caught at it.

"I was intrigued by what you said about the ceremonies," Potter began, "especially the fact that the Chief of Staff and some of his top officers were missing. Now let me tell you what I've learned."

He recounted what Ida had seen and what Girardot had told him, without mentioning the forged memcon.

"I'd like you to check on signs of troop movements with your French contacts. If landings are in the wind, we've got to ask the French to use their influence to have them called off."

"If it's all right with you, sir, I'd also like to drive up to the north coast and see for myself what's going on. There's no official restriction on photographing up there."

Potter shook his head. "They'd spot you. And since I

haven't warned them about the invasion yet, they'd think we're in on it. You might find yourself on the first plane out of here. For that matter, so might I."

"Then why can't I send the wife and kids to that beach cottage of Ida Gant's?"

Potter mulled it over. "Better than that, today is Friday. We've still got over a week. You could take them up tomorrow for a family weekend. Can you make it look innocent?."

"Absolutely. But what about Pascal? I hear he's up there now."

Potter's face hardened. "Yes, and he neglected to tell me. I'm afraid I'll have to come down on him hard this time."

"If he takes pictures, anything unusual would help us."

Potter sighed. "I would have insisted on it. The cultural officer doesn't have your stigma as a spy."

After Warnecke had left, Potter buzzed for Millie.

"What are you doing for lunch?"

"Probably tennis with Phil."

"How would you like to do some spying instead?"

He saw her eyes light up. "You mean it, sir?"

"If you don't mind giving up the tennis and Mr. Finley."

"What a sacrifice!"

"Good. I want you to have lunch at Ida's. Call her; she knows about it. I'll get you a camera to put in your purse. Take all the pictures she tells you to take, but don't let anyone see you doing it. Use the telephoto lens. And take your steno pad and write down everything she tells you. OK?"

Millie's heart swelled with pride.

"Yes, sir, Mr. Ambassador," she said, snapping to attention.

2

The Japanese Embassy Residence was set on a hillside back from the sea, with a commanding view of the coastline. A broad lawn stretched downward from the house among clumps of bushes and trees in the tropic sun. Wherever shade was offered, the guests clustered together in the midday heat, giving the lawn the appearance of a playing field with teams huddled in small groups. Individuals would brave the sun's rays and move from one group to another in the routine greetings of a diplomatic corps whose members saw each other regularly. Sprinkled among them were Foreign Ministry and other officials whose presence was based on the state of relations between the GDRS and the day's host.

The Potters arrived a few minutes after eleven, when most of the guests were already present. Even as they offered the obligatory good wishes to the Ambassador and his wife on the veranda Potter's eyes were scanning the lawn below in search of a tall, slim silhouette with a shock of wavy, blue-white hair and lined but still-handsome features who would be surrounded by lesser figures eagerly paying court to the French Ambassador. Catching sight of him beyond a group of guests, he unobtrusively made his way toward him as Catherine spotted friends and broke away.

Thierry de la Châtaigneraie was of that race of Frenchmen destined by birth and upbringing for the *carrière diplomatique*. He had been sent to Sharqiya to salvage what he could from a débâcle of French colonialism, when inattention and overconfidence had resulted in a night of horror, with the throats of pro-French government members cut and their blood allowed to run in the gutters of Al-Bida. A new set of leaders, trained in France but imbued with Marxist theories as well as religious fervor, had taken over, and the expulsion of French advisers had begun.

The stores were nearly empty now of Western goods, and academic standards had taken a precipitous dive. But most Sharqiyans couldn't afford Western goods anyway, and technical training would come from the more radical states. What did it matter if there were daily cuts in electric current and deterioration of the roadbeds and breakdowns in all sectors of urban life? Few Sharqiyans had automobiles, not many more had electricity, and here again friends would help.

Now, however, after only a few years it was apparent that these friends were unable to fill the technological gap and wanted payment for the services they did provide. And so, in the minds of French diplomats the scene was laid for the return of the "real" France, offering the hand of brotherhood and shared ideals and respect for human dignity, in the person of Thierry de la Châtaigneraie.

He had his work cut out for him, but he was making progress. Potter could not believe the French government would allow anything so crude as a mercenary invasion to upset its carefully orchestrated campaign to reassure not only Sharqiya but other francophone states that France was a sincere partner in development.

Potter made his way through the crowd of non-official guests, Sharqiyan or French for the most part and at least half of them the same from reception to reception, a sort of floating delegation from the business and cultural communities. He was about to reach his French counterpart when a woman of generous proportions in an expensive caftan barred his way.

"Monsieur l'Ambassadeur! What a pleasure!"

Oh God! It's Nadia! he groaned behind his professional smile, watching his prey drift away toward another group of guests.

"Madame Busheira! How nice to see you here."

He knew Nadia Busheira only too well as the wife of the head of Sharqiya's largest construction firm and a survivor from pre-revolutionary days. "Have you any news?" She asked him breathlessly.

This, Potter remembered, was the lady who was convinced that her feckless son, who had no *baccalauréat* and so couldn't enter a French university, could now, with one word from Potter, pursue his studies in the United States on a scholarship and gain the degree which the revolutionary government would require of him before allowing him to assume management of his father's business should they decide to nationalize it.

"News?" he asked blandly as he saw the French Ambassador come to rest amid a covey of sycophants. "About what?"

"About my son, of course. You promised to get him a scholarship at an American university. Don't you remember?"

"How could I forget, Madame?" he smiled. "As a matter of fact, I asked our cultural attache to look into the possibilities. Hasn't he contacted you yet?"

Poor Pascal, he thought. I'll have to make it up to him.

"Mr. Ambassador," said Nadia Busheira reprovingly, it's *your* intercession we need. *You* must write the letter."

As she spoke, he watched the Frenchman excuse himself and break away deftly from his admirers and join the Russian Ambassador for what surely would be a more substantive chat. Oh, if only he, Potter, could do the same as smoothly!

"I've asked Mr. Pascal to draft a letter for my signature. I promise you I'll get after it today." he said hurriedly.

Coward, he thought. Then out of the corner of his eye he saw de la Châtaigneraie laugh at the Russian's joke and raise his glass. He tried to break off but felt Nadia Busheira's stubby fingers on his arm.

"That's another promise. I hope you'll keep this one."

"Oh, I will." He freed his arm and bolted. The Frenchman had reached another group and was shaking hands. Potter joined them.

"Cher ami!" cried de la Châtaigneraie as if he had not seen him in a year. Then, in English, "How's it going, Hal?"

"Pas mal. But I'm afraid I must have a word with you."

"Then we'd better hurry, old man. I leave for Paris this afternoon."

Potter's poise almost left him, but he managed a casual, "Oh? What's up?"

"Not affairs of state this time. Something far more important—my youngest daughter's fiançailles."

"Congratulations!" Potter said brightly. "When is the big day?"

"Tomorrow, the fifth. We would have preferred a Friday the 13th, which as you know is our lucky day in France. But unfortunately one cannot change the calendar. So we shall have to be content with Saturday the fifth."

"Ah, Friday the 13th," Potter laughed. "I always used to buy a lottery ticket, but I never won a franc."

De la Châtaigneraie chuckled and led him away. "But that's very serious. You have to have luck to be a diplomat, my friend. The first thing Talleyrand used to ask a job applicant was, 'Are you lucky?'"

"And when your luck is only so-so, as mine is, you have to be twice as careful."

As they moved, Potter thought he saw, among those who had been abandoned but wearing a broad smile nevertheless, the round frame of Gaston Girardot. He lowered his voice and spoke to the ground. "I have it on pretty good authority that an invasion and a coup attempt are planned here for the 13th."

The French Ambassador's eyebrows went up.

"Ah, yes, May 13th is next Sunday, isn't it? And who is behind it this time?"

"I don't know yet," Potter admitted. "But mercenaries are supposed to be coming in by sea on the north coast, and perhaps by air too."

De la Châtaigneraie broke into laughter.

"Excellent! But where would they be coming from? Djibouti is fifteen hundred kilometers away."

"I didn't mention Djibouti," Potter smiled. "They might be coming out of the Gulf, for all I know. But I'm asking you to take the warning seriously for a good reason. The Sharqiyan government in all probability knows about it and will be waiting for them."

The French Ambassador immediately became serious.

"Really, Harold, I do not believe it. Not because we hear so many rumors of right-wing coup attempts, but because this one appears impossible. After all, we do know a few things about these gentlemen. Some of them are Frenchmen, alas. But we also know their capabilities, and believe me, they hardly include amphibious landings on well-defended islands."

"…whose defenses may be well known to them. And amphibious equipment can be bought with oil money and assembled in no time. Seriously, how long has it been known you were leaving the country?"

"Here? A few days, at most. In Paris, longer. My wife has been making preparations for three weeks. Why?"

"Just that if I were planning a landing I'd be happy to have you out of the way." Potter did not add that rogue elements in France would also want the French Ambassador to be away from his post to avoid embarrassment for both. Instead, he repeated his warning.

"Nevertheless, I beg you to tell them at the Quai. If it were to go the other way, a regime radicalized by a failed counter-revolution would have as little sympathy for an American mission here as for a French one."

"Very well. Just to reassure you, I promise I shall inform them. But between us, Harold, don't worry. There's nothing to it. Now let us rejoin the others before they decide *we* are planning an invasion."

They returned casually, the Frenchman's hand on Potter's shoulder.

"Messieurs, America and her oldest ally have just solved the problems of the world. Did we miss the canapés?"

Potter hoped the worry was not visible on his features as he spotted Gaston Girardot, round as a mandarin, approaching with the most innocent smile in the world. But then, from the other direction and also heading toward them, was Mohamed Qasim, the Minister of the Interior and head of the Secret Police. Here's the guy who may turn out to be our nemesis, Thierry old boy, he said to himself, the guy who in the event of a left-wing takeover not only would survive but prosper, maybe even ending up as President. Now all he has to find out is whether the American Ambassador will report what he knows to the GDRS, or whether the United States by its silence will associate itself with the planned invasion of a friendly nation.

The conversation was jovial. Châtaigneraie described the trials of being father of the bride in France, while Qasim set out to recount the peculiarities of weddings in Sharqiya. Potter laughed along with the rest, but felt alone with his questions.

Nothing could have been better for Millie Novak's morale than Potter's request. She called Ida, made the date and cancelled her tennis plans with Phil. Just before noon she received a call from the Foreign Ministry summoning the Ambassador to the office of the Director of Bilateral Relations, Mr. Smaili, that afternoon. She noted the name correctly, and her lips twitched. She remembered writing "Smiley" phonetically the first time she'd heard it spoken.

Ida, her hand on the railing for support, was waiting for her at the top of the steps to the piazza. They embraced.

"My dear, it's been a long time."

"Not so long, Ida. I came for luncheon just a few weeks ago with Phil Finley. Remember?"

"For me, a few weeks is a long time. Time means nothing in the middle of life. At the beginning and at the end, it means everything."

"You look pretty healthy to me."

"Perhaps. But who knows for how long?"

The table was set on the piazza overlooking the city. It was a simple meal of melon, cold seafood, salad and strawberries, with a bottle of Alsatian Riesling.

"Not your typical luncheon menu in turn-of-the-century Missouri," Ida said, "but we do have to make a few concessions to the climate."

"Ida," Millie asked as they finished dessert, "what do you know about Maître Girardot?"

Ida smiled. "A lot more than you think, and perhaps a lot more than I want to know. There was a time years ago when we were lovers."

Millie's spoon dropped to her plate. "I'm so sorry. I didn't mean to intrude."

"You're not intruding. It's common knowledge, at least in his generation and mine, what few of us are left. And remember, we're not talking about the old corn husk you're looking at right now, or the rotten pumpkin he's turned into either. We cut quite a figure in those days."

"Honestly," Millie protested, "I knew nothing about it."

"Of course not. Who cares, nowadays? I did it to take my revenge on a husband who'd been doing it to me for years. Just like the French boulevard comedies. Gaston Girardot was in his twenties and just starting out. He worked for my husband in those days. He's come a long way since then."

Seeing Ida was willing to talk, Millie shed her inhibitions.

"You mean because your husband had love affairs you did the same? Isn't that somehow demeaning? I mean, shouldn't you have just walked out on him?"

"And left all this to go back to Missouri? I should say not. Not that people didn't get divorced in those days, but I had and did what I wanted. Why give that up for alimony?"

"But if you didn't really love Maître Girardot?"

"I enjoyed the affair. I didn't have to be in love with him for that. I paid for it too."

"How?"

"By letting him rob me and my husband too. I gave him jewelry which he sold or later gave to other women. My husband placed his confidence in him and gave him business contracts. When war came in '39 my husband was mobilized, while Gaston stayed here, opened his own business and enriched himself with my husband's customers. I was in London with de Gaulle and then in North Africa and Italy, and when my husband returned from a German prison camp, he was an old man. But he built up his business again and left it all to me. He never spoke to Gaston Girardot again."

"What happened to Girardot's firm?"

"Oh, he saw the way things were going and went into

partnership with a Sharqiyan. When my husband died, they bought out his business, and by the time it was nationalized after the revolution, Gaston had his money where they couldn't touch it. He can't take most of it out of the country, but he's living very well on it here."

"And what about his partner?"

Ida smiled. "He's Minister of Finance."

"In other words, Maître Girardot has always played both ends against the middle."

"And come out a winner too. I suppose you have to admire him. How else can you survive under a regime like this one?"

Millie phrased her next question carefully. "Whose side do you think he's playing on now?"

"Both. Or whichever serves his interests. With a little money in France and an ex-partner in the government, he can jump either way."

"Don't the French know he can't be trusted?"

"Of course. But he does give them information about the government, just as he gives the government information about the French."

Millie asked the key question. "Do you think he would pass on information to us?"

"Not out of loyalty to us, certainly. It's more likely he'd take someone else's money and pass on what that person wanted us to know, hoping it would work out to his advantage."

Millie wanted to tell Ida how she'd made the pieces fit together, meshing the roly-poly images in her memory with the reports she had typed, the conversations she had overheard and the words of one of the best sources of all. But this was Embassy business, and Millie was too security-conscious to tell even Ida of her Ambassador's interest in Girardot.

"Ida, you do realize this is not why the Ambassador asked me to see you."

"Maybe not, but he's welcome to what I know. That is, if you are indiscreet enough to give away my secrets."

"I wouldn't do that."

"You'd better, or I won't invite you back. As for what I told him last night, you can see the harbor for yourself."

Millie took pictures through the telephoto lens at Ida's direction and put the camera back in her purse. As she was leaving, Ida said:

"I didn't realize what I told him last night would bring me all this attention. First the Pascal boy, and now you. There must be something going on."

Millie was puzzled. "You mean Pete Pascal was here too?"

"Yes, and he'll be spending the night at my beach house on the north coast. Uncle Sam's really got his spies out today, hasn't he?"

Millie left confused, her triumph marred by a new enigma.

Marilyn had slept later than usual, borne dreamlessly in the palm of a hand so cool and soft she had not even felt the need to roll over or shift the weight of her hips. The sunlight streaming in had awakened her, and stretching gloriously she had turned over and closed her eyes again. There was no reason to get up. The beast had fed its full. Its yellow eyes had found their prey and now were closed in sleep. Later, it would emerge to feed again. But not yet, not for a while. For the morning at least, and perhaps for the afternoon as well, it would leave her in peace. She was going to be fine today.

Downstairs her breakfast was waiting for her: a cool glass of fresh orange juice thick with pulp, a good cup of black coffee lightened with cream and French bread sliced lengthwise and buttered before toasting, and afterward a stroll in the garden protected from the view of strangers by an eight-foot hedge.

She looked out past the veranda. It was a day to play tennis or swim in the pool or just lie in the sun, though here in the tropics she had to be careful. Her fair skin couldn't take it.

But that was something she had no intention of thinking about today. She could play the piano. It was Friday, the Muslim sabbath, but the French work week was still in force, and she wouldn't have to be at the Center before six for her date with Pete.

She heard the horn and then the chimes. The old man was bestirring himself to open the gate, while Ali the gardener, skinny and austere, leaned on a rake and watched. Ali was younger. He sometimes worked in the garden in his undershirt, which was torn though he seemed to wash it frequently. Some day she would have to give him an undershirt.

The black office sedan pushed like a huge shark through the open gate. She retreated to the living room and noticed that Lou appeared solemn and avoided her gaze.

"So what's new today on the front lines of American diplomacy?" she asked brightly as they sat down to lunch, not giving a damn but hoping to cheer him up.

"Not much," he said. "The Regional Security guy is coming in Monday; so you'll have to give a luncheon for him. Invite the Warneckes maybe, or even the Ambassador."

"And Her Highness too, I suppose. Who is this guy anyhow, that he rates such high-powered company?"

Cross ignored the sarcasm. "Dan Boyle. You remember him. He covers the whole area."

She snorted. "Boyle? Yes, I remember him. A tub of lard with a file of dirty jokes gathered in all the capitals of the world. Why would I have to subject Her Highness to him?"

Evasively, Cross said, "Well, you know. Security's a big thing these days. We've got to make sure we don't overlook anything."

"Security!" She recalled Boyle's last visit. She'd asked him what his wife did all day. "I'll bet there are all kinds of things to do where you are: concerts, films, tours, shops."

Boyle had fixed his napkin to his shirt collar. "People don't live in the city if they can help it. "Most of the Embassy personnel are out about five miles in their own housing area, with plenty of security guards. They've got a club with a pool and tennis courts. There's a wives' club and a bridge club, and a Little League for the kids. You know, just like here. I don't think my wife has to go into town once a month."

"What a shame!" she'd said. "With so much to see and do! Monuments, museums, everything."

"Yeah, but once you've seen them, why see them a second time. What's the point?"

That was Dan Boyle. And those were the Embassy wives in one of the great capitals of the world. What was she, Marilyn Cross, doing anywhere in the Foreign Service?

"You see, Dan," Lou had explained, " my wife's a culture bug: painting, piano, singing and all that. It makes it tough for her in an isolated post like this."

"Oh, I'm not complaining," she'd said. "I find things to do."

"I suppose you'll be taking this Boyle around to see Pete's Center on Monday," she said now.

"Sure, and I hope he'll be back from his little jaunt."

"Jaunt?"

"That's right. It seems Mr. Pascal left this morning for a drive to the north coast for a couple of days. He didn't bother to tell the Ambassador and he took along one of his Sharqiyan artist friends."

Marilyn's smile faded. "You mean Pete's gone? For two days? I didn't know that."

"Why? Was he supposed to tell you too?"

"No, I'm just surprised. I didn't know. Yes, I did, in fact. He's having an art exhibit, and he was going to take photographs of the places in the paintings. He mentioned that."

"Then you're privileged. He didn't mention it to the Ambassador. And now he's got himself in real trouble."

"What trouble?" Marilyn asked faintly.

"Well," said Cross, his voice tense and his eyes watching hers, "it seems a highly classified document was found in his in-basket the night before last. He claims he didn't put it there, but that's where it was found."

Marilyn was suddenly quiet.

"What kind of document?" she asked vaguely.

"Just a single sheet of paper in an envelope."

"In an envelope?"

"Yeah, a white envelope with his name on it. Why? Does that mean something to you?"

"No. Of course not. I was just curious."

"I'm sure he's got an explanation. But don't worry. I'll find out who put it there."

"Well," she said, rising abruptly as a dessert spoon dropped to the floor, "after that nice meal I think I'll have a drink."

Cross winced. "Aw, come on, Marilyn. You promised."

"Yes, but just one won't hurt. Besides, we have no luncheon guests before Monday. And you're on your way back to the office. So no one will see me."

"Please, Marilyn."

"I said it won't hurt. Now pour me a cognac, or shall I ask the houseboy to?"

He went to the liquor cabinet and poured the cognac into a snifter, fully aware this was no drink for a hot day in the tropics but unwilling to make a scene over it.

She finished it in two swallows and handed it back to him.

"Please, Marilyn, don't," he begged.

"All right," she said brightly. Just leave the bottle there. I may have one more."

At least one more, she thought as the black shark pulled out of the driveway and back to the embassy. She had regained her composure. She would go out. Not to the Center, since Mr. Pascal had left without so much as a word of explanation, and on a Friday too, but to the Gallery, where she would have something to say to a certain art dealer named Brahim Zerkaoui.

Pete Pascal lay flat on the bare ground, the pebbles swept out from under him to soften the bed of dry earth and rock, looking through the glasses far off and downward toward the turquoise depths below. Beyond the white rocks of the promontory forming one arm of the sandy cove he could see the boats approaching along the coast. There were two of them, and they came fast, faster than fishing boats. They seemed to be painted gray, with numbers at the bow, like patrol vessels.

The sight irritated him. "Damn!" he muttered. "I'll have to let them pass. That means at least ten more minutes."

He placed the binoculars on the ground and rolled to one side, looking at the aquiline profile of the little man squatting beside him, his face burnt a deep coffee color in response to and in protection from the harsh sunlight which seemed to have burnt skin and flesh from everything else in sight, leaving only whitened bones protruding from the sea.

"Larbi, les photos," he said.

The goatherd passed him a knapsack with a loose-leaf binder inside. He opened to a black-and-white photograph of a painting, which he held in front of him now as he peered across the top of it toward the coast.

"The exact spot," he said. "Couldn't be closer. And it's the right time of day too. Even the shadows are identical."

He swung his legs around and sat with knees between his elbows, glancing impatiently at his wristwatch.

"But I can't take a picture with those boats in it, old boy," he said in English to his companion. "What would the critics say? 'They're not in your painting, so they can be in the photo,' that's what. To say nothing of the authorities, who don't want their military hardware photographed any more than I want to photograph it."

Larbi grinned uncomprendingly and sniffed the wind, touching his nose. "Matar."

"Go on, it won't rain. There isn't a cloud in the sky."

The other, still grinning, nodded his head insistently. "Matar!"

"If you're right, that queers us for the rest of the afternoon. And I've still got a half dozen pictures to take."

The patrol boats were nearing the promontory now, looming larger in the picture he would not take. From dots in the upper left hand corner of Larbi's painting, they had grown to ugly gray blotches in the very center, distracting the eye from the focus of the turquoise bay. Until they moved off the lower right hand edge of the canvas, the photo couldn't be taken. He could only wait and hope the light wouldn't change.

He counted the unchecked photos in the binder. There were seven left to take after this one. Three were in the neighborhood of Ras el-Kebir, eighty kilometers to the west, and already the sun was well past the zenith. So he had no choice but to spend the night at the beach house. He would wait until the patrol boats were gone, take his picture and then drive down to the cove, where the house sat on a saddle on the promontory overlooking the bay, but with a view to the west if you climbed the few steps to the top of the saddle.

Then as he focused the glasses on the house and the dirt road leading up to it from the Route Nationale, he noticed that one of the boats had altered its course and was making for the cove.

"That does it. If it anchors in the cove, we're finished for the day, especially if it rains."

Cursing, he flipped through the pictures remaining to be taken. Of the three at Ras el-Kebir, two showed gorgeous sunsets with heavy clouds undershot with gold, and the third showed a stormy sky. He waited until the boat entered the cove and dropped anchor. Then he said, "C'mon, Larbi, we've got driving to do if we're going to get to Ras el-Kebir before sunset."

They gathered their things and scrambled down the reverse slope of the hill to where the jeep was parked at the extreme limit of a road which was hardly more than a goat path. It was hot now. The ridge on which they had lain cut them off from the sea breezes, and both of them were in sweat as Pascal agreed it would rain before long.

They reached a switchback in the trail which allowed the jeep to move more easily down the remainder of the slope. Within ten minutes they would be on the tarred Route Nationale near the cove. But from there it would take them a full hour to get to Ras el-Kebir along the winding highway, and the afternoon sun would be in their eyes most of the way.

Pascal cursed his luck. Now they would have to drive back by night to get to the beach house, after which there would be only a hundred kilometers over the mountain to Al-Bida. The last leg could be done in two hours, but if he wanted to get the shadows right he would have to wait until afternoon the next day and hope the sky would be clear. He began to ask himself if it was really worth the trouble.

They were coming now to a low ridge beyond which lay the cove and the Route Nationale. Suddenly, as they reached the summit, the cool breeze hit them and they saw the cove.

Pascal swerved the jeep off the trail and behind the rocks. Then, motioning Larbi to remain quiet and follow him, he climbed out and made his way to an observation point between two huge boulders.

The boat had anchored in the cove, and a dinghy was tied up at the dock. Three men in uniform were climbing single file up the path to the beach house. The first one had already reached the porch and now was pounding on the door with his fist. Getting no answer, he tried the latch, then tentatively put his shoulder to the door.

"They're breaking in!" Pascal cried.

The second man had joined the first one on the porch and was going from window to window attempting to force open the French shutters. The third man had gone to the back of the house. In a minute he returned with a pole. He placed one end of it into the crack between the shutters of a window and leaned against it. The shutter snapped open. Without hesitation he smashed a pane of glass and opened the window. A few seconds later two of them were inside, and the third was working on the front door. With the inside locks open, it gave easily. The first man reappeared and signaled the patrol boat.

Pascal whistled between his teeth.

"The bastards are moving in, just like that!"

He turned to Larbi, who grinned self-consciously. "How about you and me putting a stop to that, Larbi? I don't care who they are. That's private property."

He motioned to the goatherd to drive with him over the ridge and surprise the burglars. Larbi's grin broadened, but he shook his head violently.

"What's the matter? Come on, before they do real damage."

But the little man would not budge.

"All right, then I'll go alone."

This time Larbi grabbed him by the arm to hold him back.

"You mean I can't go either? Are they going to shoot me?"

Pascal considered his position. Ida had entrusted the place to his care, but on the other hand, these guys were armed.

"All right, then what do we do?"

"Ras el-Kebir," Larbi said. "Après, venir ici. Eux partis, p't'être."

"Or maybe we drive back to the city and get help. But you're right, they may be gone by the time we get back. OK, Larbi, you win. But we'll have to drive right past them along the cove."

Larbi clicked his tongue in the negative and motioned him to turn the jeep around. Once more they found themselves in an airless defile. The jeep began to kick up dust, but after a few kilometers they were in view of the coast once more. The promontory was well behind them and Ras el-Kebir far ahead in the afternoon sunlight. Clouds were gathering. If they were lucky they might have a sunset like the one Larbi had painted. Then if the patrol boat was gone, they could still spend the night at the beach house, do some skin-diving and in the afternoon take that last picture and drive back to Al-Bida.

He looked back at the promontory. In the middle was

the saddle behind which stood Ida's beach house. It was protected from the wind yet handy to one of the most glorious views on the whole island, looking all the way up the coast to Ras el-Kebir, eighty kilometers away. What an observation point!

Vaguely, he wondered if that might be why the Sharqiyan Navy was taking an interest in Ida's beach house.

When Harold Potter arrived at the Ministry of Foreign Affairs he was ushered through the familiar corridors to the anteroom of the Director of Bilateral Relations.

Meeting Suleiman Smaili was always an amusing experience. A small man with jet-black eyebrows and a fringe of beard, Smaili greeted each visiting member of the diplomatic corps like a lost brother, coming at him from across his large office with arms outstretched and moon face open in a transport of joy. It made no difference what ideological, political or religious camp the visitor belonged to. To Smaili he was a member of the family. Each ambassador had the impression that, whatever dull business or even clash of interests might set their countries at odds, heartfelt friendship lay at the foundation of their relations with Suleiman Smaili.

But not today. Today the atmosphere in the office was frigid. Smaili had pinched his jovial features into a mask of comic severity. He waved Potter not to the divan with its big cushions around which Sharqiyans, their slippers removed, would wrap arms, legs and feet in joyful abandon, but rather to the straight-backed chair facing his own desk.

"Monsieur l'Ambassadeur," he began in a strained effort at severity, "my government has instructed me to call to your attention an incident of shocking brutality perpetrated last night by a member of your staff."

Oh God, thought Potter, so Corker got into a brawl in a bar. "Monsieur le Directeur," he said, "I can't imagine what could have happened to cause your government to give it your notice. It must be something of which I am completely unaware."

Smaili was taken aback by Potter's quick reply and lost the thread of his carefully rehearsed protest. He caught himself after an instant of hesitation, however, and went on without replying.

"This man, Monsieur l'Ambassadeur, was seen by witnesses entering a public place of relaxation where civilized patrons were innocently engaged in tranquil conversation, and assaulting without provocation a young Sharqiyan couple, both of whom are now hospitalized. This barbaric behavior on the part of one of your subordinates is regarded by the government of the Democratic Republic of Sharqiya as typical of the attitude of the American imperialists toward the peace-loving citizens of progressive nations, and the challenge which it represents to the civilized world cannot go unanswered."

My poor Smaili, thought Potter, you were not born to issue diatribes of this kind.

"Monsieur le Directeur," he began, "it is true that one of our guards may have misbehaved last evening, according to reports I have received. Whatever the provocation, he may well have caused some damage to property. The United States will of course give favorable consideration to any claims duly forwarded to it by the injured parties, should our own investigation confirm these allegations. I'm afraid such incidents do occur, but this one hardly constitutes a diplomatic incident. Surely it can be resolved amicably between friendly governments such as ours."

"Compensation for actual damage done," Smaili replied, "will not be sufficient considering the injury to citizens of the Democratic Republic of Sharqiya. My government demands, first of all, that this American brute be turned over to it for trial by a people's court, and second, that the United States government issue a public apology and pay damages to the Sharqiyan people for this unwarranted attack on its sovereignty."

So they're really trying to make something of it. He recited his official answer: The United States had always wanted good relations, but had learned that this was in fact a lovers' quarrel and should be given no more importance than a brawl among sailors in the port.

"We attach far more importance to it than that," Smaili insisted, "and we demand that you turn over the individual immediately to the Sharqiyan authorities."

"We agree," he answered, "that the boy does not enjoy diplomatic immunity and therefore is subject to the jurisdiction of the local courts. However, it is common practice for governments to allow us to dispose of such cases ourselves. You may rest assured he will be adequately punished by our courts."

"Monsieur l' Ambassadeur, I ask you once more, will you turn this man over to us immediately?"

Potter feigned surprise. "But I thought you knew I was speaking generally, Monsieur le Directeur. Unfortunately, we are unable to do so because the boy has not reported back to the Embassy."

Smaili frowned. "Are you saying he is in flight?"

"Apparently, unless he is lying injured somewhere in the city. It may be that he received injuries as well, since he is small and weighs no more than the average Sharqiyan."

"Then my government will have to consider what further steps it will take."

These words amounted to a dismissal. Potter seized the moment to offer the hand of friendship.

"Monsieur le Directeur, when you asked to see me, I was myself about to request a word with you on a far more serious matter."

Smaili, vexed and taken aback, had no choice but to listen.

"Yesterday I was told that an invasion of your country by foreign mercenaries was being planned. Obviously, I have no way of judging the accuracy of the information, but it is said that armed landings are to take place on the night of May 12th to 13th along the north coast of the island with a view to overthrowing your government. The United States deplores any such action, it goes without saying, and in the event it takes place, I feel confident we would stand ready to assist your government in any way possible."

That should hold him, he thought. Poor Smaili. After this, he must be ready to embrace me.

But Smaili's expression did not change.

"I shall convey the information to my superiors. Good day, Monsieur l'Ambassadeur."

Back at the Embassy Potter ran into Lou Cross.

"Come on upstairs to my office, will you, Lou?" he said.

Cross followed him wondering how he was going to explain what he'd learned about the connecting door at the Center. They passed Millie at her desk without a nod in her direction. Inside the office, with the Stars and Sripes on a staff behind a big mahogany desk and photos of the President and the Secretary of State on the wall, Potter nodded to Cross to close the door.

Cross braced himself.

"Well, the news isn't good, Lou. I've just been called to the Ministry to hear a protest over our Marine Guard Corker and a demand that we turn him over to them for trial--and all because of the brawl he got into last night."

"But we can't turn him over, sir. He's AWOL."

"That's what I told them. And that makes one more potential problem for us. If things turn nasty next week and they catch him, we could have a hostage situation on our hands. So I want you to tell the Marines to keep an eye out for him and haul him in here for his own good. I was a platoon leader in Korea, and I took care of my men. I plan to do the same here whether they have diplomatic status or not. They'll have to convince Corker he'll be better off here than in any Sharqiyan jail. Now, have you found anything out about that forged memcon?"

Cross began to stammer.

"Well, sir, not much ... That is, I questioned Mrs. Henry, and she told me...Well, maybe I ought to start at the beginning."

Cross stumbled through the tale of the locked connecting door but avoided any mention of possible users of the other bathroom. When he'd finished, he looked at Potter's impassive face and added lamely, "...So I guess anyone with a key could have gotten in..."

"Is that all?" Potter shot back. "Couldn't Marge Henry tell you who uses the bathroom after duty hours? That's the time we're interested in, not when the building is full of staff and visitors and the PAO's office door is open."

Cross half knew this question was coming, yet he had no quick answer.

"Well, she did say the teachers all used it before their six-thirty classes. But which ones I guess she really didn't know for sure..."

"Marilyn has a six-thirty class, doesn't she? Have you asked her?"

Cross squirmed. "No, sir, not yet. But I will. I'll ask her as soon as I see her."

"I think you'd better. I'm sure she'll be able to throw at least some light on the mystery."

Cross left the office in complete disarray, feeling the Ambassador's gaze boring into his back.

My God, he suspects something already. He may even know the truth!

When Marilyn Cross reached the art gallery, second thoughts were gone. Zerkaoui had used her to hurt Pete Pascal, and she was going to tell him so.

"Where is Mr. Zerkaoui?" she demanded, paying no attention to the customers inside the shop.

The clerk spread his hands helplessly and smiled. "He is out. Perhaps later."

"Perhaps now."

She lifted the trap in the counter and forced her way through.

"But Mr. Zerkaoui is out!" the clerk cried, trying to intercept her. He failed, but his protests gave warning to anyone in the storeroom.

It was a warehouse, with cement floor and sliding metal door large enough to permit a small truck to back in and unload. To Marilyn it seemed unoccupied until a narrow beam of light followed by a click told her the side door behind the stack of rugs had just been opened and closed.

"I know you're there," she said evenly. "Come on out."

Brahim Zerkaoui appeared from behind the stack, dressed as neatly as if he had been in his gallery welcoming local dignitaries to the annual art show. Not a hair of his head was out of place; not a drop of perspiration shone on his brow; not a wrinkle was seen in his jacket or trousers.

"Why, Madame Cross. I didn't expect you today."

"I can see that. I want a few words with you."

Seeing she was alone, he went to her with arms outstretched. "Marilyn, my dear, something has upset you. What is it?"

"Don't sweet-talk me, Brahim. You tried to make a fool of me."

"How? What did I do?"

"You gave me a letter for Pete when I was here last Wednesday. Don't deny it."

"Of course I did. Why should I deny it? Did you give it to him?"

"You know I did. I took it to his office and put it on his desk, exactly where you told me."

"I didn't tell you where to put it. I merely said give it to him. Don't tell me it's lost."

"No, you said not to give it to him, to put it in the stack of papers where he'd find it in the morning."

"And did he find it there in the morning?"

"No, he found it Wednesday evening, or someone did."

Zerkaoui frowned. "Wednesday evening? But you weren't supposed to go to the Center until Thursday evening."

"So I had an extra class and left it there a day early. You wanted him to get it, didn't you?"

"Yes, of course, but..."

"Don't change the subject. You wanted him to get into trouble over it, because you knew it was Secret and the Marines would find it."

"That's ridiculous. I gave you a sealed envelope. How could I know what was inside?"

"It was not sealed, and you know it. I didn't read it, but I'll bet you did."

Zerkaoui's face wore an expression of exasperation. "My sweet Marilyn, that letter was something he had dropped the morning he visited me. I was merely restoring it to him the easiest way."

"You're lying. Pete was never here before yesterday. He told me so. "

He released her and turned away. "I suppose I deserve it," he continued with a sigh, looking away. "No doubt you think it was an account of your secret visits here which I was sending him to make him jealous."

"No, you don't. Anything I may have done with you, Mr. Zerkaoui, is none of his business, just as what I do with him is none of yours."

He shrugged. "Then I can't imagine what was in the envelope."

She wavered. "If you know, I don't have to tell you. And if you don't, you won't find out from me."

"You see? You've just admitted I may be telling the truth. In fact, all you know is what someone told you. Who? Pascal? No, I'll bet it was your husband."

"What if it was? That just proves it's serious."

"Perhaps, but it doesn't prove I planted it. All it proves is that he was in possession of something compromising which I innocently returned to him. He may say I planted it. He's an American diplomat, and he can say anything he wants about me. But remember, I can say what I want about him too. Or about you, Marilyn."

"You bastard!"

"Why? If someone tells lies about me, can't I tell the truth about him--or her?"

"You are a stinking bastard!"

He shrugged again. "I am sorry you feel that way, Madame Cross. And I am sorry you didn't find what you were looking for this afternoon. Now may I show you out through the front of the shop? Or would you prefer to use the side door, as you have in the past?"

She turned and stalked out the way she had come in. Once in the street, she began to walk rapidly, her heart pounding, holding back tears of rage. Why did he do it? What has he got against me? He's probably jealous of Pete. He wanted me all to himself. Well, no chance of that, Mr. Zerkaoui. You're lucky you got what you did.

Suddenly she realized she had passed her car and walked an extra block. She retraced her steps and replayed the scene in her mind. It made her feel better to think Zerkaoui had framed Pete out of jealousy. It gave her a sense of worth to think that men might fight over her. And she wasn't that bad to look at, even if she was almost forty. She still had her figure, and she knew how to show it off.

A man had stopped and was watching her. He was standing almost beside her car. With frozen features she returned his gaze. He was in Western dress, but otherwise he was just another macho Sharqiyan with a black mustache.

Abruptly she stepped off the curb and around the front of the car to the driver's door. She jerked her hip in his direction with a slight but unmistakable movement if you were looking at her. He was. As she turned on the ignition, he looked in the right front window at her, a broad smile on his face. Then, as the engine roared, she looked at him again with the same ice-cold stare and sped off, the man a diminishing silhouette in her rear-view mirror. She laughed. Any man was hers for the asking. Brahim Zerkaoui needn't think she was going to miss him. In fact, he might be sorry for treating her the way he had.

Catherine had spent the morning at home. She was free today. She would putter about in her garden, inspect the residence for dust and dirt and plan the noon meal with the cook.

But above all, and without seeming to do so, she would keep her eye on Hanifa.

She watched her make the beds and dust the living room, noting carefully the hour and duration of each function. She saw her take the large straw basket and go off to the market with the driver, and she noted the time of her return with the basket full of fruits and vegetables. Finally, after lunch when Harold was back at the Embassy and she was alone again, she called Hanifa and took her to the study, where she pointed to the typewriter.

"Where did you take this machine on Wednesday, Hanifa?"

The girl lost her composure completely. "Nowhere, Madame. I just put it on the floor to clean the table."

"You put it in the shopping basket and took it downtown. Don't deny it; you were seen. Now tell me where you took it."

The girl began to cry.

"I took it to be fixed."

"Who told you it needed fixing?"

"Someone at the market told me. He took it and gave it back to me an hour later all fixed."

"No one at the market even knew about this typewriter. Now tell me the truth. Who asked you to take it there?"

"A man. I don't know his name. He said the Ambassador told him to fix it, and I was to bring it in. He said the Ambassador would fire me if I didn't."

"But you knew that wasn't true. You knew he wanted to steal it."

"No, Madame, because he gave it back after only one hour. That isn't stealing, is it?"

"And he told you not to tell anyone or you'd lose your job, didn't he?"

"That's right, Madame. That's what he told me."

"All right, Hanifa. We're going to the market now, and you're going to find that man for me."

"I can't," the girl wailed. "He'll kill me."

"Nonsense. He won't even recognize you. You'll he wearing your jellaba and your veil."

Catherine knew the market area. She shopped there often for specialties. The main shopping district, with what was left of its Western boutiques, was only a block away on a palm-lined avenue.

"Now show me the shop where you left the typewriter," she told the girl as they reached the edge of the crowded square.

"I didn't leave it at a shop, Madame. Someone took it from me at the market and brought it back an hour later."

"But you took it where he told you to take it, and that's where you're going to take me."

They edged through a sea of bodies, women in tent-like jellabas and hawking vendors and porters and donkeys and wagons. The street was parallel to the main avenue. Dingy shops lined one side, and the rear entrances of the more elegant Western shops on the avenue formed the other side. One of these was on a corner, with a heavy metal door on rollers at the rear and a smaller door opening onto an alley on the side. The building seemed vaguely familiar to Catherine.

"That's it," said Hanifa, pointing at a tiny shop across the street from the metal door. "That's where he told me to take it."

It was a bicycle repair shop, with spare parts of all kinds affixed to the inner walls.

"You mean you left it here and didn't even know whether you'd get it back or not?"

"But I did get it back, Madame. Just one hour later I came back with my basket full of food, and they emptied it and put the machine in and covered it with the food. I went to the car and brought it back here and put it on the table."

"And wiped the table afterward, idiot."

"Oh Madame, the machine is fixed, isn't it?"

As she spoke, the side door of the corner building opened, and a man in a natty tan suit stepped out, crossed the street and spoke to someone outside the bicycle shop. Hanifa gasped.

"What's the matter, Hanifa? Who are you looking at?"

"No one, Madame. I'm not looking at anyone."

"You certainly are. It's not that man in the tan suit, is it? Is it? Hanifa, look at me."

"No, no, it's not him. I swear it's not him."

Catherine shifted the car into gear and navigated through the crowd and out onto the avenue. She spoke not another word to Hanifa on the way home. She didn't have to. She'd found out what she wanted to know, for she recognized the man whose appearance had struck terror in her maid. It was Brahim Zerkaoui, the art dealer who only a week before had been at the Residence with Catherine's new painting.

A bloody and tattered Corporal Ronald Corker, USMC, woke up sore and hungry. His head ached, his shoulder felt as if it had been wrenched out of its socket and his wrist was so swollen he could hardly move his hand. He was filthy, and with his shirt torn up the back and his pants a mess he knew there would be no chance of walking away without being noticed.

He had no memory of how he had gotten into the clump of bushes where he had been sleeping. It must have been just before dawn, because he did remember running in the darkness and then seeing the sky get lighter and realizing he would have to hide somewhere or be caught. He must have simply fallen there in exhaustion.

He crawled to an opening in the bushes and rose to his feet. Peering through the foliage, he saw what looked like a vacant lot in a residential area, with walls and high hedges around the houses whose roofs and second stories he could see. The sun wasn't overhead; so it must have been either mid-morning or mid-afternoon.

Maybe if he could crawl through one of the hedges he could find a kitchen and get something to drink, and a bite to eat. He guessed he should've stayed in the medina. But the medina was full of rats, and there were too many people who would spot him. That was it. That was why he'd left the medina and come out this way, to get where nobody would spot him.

Like hell they wouldn't. By now everybody must know he'd hit Fatima—maybe even killed her. They'd all be after him. Sgt. Hernandez had told him many times to stay out of trouble downtown because Marines weren't protected like diplomats. The Sharkies could jail you, and there wasn't nobody crazy enough to want to see the inside of a Sharkie jail.

But he didn't do it on purpose. Honest to God, he loved her. He was gonna marry her and take her back to his family in the States. But she had to screw around on him and get him mad. After all he'd told her and after everything he'd done for her, there she was letting this Sharkie love her up, right out in public.

Suddenly he realized he was crying. The tears were running down his cheeks, and when he wiped his face he saw it was a smear of blood and grime. Some way he'd have to get washed up too.

He was looking for a brook or a water faucet when he spotted a familiar street. Jeez, I know where I am, he said to himself. I've been here before. But he didn't want to ring the bell because you'd never know how they might react. Maybe if he could get through the hedge near the kitchen they might let him wash up and give him something to eat. Then he could decide whether he should turn himself in at the Marine House or catch a boat or a plane off the island, or maybe just hide here if they'd let him.

He felt his way along the edge of the bushes. The hedge must have been eight feet high, and there was chicken wire running along it. Some chance of finding a hole through that stuff.

But he did find a hole, and in a few seconds he was under the hedge and inside. He could feel a long scratch down his back, but it didn't matter now because he was safe.

He was behind a piece of lawn furniture, and when he looked out he saw this babe on a lawn chair in shorts and a halter, stretched out in the sun.

It's her! he thought. What a piece of ass!

Then his foot hit something, and she jumped up.

"Who's that?"

He could see she was scared. "It's only me, ma'am. Corker."

"Corker?"

"You know, one of the Marines."

She came over to him in her shorts, with her legs and her arms all greased up, with a big hat and dark glasses. "What's the matter with you, kid? You're all covered with dirt. And you're bleeding."

Now he was scared. "I just need something to eat and drink, Mrs. Cross. Then I'll get out, I promise you."

"Don't he silly. You look exhausted."

"I'm in trouble, ma'am. The Sharkies are after me. I think I killed my girl."

She came up to him and took him by the wrist and pulled him toward the house. He winced with pain. He noticed she had alcohol on her breath.

"You're coming in the house to get cleaned up," she said. "Then we'll get you clean clothes and something to eat. As for your girl, they said she'll be OK. Now keep quiet so the cook won't hear you."

He started to cry. He couldn't help it. She was alive! Fatima was gonna be OK!

She had him take off his shoes and walk barefoot around the rug and up the stairs. His feet were as dirty as his hands. But then she showed him the bathroom, and a minute later there he was, under a cool shower with a big bar of soap, watching the dirt and the blood go down the drain.

"When you're ready, here are some clothes," he heard her say.

Then he was clean and dry and sitting on a lawn chair on her upstairs balcony sipping a coke and eating a sandwich. She was in the other chair, and she had a drink too, but it was a clear one. Boy, was she a dish! She was taller than he was with her sandals on, and she was built big in the ass, the way he liked them. Her legs and her chest and her face were all pink under the grease. The guys wouldn't believe him when he told them about it.

"So you're Corker," she said. "What's your first name, honey?"

"Ronald, ma'am."

"Ronald. You've made a lot of trouble for people, you know that?"

"Yes, ma'am, I'm afraid so. But I didn't mean to."

"How old are you, Ronald?"

"Nineteen and a half, ma'am. I'll be twenty in December."

"You don't have to call me ma'am. My name's Marilyn."

That made him nervous. "Yes, ma'am. But maybe I oughta call you Mrs. Cross."

"Don't be silly. I like Marilyn better."

He tried to change the subject. "What time is it?"

"About three-thirty. Why?"

"I was just thinking, if Fatima ain't dead, then maybe things aren't as bad as I thought. Maybe I could go back to the Marine House and turn myself in."

"Why didn't you do that in the first place, honey?"

"I guess I was scared, is all. But now maybe it's OK to go back. I'm AWOL, but I ain't no deserter."

"You'll have to make up you're own mind on that, Ron. Now why don't you sit here for a minute while I go change? That sun is hot."

She finished her drink and went into the bedroom. He watched her go. Man, look at that ass. Old Cross must go ape over that. Fatima's ass was all right, but it was nothing like that. He wished he could see Fatima again. Boy, would he have a few words to say to her. She wouldn't fool around on him again, not Ron Corker. He kinda wished she was here, though. Looking at Mrs. Cross made him horny, and Fatima sure knew how to take care of that.

"There, that feels better," he heard her say.

She hadn't changed her clothes at all. All she'd done was wipe the cream off and put on a shiny dressing gown with cord pulled tight so you could see how thin her waist was and how her big butt spread out below it, rolling like a boat in the water when she walked. She'd fixed her hair too and put on makeup. But he could still smell the alcohol, and darned if she didn't have another drink in her hand.

She went to the balcony and then turned and smiled. "Poor kid, you must be tired. You should lie down and take a nap."

"No, ma'am, I'm fine," he said. "I was sleepin' in the bushes."

She didn't seem to hear him. "We've got four bedrooms in this house, so you've got your choice of beds."

"Gee, honest, I'm not tired, Mrs. Cross."

"Marilyn."

" ...Marilyn."

"Let me show you."

She took him into her bedroom. The bed was king-size. "This is where I sleep," she said. "And over there is the guest room, with the twin beds. The other rooms aren't made up."

She went to one of the twin beds and pulled back the slip cover. "It isn't made up either. Well, back in here then."

Back in the master bedroom, she finished her drink and set the glass on the dresser. She took a pack of cigarettes.

"Smoke? "

He shook his head.

"Do you mind?"

She handed him the lighter and held his hand to steady it and pushed the cigarette into the flame. Then she inhaled and blew smoke in his face.

He coughed. " Hey, that's no fair."

She laughed and put the cigarette down. She was a little unsteady, but she walked up to him and wrinkled her nose at him.

"I'll bet Ronnie has never smoked a whole cigarette in his life."

"Sure I have. I just never got the habit."

"I wish you didn't have that shirt on," she said. "I don't like it on you."

"Gee, you gave it to me. I seen it on Mr. Cross."

"Maybe that's why I don't like it. Take it off, and I'll give you another one."

He took the shirt off. The bruises and cuts on his shoulders made him wince, especially when she ran her fingers over them. "You're a nice boy, Ronnie," she said. "You deserve something nice."

He couldn't believe she'd do it, not with him alone there in her bedroom and her with her hands on the belt of her dressing gown, standing right there in front of the bed and smiling at him.

But then she did do it, and he still couldn't believe it. She undid the belt, and the dressing gown just opened by itself and fell on the floor, and there she was, Mrs. Cross the wife of Mr. Lou Cross the Second Secretary and Chief of Administration standing there right in front of him bare-ass naked.

"Mrs. Cross ..."

She wrinkled her nose at him and came right up and put her arms around his shoulders.

"Call me Marilyn, Ron honey. And be real good to me, you hear?"

He didn't know how he got downstairs and out of that house. But he did remember the old guard's face as he ran past him and out the gate in his undershirt, with Cross's shirt in his hand, heading toward the Marine House. He'd turn himself in and take his punishment. Anything they wanted to do to him was okay, but that was one thing they couldn't hang on him because he didn't do it even though she wanted him to. That's right, she actually wanted him, Ron Corker, to screw her. Honest, guys, you don't hafta believe me, but I coulda screwed her. I coulda screwed Mrs. Lou Cross, the wife of the Second Secretary and Chief of Administration!

By day's end Potter's worries were directed toward security. Boyle had recommended safety doors and secure areas inside the Embassy, including the top floor vault, where the entire staff could hole up in the event of an attack. But Potter had asked, " What if they torch the building? What do we do then—fry?"

Boyle's only answer was that the vault was where the communications equipment was, and besides, it could be made fairly comfortable in the event of a siege. Barring a fire, of course.

But Potter favored safety in dispersion and distance from

the Embassy. If a mob formed in front of the building, he wanted as few people inside as possible and a way out for the rest.

"Mr. Ambassador," Boyle had said, "my job is to see that you personally get the best protection I can give you. You're the President's man here, and the Marines are here to protect you first. The rest of the embassy comes afterwards."

But Potter assumed an assassin bent on killing an American ambassador would find a way to do so. "You can avoid narrow, crowded streets and vary your time and route," he'd told Boyle, "but there are limits. There comes a time when you just have to trust to whatever you believe in."

Besides, his infantry training at Fort Benning OCS had taught him to think about his men. They might not be targeted individually, but they were as vulnerable as he was--the Marines especially, since they had no diplomatic immunity. And he didn't want any of their names inscribed on that plaque in the Diplomatic Lobby at the State Department.

Catherine, of course, didn't agree. "You, darling, are the President's personal representative. You're the one accredited to this government, and your life comes first."

He'd nodded when she'd said it, but the notion went against not only his military training but his estimate of his own worth.

And now Lou Cross was here with his report on security at the Cultural Center. He motioned Cross to one of the big leather chairs and took a seat opposite him, expecting him to heap his criticism on Pascal's back.

Instead, he got a detailed account of measures Cross had taken since that morning.

"So you're putting mylar on the windows and pushing books to the back of the shelves," he said when Cross had finished. "You know, Lou, that may satisfy Dan Boyle and help against hidden explosives. But I still want to know how that forged memcon got into Pete Pascal's in-basket. What did Marilyn have to say about that, or haven't you gotten around to asking her?"

Cross was ready with an answer. "As a matter of fact, I haven't been able to. She was out when I tried to call. But I'll certainly ask her tonight."

"In any case, you're saying someone with a key could lock himself in the outside toilet, enter Pascal's office through that door, deposit the memcon and retrace his steps. Right?"

"Yes, sir, if he had the right key."

"Who does have the right key?"

"I do, locked in my office with all the other keys. No one has access to them but the Duty Officer, Sgt. Hernandez and myself."

"When are they taken out?"

"Only for inspections. The Marines take them with them every night and lock them up when they get back."

"Which means every officer and Marine has had access to them at one time or another. Is that door on the Marines' list to be checked every night?"

Cross had a ready answer. "No, sir, but even if they checked it every night, Pascal could be letting in anyone he wants to after hours and letting them out the same way."

Potter mulled this over. "And Pete's not here today to tell us whether he does or not. Then we've got to ask ourselves whom he might be letting into his office after duty hours, and why."

He watched Cross freeze. He'd turned his explanation against him, and he thought he could detect sweat on his brow.

"Unless, of course," he added casually, "he let the person in not knowing he–or she–had something to place in his in-basket when he wasn't looking."

Cross seemed to recoil. His lips moved, but no sound came out. Potter remained silent, his eyes not leaving Cross's.

"I wonder..." he mused. Then, his brow clearing, he said, "Well, it's obvious we can't solve the mystery today. When Pete gets back, I'll put the question to him. Perhaps we'll have the answer before our security officer gets here, after all. Thanks, Lou. At least you're cleaning up the Cultural Center. I'm glad of that."

Potter watched him leave and then sat looking out the window, past the white rooftops and the minaret toward the cranes in the port and the sea beyond. Well now, he said to himself, why should Lou be so uncomfortable at the possibility of someone entering Pete's office through a locked door? Why indeed, unless that someone was Marilyn?

Poor Lou, he concluded. This is one he may not be able to ignore. And for that matter, I may not be able to either.

Marilyn Cross stood on the upstairs balcony with her robe pulled together in front, looking out over the hedge at Corker running up the street and laughing lightly to herself.

Scared him off, that's what I did. Twice his age, and I scared him off. Maybe I reminded him of his mother.

She looked down onto the lawn where Ali was on his knees in the roses and the old man was at the gate in his jellaba. Everything was the same again. The excitement was over, and she was alone.

She reentered the bedroom and stood in front of the full-length mirror, letting the dressing gown fall from her shoulders. Not bad, she thought, just like a photo negative—white where there ought to be color and red where the skin should be white. A new personality, a positive instead of a negative. A new woman maybe. She wondered it would be like to be different from what she was.

She put on the dressing gown again and poured herself another drink. Good thing she kept a supply here so she wouldn't have to go downstairs where the cook might see her.

She was finished with Zerkaoui, but she still had Pete, except he'd gone off without telling her. She'd fix him, though. She wouldn't go to the Center tonight. Let Marge find another teacher. If she wanted to blame someone, she could blame Pete.

She set down her drink and made her way to the telephone.

"Marge? Marilyn. I won't be able to make it tonight...I've

got a headache...Well, I'm sorry. I didn't plan to have one...Then why don't you cancel the class?...Then teach it yourself...Look, I'll be in Monday as usual...That's right. Have a lovely weekend."

Damn Marge, anyhow. After I go to the trouble of telling her I'm not coming, she tries to give me a hard time. Well, that's my good deed for today, whether she likes it or not. That and giving the kid a bath and a shirt and something to eat. As a matter of fact, she'd done nothing but good deeds today. For that she deserved a reward.

She walked very tall and straight across the living room and slid open the glass door to the terrace. Ali was still on his knees, raking the dirt around the roses. He was in the white but torn undershirt he'd washed that morning, though it was soaked in sweat now. He wore a skullcap on his bald head to protect it from the sun, but his skin was almost black anyway. He had Arab features, but he was darker than Pete.

"Ali, come here," she called.

He jumped to his feet and scampered over to her with that idiot grin on his face.

She motioned him into the house, using the gesture she had learned here instead of wiggling her finger, which was considered obscene in Sharqiya. He didn't speak French either. Too bad. You'd think a man with six kids would learn a trade instead of working as a gardener, but not in this country.

He left his sandals at the door as if entering a mosque. It was Friday, wasn't it? She led him upstairs and into her room, where she indicated the rolldown shutter outside her window. "You fix, Ali."

She made a cranking movement with her hands. He nodded brightly, detached and began to crank the handle. The shutter began to descend, blocking out the daylight. She turned on the lights and closed the bedroom door, watching his shiny shoulders ripple as he worked the handle.

The shutter was down now. Ali replaced the handle and turned toward her, hoping no doubt for a tip.

She watched the eager smile fade as his brow darkened.

It was comic to watch, but to reassure him she was smiling, with the friendliest smile she knew how to give, leaning back against the dresser with her gown wide open and a ten-dinar note between her fingers, offering him peaches and cream.

She dropped the gown and walked around the bed to pull back the covers. She smiled again.

His face registered surprise, but his body stiffened and his eyes hardened as if she'd slapped his face.

"No, Madame," he said. "I no want."

"Sure you do, Ali," she smiled. "I won't tell."

But he shook his head vigorously. "No, Madame. Ali only do gardens, no want trouble."

And with a curling of his lip in fundamentalist outrage at this attempt by a drunken infidel woman to lead him astray on his day of prayer, he strode past her and out the door.

5

It started to rain at five o'clock, and by the time the Embassy closed at five-thirty it was coming down in sheets. For those who made the traditional TGIF stop at the Marine House next door, there was no choice but to get wet.

TGIF was an important occasion for Charlie Agar . He closed down his circuits at five, and the Marine House bar was his next stop. Friday was special because that was when everybody turned up—Marines, their girls, other outsiders as well as Embassy employees. There were no security checks as such, but all were warned not to discuss Embassy business.

Charlie wasn't a talker, though he handled more words than all the rest of the Embassy combined. He would buy a beer, shoot pool with one of the Marines and then retire to the last bar stool and observe what for him was the comedy or the drama of life at Amemb Al-Bida.

A Marine gave him a towel to dry his head, and the game of pool kept his blood circulating until his shirt dried. Then, plastering his few strands of blond hair laterally across his skull, he withdrew to his observation perch.

The same half-dozen Marines were there with their girls and a few hangers-on from the European and Sharqiyan communities. One or two of the officers usually turned up, and when they did the evening news took on a new dimension. In the absence of an American TV network news program, it kept him up on local events, especially those nuggets that didn't go out in the cable traffic.

Beyond that, Charlie's life was one of fantasy in the midst of routine. He read paperbacks by the dozen, and hidden under the leg of his jeans he kept a long, slender knife strapped to his calf. He had never used the knife and had never thought out how he might use it in case of need. But he loved the feel of it, and he stroked it through his jeans as a matter of habit.

He was stroking it now as he sat on his bar stool and heard the first order of business discussed.

The subject in everyone's mind, if not on their lips, was

the disappearance of Corker. Drew, who had been with him at the time of the brawl, asked Sgt. Hernandez what was new "on our boy."

"Not a word. Negative," said the Sergeant.

"Well, he's just a kid with a temper and no brains. And that haybag of his was nothin' but an old hoor anyhow. He's better off without her."

"He won't want her no more after he sees what he done to her face," said Corporal Ricci.

"Where do you think he went?" Agar asked in a low voice, glancing around on the lookout for unauthorized listeners. "Was he shackin' up with her in town?"

"Hell, no," said Drew, "and he'd be crazy to go there. Her family'd turn him over to the cops, if they didn't kill him first."

"They catch him, he's in real trouble," Sgt. Hernandez said from behind the bar. "You guys better believe it. You screw up like him, they ain't nothin' Uncle Sam can do to help you."

Lou Cross had just arrived. He looked around the room and spoke in lowered tones.

"Men, this is a public place. You've got Sharqiyans and French and I don't know what else in this room right now. So I don't want to hear any more talk about the guy. It'll only make matters worse. Understand?"

"Mr. Cross is right," Hernandez said. "Did you guys hear him?"

So that ended the story of Ron Corker, Agar thought. It was like switching channels on TV, except that the program on the new channel didn't interest him. He knew Cross was right. His last outgoing of the day was a message from the Ambassador telling how he'd got called into the Ministry to get his ass chewed out. The Sharkies were using Corker to make trouble for Uncle Sam, but of course Charlie mentioned this to nobody. When he was outside the vault, he always said, he was a receiver, not a transmitter.

At that moment Drew spotted Commander Warnecke entering. He winked at Hernandez, and the Marines went on their best behavior. As Defense Attaché Warnecke had no authority over them, but he was the equivalent of a lieutenant colonel, and they respected that.

He joined them at the bar and began talking about the weather, loudly enough for all to hear.

"If it clears up during the night, I'm taking the family out to Ida's beach house for the weekend," he said.

"Isn't that pretty isolated?" Cross asked.

"That's just what I want, a quiet weekend with sunshine and skin-diving, and only two hours drive from here."

Charlie listened with mild interest, noting how Warnecke could put an innocent face on sensitive matters. He remembered the Ambassador's morning cable on plans to scout the coast, and Warnecke's own report. Maybe Monday morning the Commander would have something interesting to send out.

Five minutes later the door slammed open and a drenched Pete Pascal appeared, his hair and beard glistening with rain. His shoes squished, and the raincoat over his shoulders had done nothing to keep the water off his bare legs and T-shirt.

"You look like you've been in for a swim," Cross said, eyeing the man with hostility who not only disobeyed regulations but, worse, helped himself to another officer's wife.

"I feel like it. Gimme a shot of bourbon, will you, Hernandez?"

"Where've you been?" asked Cross as if he didn't know.

"Oh, on the north coast and up on the mountain taking pictures for an exhibit. Why?"

"You could have asked the Ambassador's permission."

"What for? It's part of my job."

"Because I was looking for you. I went over to the Center to see if you'd followed the RSO's recommendations, especially with Boyle coming in, and I see you haven't."

Pascal frowned. "Why didn't you tell me? I'm not clairvoyant."

"No, but you've got a responsibility to keep the Ambassador informed of your whereabouts. So take it from there."

"What kind of pictures were you taking?" Warnecke asked mildly as Cross left.

Pascal relaxed, sensing an appreciative audience.

"Look, I've got this guy who is one of the greatest primitive painters I know. He paints typical, authentic scenes as good as any I've ever seen. In the States no one would bother; they'd take a snapshot. But this guy's eye is his lens, and a piece of cardboard out of the city dump is his film. I wanted to take photos of the background to display next to the paintings to show what an eye the man has."

"Didn't the rain cramp your style?"

"Not too much. I got almost all my pictures before it clouded up. You see, I was going to spend the night at Ida Gant's beach house and take one last shot of the cove tomorrow morning. But they not only screwed up my picture; they broke into her house, and I had to drive all the way back here in the rain in an open jeep."

"What? Who's 'they', and what did they do?"

Pascal drew a long breath. "A perfect shot of the cove, and these two boats had to come right into the picture. One of them parked there in the cove. I was waiting for them to move out so I could take the shot I wanted. But instead they stayed right there."

"What kind of boats were they?" asked Warnecke, keeping his voice lowered.

"How should I know? Some kind of naval craft."

"I'd like to see your photos of them."

"I tell you I didn't take any. They ruined the composition, and I wasn't about to waste my film."

Warnecke's jaw tightened. "Then what happened?"

"They broke into the house."

"Into Ida Gant's house? You saw them do it?"

"I sure did. I took the jeep and drove up to Ras el-Kebir and took a couple of pictures there and came back, hoping they'd be gone. But they were still there, and it was raining. So I drove home, and tomorrow I've got to give Ida her key back and tell her what happened."

Warnecke was fidgeting with rage. He looked over his shoulder to make sure there was no one within earshot but Agar. Then he pulled Pascal up to him and lowered his voice.

"Now let's get this straight. I want to know what kind of boats they were and who was in them."

Pascal frowned. He had just downed his second bourbon.

"How the hell should I know? I'm not an expert on boats. I was in the Army. If you want to know about booby traps, I'll tell you. But I don't suppose the Navy ever ran into them."

Warnecke spoke with great care.

"Pete, I want to know who these people were. Were they Sharqiyans or Europeans?"

"They had to be Sharqiyans. They were in uniform, and the boats were Sharqiyan."

"You're sure this was the Sharqiyan Navy?"

"Who else's navy would it be? The boats had numbers on them."

"Do you remember what the numbers were?"

"No. How could I?"

"And you didn't take any pictures?"

"Of course not. I told you why."

Warnecke' s eyes narrowed. He spoke very evenly.

"Didn't you think the Ambassador might be interested?"

Pascal bridled. He downed his third bourbon.

"I'll tell you why I didn't take pictures for you, Commander. Because I'm not one of your goddamned spies."

Warnecke flushed. "Pete, we all work for the same uncle."

"My work is cultural. I don't work for the military. I served my time in Nam, Commander."

Warnecke pulled back and pretended to relax on his bar stool. He took a swallow of beer and smiled patiently.

"OK, we all served our time. But we're still on Uncle Sam's payroll, both of us. Now why don't you let me develop the pictures you did take, and then let's have a good long talk about what you saw today. What do you say?"

Pascal was drunk now. He set his glass down carefully

on the bar, picked up the camera and the attache case and with narrowed eyes looked Warnecke straight in the face.

"What do I say? I say, 'Fuck you, Commander.' "

With that, he slid off his bar stool and weaved his way out of the room.

Hernandez, who had been wiping a glass, stopped and followed him with his eyes but said nothing. Charlie Agar kept silent.

"OK, fella," Warnecke shrugged. "We'll see."

He rotated on the bar stool and set down his empty glass, motioning for a refill. "So what else is new?" he asked Hernandez.

"Not much, sir," mumbled the sergeant, visibly embarrassed at the insult to an officer. "Our man's still missing."

"Your man's the least of our troubles," Warnecke said. "He should stay missing." He stood up and moved to the balcony to look out. "What do you know?" he called back. "The rain's stopped. I guess I'll be able to take the family out tomorrow, after all. Yep," he said for all to hear, "there's a hotel in that village off to the east. Guess we'll get a couple of rooms there and do our skin-diving in that cove. Well, got to get back home."

The telephone rang before he could leave. Hernandez took it. "No shit?" he said. He motioned Warnecke back to the bar, leaned across and whispered, "Corker just turned himself in."

Warnecke snorted. "So every cloud does have a silver lining. I guess I'll just mosey over and have a look-see. Don't go away, Sgt. Hernandez. You may be hearing from me."

Charlie Agar had not budged from the last bar stool. He was thinking about what he had just witnessed and smiling with quiet satisfaction. Not that he would have anywhere else to go, but this was one TGIF he was sure glad he hadn't missed. No doubt about it. It was the only way to keep up with what really went on at the Embassy.

6

Now, with three shots of bourbon in him, Pascal returned to his top-floor apartment a few blocks from the Cultural Center. He no longer felt the dampness of his clothing, only the sense of outrage that Uncle Sam's official spy in Sharqiya would try to use him.

Well, he hadn't succeeded. The shots in his camera were his to use the way he wanted to use them: to bring people closer together by showing Sharqiyans that Americans cared about their arts and their country, not for purposes of spying on Sharqiyan military defenses.

Inside his darkroom he went to work. If he could stay on his feet until the film was developed, he could grab a bite while the negatives dried and then start printing the enlargements. Tomorrow he would take everything to the Center and set up the exhibit. The posters would be back from the printer's. He could start distributing them immediately.

He looked in the refrigerator and saw there was nothing to eat, not even fruit. Damn that maid. She was supposed to do his shopping for him after she cleaned his apartment. She didn't have to cook. All he asked was that she keep the place stocked, for which he paid her well.

Then he noticed she hadn't been in at all. Last night's dishes were still in the sink. That was funny, because she never missed a day. Brahim Zerkaoui had found her for him, and she was a jewel. Well, so be it. It was eight o'clock and the rain had stopped. He could eat at the sidewalk restaurant downstairs and watch the world, such as it was in Al-Bida, go by.

He chose the châteaubriand, string beans, with good French bread and a carafe of red wine. There were some aspects of French colonialism that no one should complain about.

He was feeling better already. The fresh evening air was bracing, and the sight and odors of food had awakened his appetite. The effects of the bourbon had worn off, and the tension he had built up while driving was melting away. He didn't remember feeling this good on a Friday evening in months. Was it the TGIF? No, it was a Friday evening without Marilyn!

He laughed aloud. Usually he got home so pooped he went to bed or just sat around, all so she could be at her best in the classroom.

He noticed a girl just sitting down at a table by the wall. Any other Friday he wouldn't even have noticed her, but now...

She had noticed him too. She was sitting with another girl, and they were both in Western dress though both looked like the local product: long, straight black hair and ivory skin, and not too fat either. Probably hookers, and high class ones or they wouldn't be eating in a place like this.

He raised his wine glass to her. She turned her head away haughtily, but a smile played on her lips. For a few minutes she was careful not to look at him, but during dessert he had a chance to do it again. He held up his coffee cup and pointed to it. She shook her head, frowning in the direction of her companion. Pascal couldn't tell what the other one looked like, but he rose as if to join them. When she glared and shook her head, he sank back in puzzlement.

Waiting, he read a newspaper and watched them finish their meal and pay their bill. Then they both rose, and Pascal saw that the other was an adolescent. So that was it. Mama was raising her daughter to be an honest woman, and so she had to be on her best behavior. Well, better luck next time. He watched them hail a taxi.

The taxi drew up, the door opened and closed and he heard it chug away. Too bad. He'd have to keep that one on file.

He had just settled down to his paper, however, when he looked up once more and saw the woman standing alone on the sidewalk, looking in his direction.

Pete Pascal, man of action. He left an adequate banknote on the table behind him and walked up to her on the sidewalk. She frowned slightly and turned away, walking to a corner where the patrons of the restaurant couldn't see them. Then she turned to him with a hint of a smile on her lips.

"My name is Ayeesha," she said in good French. But for Pete Pascal she was a woman of mystery out of the Arabian Nights. Five minutes later she stood beside him on the balcony of his apartment looking out over the rooftops of Baghdad. It wasn't quite like that, he admitted, and Al-Bida wasn't Baghdad either. But beggars couldn't he choosers, and he needed a change from the usual Friday night routine with Marilyn.

Ayeesha was that. As dark as Marilyn was blond, she had a finesse that Marilyn lacked, and there was not a trace of alcohol on her breath. Even now, she refused all but orange soda. She was interested in his books and his stereo and was curious to know what lay behind the darkroom door.

"My secret collection of women," he whispered. He opened the door to check the negatives, then turned on the light and showed her a drawerful of glossy prints of nudes he had taken, among them several of Marilyn Cross. They were not badly done, even those where Marilyn leered out at you from an alcoholic haze, posing on the divan in his office.

"You like?" he asked. She shrugged and pouted. "I know they're not as beautiful as you," he said. She squeezed his hand. "I take pictures of you, yes?" he pursued, pointing to his camera. She smiled. "If you like."

After the picture-taking they made love, and after that he went to the kitchen to make coffee. When he returned, she was dressed and ready to leave.

"I go home to my niece," she said, finishing her coffee.

"I'll bet your niece isn't used to having Auntie send her home alone," he lied, offering her a bill from his wallet.

She refused it. "I no come for business," she said. But she allowed him to place the bill in the pocket of her jacket nevertheless.

Oh, baby, what an act! And what a waste of time!

He returned to the darkroom, really tired now, and finished his work. He looked at the camera and thought of Ayeesha. Man, with that black hair and white skin, the pictures should he gorgeous. Without looking at it, he opened the camera to remove the film for development later. He pulled the spool handle and tapped the front to let the roll drop into his hand. Nothing happened. He looked down at the open camera. There was no film in it. But there had to be; he'd felt it when he'd advanced the frames. He looked on the floor. It wasn't possible.

A thought occurred to him. He opened the drawer where the nude photos were kept. The box seemed untouched, and yet when he opened it he could see that the stack of prints was not as thick as it had been. He flipped through the pictures frantically, then flipped through them again, then counted them twice.

There was no doubt about it. The nude photos of Marilyn Cross were missing.

Lou Cross had barely reached home when the walkie-talkie in the den began to make sounds. Lou took the emergency radio seriously. It was his only means of contact with the Embassy when the phones were out, which happened whenever it rained in this season. Each American at the Embassy had one at home, usually in his bedroom. But Lou took pains to keep his within earshot wherever he happened to be. Tonight he was unusually careful because he was duty officer and because of the special circumstances.

"Three-zero-two," the voice called. "This is control calling three-zero-two. Can you hear me?"

Marilyn was playing a Schubert Impromptu. Her fingers were stumbling repeatedly in the arpeggio, forcing her to go over the phrase again and again. She paid no attention to the sounds coming from the radio.

"I hear you loud and clear," Cross called into the instrument, recognizing the voice of the Marine on duty. "Over."

Warnecke's voice came on. "Sorry to bother you, three-zero-two, but I think you'd better come in again. We've got something to show you. Over."

Lou was tired, but duty called. "I'm on my way. Over and out."

Marilyn had just completed the passage almost without mistakes and had gone on to the next part.

"I've got to go back to the office," he said. "Do you mind?"

"Go ahead." She said it without stopping, then missed a note and swore as she returned to the previous page.

"You're sure you don't mind?"

"Didn't I say so?"

"You didn't teach tonight."

"In this rain?"

"The rain has stopped. Don't you always teach Fridays?"

"Not when I don't feel like it."

He hesitated. "I'll be back as soon as I can."

"Don't hurry." She had stumbled again and was repeating more loudly and insistently.

Cross gave up and left. At the Embassy he found Warnecke and Hernandez with the Marine on duty. "Corker turned himself in," Warnecke said. "Sorry I couldn't tell you on the phone, but the Sharkies are after him, and they could be listening in."

"I'm glad you called," Cross said grimly. "Where is he?"

"We've got him at the Marine House getting a shower and dry clothes."

"Did you call the Ambassador?"

"He's out to dinner."

"Then I'll call him on the beeper." Cross was glad he would be the one to inform the boss.

"Is it that important?"

"It was important enough to get him chewed out at the Ministry this afternoon. He'll want to know."

"Sir, he won't turn Corker over to the Sharkies, will he?" Hernandez asked.

"Probably not. But we have to get his OK to keep him here. In the meantime, let's hear what Corker has to say for himself."

At the Marine House next door, Corker was just getting

into dry clothes from the dresser in his room. At the sight of Lou Cross he froze to attention.

"Take it easy, Corker. I'm not going to eat you. I just want to ask you some questions."

"Yes, sir," said Corker, as stiff as before.

"Did they tell you what you did to that girl?"

"Yes, sir. But I didn't mean to hit her hard."

"But you did. You broke her jaw, and you're in beaucoup trouble on account of it. You know that, don't you?"

"Yes, sir. I'm sorry about what happened."

"Where've you been hiding out?"

"I tried to sleep in the medina, sir, but the rats were so bad I had to get out. I just sorta wandered around till I found some bushes to sleep in."

"Where was that?"

"On the edge of town, sir, where the big houses are."

"You mean where I live?'

"Yes, sir."

"Did anyone spot you?"

"I don't think so, sir."

"Did you see anyone you knew?"

"No, sir. I was just waitin' for a chance to turn myself in."

"And you walked all the way back here?"

"I guess I ran, mostly, sir."

"Well, you're wanted by the police, Corker. We're going to hide you somewhere till we decide what to do with you." He turned to Warnecke. "Got any ideas?"

"We can't leave him here. He may have been seen, and the police may come asking. How about the vault?"

"Perfect. There's a john and a refrigerator. We can fix up a cot and bring food in when no one else is in the building, at least until the Ambassador decides what to do with him. You understand that, Corker, don't you?"

"Yes, sir. I guess I'm better off locked up. I done enough damage already."

"Then get your things together. I want this place cleaned up so the maid won't know you've come back."

When Corker was ready, Cross took a last look around. At the sight of a shirt, trousers and underwear among the dirty laundry, he stopped.

"What's this?"

"That's what he showed up in," Warnecke said. "Soaked to the skin."

"Where did you get these clothes, Corker?"

"I dunno, sir. That's what I was wearing all day."

"This shirt too?"

"Yes, sir."

"You didn't by any chance pick these clothes up this afternoon at one of the houses out there?"

"No, sir. Honest, that's what I was wearing all day."

Cross was suddenly nonchalant. "That's all right, Corker. It'll be easy to check where you got them. Leave them here."

Back at the Embassy, Cross called the Ambassador via his beeper. "The missing package has turned up, sir. I think we'd better put it away for safe keeping."

"Good man, Lou. That's one less worry."

Cross returned home glowing in the Ambassador's praise but with his suspicions aroused on another score. Marilyn was reading in bed.

"The Marine turned himself in," he said casually.

"What Marine?"

"Corker, the one that went AWOL last night. You know about him."

And they called you in just for that?"

"You bet they did. It was important. They needed me to tell them what to do with him. And by the way, he was wearing a shirt and pants that looked a lot like mine."

"So?"

"So I'm asking you if he was here today."

"I would have told you, wouldn't I?"

He felt relief. She rarely lied any more. She didn't seem to care.

"By the way," he said, changing the subject, "Ida Gant's beach house was broken into."

"How do you know that?"

"Warnecke said Pascal told him. He saw the whole thing."

Marilyn looked up from her book. "Is Pete back?"

"He was at TGIF. He couldn't very well stay at Ida's if it was occupied by burglars, could he?"

"What time did you see him?"

"Just before six. We didn't stay. He was soaking wet."

"Good. Maybe he'll catch pneumonia."

He looked at her. "What have you got against him?"

"Not a thing." She returned to her book.

He yawned. "It's been a long day. I guess I'll turn in."

He pulled back the bedcovers, looked at the side of the bed for a moment and said, "How come you changed the sheets? It's only Friday."

"I just felt like it," she said without looking up. "There was a tear on my side. Do I have to explain?"

He sat on the bed facing away from her. "Honey, I want to ask you something." She made no response. "You won't get mad if I ask you a question, will you?"

"How do I know? Ask it."

"Well, you know... I just hope what happened at our last post...you know...isn't going to happen here."

He felt her eyes on his back. "Is that a question?"

"You know what I mean, honey, why we got sent here in the first place when I tried to extend where we were."

"So being in this dump is my fault? Is that it?"

"Maybe not entirely. But you've got to admit we left kind of under a cloud. And this place is so small everybody knows everything you do. You can't get away with things here."

"And so you want me to spend my time pushing cookies with Her Ladyship?"

"It wouldn't hurt once in a while."

"You make me laugh. Say, why don't you and she have a hot love affair? It'd do wonders for your rating."

"Cut it out, honey. Don't say things like that."

"You started it. You brought up our last post."

"OK, I'm sorry." Silence, then, "Honey, it's Friday."

"So?"

"Don't you remember? We always did it on Friday nights."

She made him wait, then, "I don't feel like it tonight."

"You always used to."

"Well, tonight I don't."

"OK, OK. I just thought you might want to."

He turned out his light and lay flat on his back while she continued reading. When she finally finished her chapter and switched off her light and turned over onto her side with her back to him, he still lay awake, though now his eyes were wide open in the darkness. After a few minutes he heard her regular breathing, and this relieved him because now he could say to himself over and over again, "But not with just anyone. With Pascal was bad enough, but not with a goddamned Marine."

Day Three
Saturday, May 5

1

The Warnecke Family—ranch wagon, ice chest, beach balls, flippers, masks, snorkel, frisbee and all—pulled out of the yard of the Defense Attache's residence at six a.m., just as the tropical dawn was breaking. The wife, the kids, the dog, even the driver himself seemed no more than an escort for the huge shipment of materiel being transported from the south coast to the north coast of the island of Sharqiya. But Jack Warnecke was used to this mode of travel. His caravans had navigated the highways of Europe, the Middle East, Korea and Japan, and the twisting mountain roads of Sharqiya were not about to daunt him—or his brood.

They were well up on the mountain before the full warmth of the sun hit them, and except for those pockets where no breezes off the sea could penetrate they were comfortable in the big car, with its air-conditioning on.

When they reached the top of the pass opening onto the cove where Ida's beach house stood, he stopped in the old French parking area with its weathered *table d'orientation* and ostentatiously had everyone get out and stretch. He even handed his camera, with telephoto lens attached, to his elder son Mike, age twelve, and told him to take pictures of the cove and beyond. The boy snapped away gleefully while younger son Steve lined the family up against the orientation table for an instant family shot. Then, after a good look up and down the coast, they all piled back into the car and began the descent.

Warnecke's mind had retained an image as sharp as any photo. He had seen a Soviet-built P-6 patrol craft in the cove, anchored to remain out of sight to any vessel approaching from the sea and yet ready to get under way at a moment's notice. He had also seen on the ridge above Ida's beach house a scanning device to warn the patrol boat at night of the approach of another vessel. There was no doubt in Warnecke's mind now that the Sharqiyans were aware of the threat and were taking precautions. So, reaching the coast, they turned right without another look at the cove and headed for the hotel fifty kilometers farther on.

The drive was beautiful but uneventful. They scanned the mountain to their right for signs of other installations, but the morning sun was in their eyes, and the kids were getting restless. Once or twice they stopped for more pictures, but by now they were all anxious for a swim.

At eleven o'clock they arrived in the small fishing port where the Hôtel de la Plage stood. It was picturesque, lacking the spectacular beauty of Ida's cove but more open to the sea. Here too a patrol boat was anchored offshore. Warnecke estimated that it would not be entirely invisible to ships at sea, and he concluded that their need to protect the coast was more important even than the element of surprise.

He pulled into the parking lot and cut the engine. While the family began to unload, he walked into the hotel and up to the reception desk.

"My name's Warnecke," he announced. "I phoned last night from Al-Bida and made reservations for two rooms."

"I am sorry, sir," the clerk answered. "The hotel is full."

"What do you mean, full? My car's the only vehicle in the parking lot."

"I regret, but I can do nothing about it."

"Look, I called last night. You took my name. Let's see the register."

The clerk spread his hands. "The hotel is filled up, sir. There are no rooms available."

Warnecke looked around the lobby and saw only a pair of sleepy porters. "I say the hotel is empty, and I want two double rooms. I've got my family outside, and they're tired."

At this point another man approached. Warnecke instantly recognized him as a policeman.

"I'm sorry, Commander Warnecke," he said. "The clerk obviously is not making himself clear. What he means to say is that while some of the rooms may not be occupied, the hotel is not receiving guests today. In other words, we are closed."

"Then why are the doors wide open? And how do you know my rank?"

"What I am suggesting, Commander," the man continued without answering the questions, "is that there is no room for you or your family at this hotel or in the village and that you had best be on your way back to Al-Bida."

Warnecke's anger cooled. This was not bureaucratic incompetence. "So there is something here that I am not supposed to see. Is that it?"

"You may think what you please. However, you were seen photographing military installations all along our north coast this morning, in clear violation of your proper function here as a diplomat."

Warnecke took a deep breath. "I am here with my family for a weekend on the coast. We have not been informed of any restrictions on picture-taking, but if one of my sons took photos he shouldn't have, then I am sorry. It is a very beautiful coast, and if photographs were permitted, I am sure many tourists would want to come here."

"Al Sharqiya is not seeking tourists, Commander Warnecke. Now if you will kindly turn over your camera..."

"This camera is the property of the United States government. I cannot turn it over to you."

"Then give me the film that is inside."

"Help yourself."

The man wound the film and removed it, returning the camera.

"Only three exposures have been made on this film, Commander. I must ask for the other roll."

"There is no other roll."

"You were seen taking photographs in at least six places along the coast. So please give me the other roll."

"Search me if you want," Warnecke challenged him.

"That will not be necessary. We will ask your family and search your vehicle instead. We will also want the film in your son's camera."

Warnecke was taken outside, where a police car blocked the exit from the parking lot and a detachment of police surrounded the ranch wagon.

"Don't worry," he told his wife. "They just want our film. Let's have that other roll, Mike."

The boy fished a roll out of one pocket and handed it to his father, who passed it to the policeman, then called his other son. "Steve, your camera too. Hurry up."

The younger boy gave up his camera reluctantly.

"Here," said Warnecke. "Open this up too. It's one-ten film, and it's got a dozen family shots in color. But you can't develop color in this country. We have to send it to the States. It takes a month to get it back."

The policeman watched him impassively. "You are trying hard, Commander, but it won't work. The roll of film you just gave me was unexposed." He held up the 35-mm. roll, from which a telltale strip of film protruded. "Now I fear we shall have to search your car for the real film."

Warnecke laughed. "Mike, that was the wrong film." Let's have the roll we finished a while back."

The boy went to the car and returned with another roll.

"That's better," said the policeman. " Now please be on your way. And do not return to the north coast without specific authorization from the Ministry of the Interior. You may not take the coastal road. There is a more direct road to Al-Bida leading inland from here."

"But that road isn't even paved," protested Warnecke. "It'll take us all afternoon, even if the springs do hold up."

"I'm sure that if you drive slowly the springs will hold up. Our roads may not be built for your cars, but they are perfectly adequate for our needs."

Warnecke glared at him. "Thanks."

"Let's go, Jack," said Gladys, pulling at his sleeve. "It's no use arguing. "

"Have you got sandwiches enough?"

"Plenty, and a thermos. We'll make it all right."

"Good girl. Let's go then."

Without another word they climbed into the ranch wagon and began the trip home. The sea breezes ceased as soon as they passed through the defile. They closed the windows and turned on the air conditioning. The ranch wagon groaned as it heaved over the ruts. Warnecke swore under his breath. "I almost lost my temper with that so-and-so. Very undiplomatic of me."

No one spoke until Mike said, "You know something, Dad?"

"What?"

"That film I gave him... it was all shots we took along the coast. But the ones we took of Mrs. Gant's cove from up on the pass, those were the last shots on another roll. We've still got that roll. Here it is."

He held the small cylinder for his father to see.

Warnecke grinned.

"Good boy. We may make a master spy out of you yet."

It felt like a week day. Potter flipped through the batch of telegrams which Agar had just handed him. These were the Friday cables out of Washington, the last he could normally expect before Monday. Sharqiya was nine hours ahead of Washington and pretty low on anybody's list of priorities.

The cable, marked Immediate but not NIACT, lay on top of the pile.

"DEPARTMENT HAS ALERTED ALL NEIGHBORING MISSIONS BUT HAS RECEIVED NO REPEAT NO INDICA-TIONS OF ACTIVITY SUGGESTING EARLY DEPARTURE OF AN INVASION FORCE.

"WE APPRECIATE YOUR CONCERN BUT SUGGEST YOU SIT TIGHT AND CONDUCT BUSINESS ON ROUTINE BASIS. DESPITE YOUR DENIALS, GDRS COULD STILL CLAIM CABLE IMPLIES U.S. PARTICIPATION IN PLOT, WHICH THEY COULD MAKE PUBLIC AND USE AGAINST US. SUGGEST YOU EMPHASIZE OUR PEACEFUL INTEN-TIONS AND COMPLETE DISASSOCIATION FROM ANY PURPORTED COUP ATTEMPT.

"DEPARTMENT HAS FULL CONFIDENCE IN YOUR ABILITY TO HANDLE SITUATION. WE LOOK FORWARD TO FURTHER NEWS FROM AL-BIDA ON MONDAY MORN-ING."

Potter tossed the cable aside. They still don't understand. If I'd let my first cable go the way I wrote it, it might be differ-ent, even if it did get my tail in a sling.

Oh, damn Ridgeway, he thought. He'd met the man for the first time on his arrival at the Department for his orienta-tion. A tired bureaucrat, facing early retirement, with high school French and rudimentary Arabic, and little knowledge of French colonial history. He would already have left for a weekend on the golf course or sailing on the Bay. Must be lovely this time of year, too lovely to let events in a backwater like Sharqiya interfere. So don't bother to cable back before Monday morning in Washington, which is Monday afternoon in Al-Bida. Enjoy your weekend, keep cool and don't let your imagination run away with you.

He had half a mind to send a Night Action Immediate. Ridgeway would be furious. Even if he was in bed at his house on the Bay, a NIACT would bring him back to the Department. It would serve him right. "So the Professor has caught a case of localitis already," he'd be saying.

He went to his wall map and measured the distances from the Sharqiyan crescent to East Africa and Southwest Asia. He wished Warnecke were back to estimate the time it would take for various craft to reach the coast.

Even though there were no indications from other posts of a buildup, he was convinced the Sharqiyans were taking the threat seriously. Look at the troop movements to the north coast. Look at what Ida had told him, and the photos Millie had taken. It was clear the GDRS not only didn't want American aid but was actively trying to compromise us.

He'd done what he could, and this was what he'd tell Ridgeway in the cable he was drafting. It would be on Ridgeway's desk Monday, and there would still be almost a week before any landings.

He flipped through the remaining cables and decided they could wait while he performed a minor chore. He buzzed Sgt. Hernandez. "Top, how is our boy doing up in the vault?"

"He's quiet, sir. Giving us no trouble."

"Then bring him down to my office, please. I'd like to talk to him."

Corker was brought in and left standing at attention in a fresh uniform with his face scrubbed clean around the cuts, the bruises and the nearly-closed eye.

"That's quite a shiner you've got there, Corker."

"Yes, sir. I guess I didn't duck fast enough."

"Why did you run away?"

"I dunno, sir. I thought I'd killed her at first. I guess I panicked."

"Well, you might have killed her. You realize that."

"Yes, sir."

"And you'd been warned to stay out of trouble. You in particular. What are you planning to do after this tour, stay in the service or get out?"

"Gee, I dunno, sir. I'd like to stay in for twenty. But now I'm not sure they'll let me."

"The Sharqiyan police want you, you know, and you've got no diplomatic immunity. Nor do I have a right to hold you here. In fact, if I keep you here and they find out about it, I'll be in serious trouble myself, and so will Uncle Sam. Have you ever seen the inside of a Sharqiyan jail?"

"No, sir."

"Well, I don't recommend it. For that reason, I'm going to hold you here in the vault, without their knowledge, until we can find a way to get you out of this country. I have no control over what the Marine Corps does with you, but I can try to keep you out of the hands of the Sharqiyans. Are you willing to accept that, or would you rather take your chances with Sharqiyan justice?"

Corker gulped. His bruised face flushed deeper.

"No, sir. I'll stay here if you'll let me. And I'll do anything I can to make up for all the trouble."

"All right, Corker," Potter said, heaving a sigh of resignation. "I'm sticking my neck out for you, but I may need you before we're through. You may report back to Sgt. Hernandez."

Corker snapped to attention. "Yes, sir. Anything, sir. Thank you, Mr. Ambassador."

When he had left, Potter buzzed Hernandez to return him to the vault. *Another loser. The Marine Corps won't want to retain him. But if I can keep him out of the hands of the Sharqiyans, it will be worth it. To both of us.*

Pascal dreaded informing Ida Gant Richard about the break-in at her beach house. He had enough to do to prepare for his exhibit, yet telling her was his first task of the day. He filled his jeep with gas at the Embassy garage and set out for the Watch Tower.

He found her at the railing on her piazza. She looked even frailer to him than she had the day before.

"What are you doing back here?" she cried. "I thought I told you to stay at my beach house."

"Let's sit down, Ida," he said, climbing the steps to the piazza. "I'll tell you what happened."

He did so, going into far greater detail than with Warnecke. Her face ashen, she sank back in her deck chair in a faint. The house boy brought a glass of cognac. She came around slowly.

"In sixty years on this island," she said, "nothing like this has ever happened to me. To have the government itself commit an act of burglary and vandalism! I never thought I'd see it."

"I'm sorry to bring you bad news, Ida."

"It's not your fault, and I'm glad you told me. But oh! I can't understand why they won't let me end my life in peace!"

"Maybe the Ambassador can make a protest," he offered lamely.

"Don't be silly. Harold Potter is more under my care than I am under his. When I set my mind to it, I can protest louder than anyone you ever saw."

"That's more like the Ida I know. Who are you going to protest to?"

"The Minister of Defense, naturally. He's the trespasser. And the Minister of the Interior. He's the one who is supposed to be protecting me against burglars."

"Do you know them?" Pascal asked, not without awe.

"Of course I know them. Karim al-Rashidi was a foundling who grew up in my orphanage. I helped him get into the lycée and from there into the military academy. He ended up at St. Cyr. As for Qasim, he was a police informer who nearly went to jail for taking bribes. Gaston Girardot defended him, but what really saved him was the revolution. He wasn't one of my orphans, but he owes me a few favors anyway."

"Ida, is there anyone in this country you don't know?"

"It isn't who you know, young man. It's what you know about them."

"Ida, sometimes you shock me."

"Like hell. Now get out of here and let me handle this my way. I'm going to visit my orphanage today, and I may just find myself paying a call on a couple of ministers."

From the jeep, Pascal looked up to see her standing at

the top of the steps of her piazza. She waved. She still has plenty of spirit, he thought, even if her strength is gone.

"And don't worry. In a few days I'll send you back to my beach house to enjoy yourself."

Lou Cross groaned as he switched off the alarm. As duty officer, he felt he had to be first at the Embassy to make sure everything was all right. But he'd been awake most of the night, while Marilyn had slept like a baby.

He threw water on his face and examined the dark bags under his bloodshot eyes. He could hear her snoring even from the bathroom. Some guys see a good-looking woman and think that's all there is to it. They don't know what it's like to live with one, month after month and year after year, and try to have a career and get ahead just so she can have what she wants in life.

But he knew. His two kids by his first wife were in school in the states, as if that didn't cost something. And here at a hardship post where people are supposed to help each other she falls for a wise guy who couldn't even hold onto his own wife.

Then he remembered the forged memcon. He couldn't tell the Ambassador about that, and what was worse, Boyle would be here on Monday. If Boyle guessed right, he'd be in real trouble.

All that, and then she goes for a snotty young punk of a Marine!

He nicked his chin shaving and swore as he stanched the blood. Well, he'd fix Corker. No one was going to make him the laughing stock of the whole Embassy.

He threw more cold water on his face while he heated up the coffee. He turned down the gas and opened the front door, inhaling deeply. The old man was sitting at the gate, awake or asleep he never could tell. Never says a word; just sits there and takes it all in.

The old man gestured toward the mail box. Cross withdrew a large brown envelope with his name on it but no stamp. It could be a letter bomb, he thought. He took it into the house and ran his metal detector over it. There was no indication of metal. He soaked it anyway in the sink. The envelope came unglued. He found three 8 x 10 glossies sticky from the water. He was able to pull them apart, and there she was, smiling a smile she never gave him, offering everything she had to somebody else.

A little later, Catherine Potter was eating her breakfast on the sun porch when the maid brought an envelope to her.

"Where did this come from?" she asked, noticing the rather elegant French hand in which her name had been written.

"It was in the mail box at the gate, Madame."

"But there's no stamp on it. And today is Saturday."

"I don't know, Madame," the maid said. "The gardener gave it to me."

Catherine turned the envelope over and over. It was stiff, like a photographer's envelope.

They had been briefed at the Department on letter bombs, but this one was feather-light, and there seemed to be no metal in it, not even a clasp. So she slit it neatly with a knife.

"Well!" was all she could say as she withdrew the first photo, instinctively reinserting it and pushing the envelope away from her. She felt as if she had opened the wrong door in a hotel. But then her curiosity overcame her shock. She made sure the maid was gone and withdrew all the photos. There were three of them, different views of the same subject, each more explicit than the last.

She drew a deep breath, replaced them securely and sat staring out the window. She was vexed that her breath was short and her heart was beating rapidly. Nevertheless, this had finally made up her mind for her, even if it did rather spoil her breakfast.

She finished eating, rose resolutely and took the envelope between two fingers, pinching it closed. I'm afraid, she announced to herself, that this is the last straw.

2

From Ida's, Pascal went directly to the Center to check on the exhibit. The library would be closed and the Sharqiyan employees would be off. The trip back to take more photos could wait until tomorrow.

The guard opened the gate, and Pascal drove past the broad lawn to the parking lot behind. It was a fine Center— elegant and dignified yet open and friendly. He was proud of his accomplishments there. Despite the presence of a much larger French Center and a Goethe Institut, it was gaining a reputation around town for being where the action was. He took out his key and let himself into the entrance hall.

"What the hell is going on here?" he cried out to the empty building.

Window displays lay stacked on the floor. Curtains were draped over the wrought-iron bannister of the marble staircase. Rolls of transparent plastic material leaned against the windows. Pails of dirty water rested on long strips of wrapping paper spread on the floor.

"I'll be damned!" he swore. "They're putting mylar on the windows! And they didn't even finish the job."

"Take a look at your library while you're at it."

It was Marge Henry speaking through the grill at the top of the stairs. She had heard him come in and had crossed over from her office.

He crossed the hall and opened the French doors to the library. Bookcases had been pulled away from the windows to permit mylaring, and exhibits were on the floor. Tables and chairs were stacked on one side of the room. In the cases lining the walls every book had been pushed back and protruded irregularly according to size. Those on the upper shelves were inaccessible and all but invisible.

He walked back into the hall. " Marge, did Cross do this?"

"Who else? He walked in yesterday morning with his crew and started tearing things apart."

She told him what she knew about the Admin Officer's visit.

"What I don't understand, Mr. Pascal, is why he was so interested in which doors were locked and which were open. Apparently something is missing, but they wouldn't say what."

Pascal was suddenly alert. "Which doors was he talking about?"

"The one in the corridor leading into the school. The grill at the top of the stairs. Your office door, and apparently the door inside your bathroom."

"What did he find out?"

"That nobody could come upstairs after six o'clock, but that I or any of the teachers could get in via the corridor from the school."

"What's wrong with that? They all come in to use the john."

Marge's gaze wavered.

"Not all of them, Mr. Pascal. Marilyn Cross uses it every time she has a class. She stays in there for half an hour at a time."

"How do you know that?"

"She has to pass my office going and coming. And once I tried to use it at six-twenty and found it locked. I don't know what she does in there all that time, but I'm afraid she may be hitting the bottle. There are times in class when she acts positively spaced out."

"Do the students notice anything?"

"You can bet they do. I don't want to bring my troubles to you or tell tales out of school, but Marilyn is getting to be a real problem."

Pascal's glance faltered. He took a deep breath. "In what way?"

"Her drinking, first of all. You can imagine the effect it has in a Muslim country. And then, she misses classes. Yesterday afternoon she gave me about two hours' warning, and I had to teach the class myself."

"She wasn't here last night?"

"No. Of course, there was the rain, but I don't think that was the reason. Frankly she sounded drunk over the phone."

"Oh, Christ," he sighed.

"And then, she can be abusive. Or over-friendly. One of the students told me she put her arm around him and he could smell liquor on her breath. This particular kid looks like a fundamentalist to me. He was scandalized. That's not good for the school's reputation."

Pascal was unable to answer. He raised his arms and then dropped them helplessly. "What can I do, Marge?" he asked finally. "She's the Admin Officer's wife. It's policy to give overseas wives precedence on jobs to keep them busy."

"But at what cost, Mr. Pascal?"

"I could talk to her husband, I suppose. But it' s delicate."

"Or talk to her. She seems more relaxed when you're around. "

He winced but made no direct comment. "Could you find a replacement if she left?"

"No problem."

"Then I'll see what I can do. But I can't promise anything."

Pascal sat for a long time alone at his desk, staring at the opposite wall. They're closing in on you, old boy. Better call a halt before there's real trouble.

Then another thought occurred to him. Could she be the one who put that envelope on his desk?

Ida Gant Richard called the Ministry of National Defense a few minutes after Pascal left her. On a Saturday she didn't expect to find the Minister's office open. Nevertheless, she wanted it recorded at the Ministry that she had called there first before talking the more audacious step of calling the Minister at his home.

To her surprise, however, she was told the Minister was in conference and couldn't be disturbed.

"I didn't ask you to disturb him. Just tell me what time it will be convenient for me to pay him a visit."

The voice was hesitant. "I don't think Monsieur le Ministre will be able to receive you today, Madame. He is very busy."

"Then you may tell him I'll be at his office in half an hour. We'll see then whether he is able to receive me."

She hung up abruptly and donned the white gloves and broad-brimmed hat which she always wore when in the sun or down in Al-Bida. They were a relic of another day, a reminder of fair-skinned colonial administrators now gone.

Omar brought the vintage limousine to the edge of the steps and helped her down from her piazza. He held the car door open for her.

"To the Caserne Maynardier, Omar," she said.

Under the arched entrance to the vast hollow square which was the heart of the new Ministry, she descended from the limousine. The tarbooshed guards stood at attention. The building had no elevator, and the climb to the second floor was a long one, but Ida braced herself and, with one hand firmly on the railing, climbed each marble step slowly.

At the top of the stairs she recognized the suite of offices which had once served the French military governors of the island. This visit would be no different from the others; the minister was still a small boy whose knuckles she had once rapped.

"You may inform the Minister that Madame Richard is here," she said coolly but not unpleasantly to the startled secretary.

An atavistic habit of obedience brought an immediate response. Within five minutes another official appeared at the door to the inner office and, with a bow, motioned her to enter.

Karim al-Rashidi was halfway to her with arms outstretched when she caught her first glimpse of him.

"Madame Richard! My dear Mother!"

"You're putting on weight, Karim," she replied. "You should get out from behind that desk and get some exercise."

"That is the tragedy of my life, my Mother. The higher I rise, the less I am able to do the things I want to do."

"Then quit your job and do them."

He spread his arms in despair. "How can I when I am still filled with that sense of duty to my country which you were the first to instill in me? Now please sit down and tell me what I can do for you."

"You can tell your brigands to get out of my beach house and have some respect for private property."

He frowned. "Which beach house? What private property?"

"You know perfectly well," she said, and told him all she had learned from Pascal.

He rose from his desk and began to pace his office, with his hand on his chin. Finally he turned to her and said: "My dear Mother, I can assure you your house was not entered for frivolous reasons. I can promise you that within a few days it will be restored to its original condition and returned to you with compensation and our grateful thanks."

"Thanks for nothing. You didn't ask for it, and I didn't offer it to you. You just took it."

He raised his arms helplessly. "There are times, my Mother, when reasons of state must take precedence."

"What reasons of state?"

He hesitated. "Reasons of state which I cannot divulge."

"That's it," she fumed, "give me the bureaucratic runaround. You have trespassed on my property, and I insist that you get out immediately."

"Not immediately, but soon."

Her gaze narrowed. "You're expecting an invasion, aren't you? Well, you should have built an observation post of your own. I warn you, Karim, get out today or I shall go to Mohamed Qasim and make it a matter for the police."

She pounded the floor with her cane. This time Karim al-Rashidi reacted with alarm.

"No, please. Madame Richard, you are my dear Mother. Your safety means a great deal to me. I beg you to stay out of this affair and let my men occupy your house a few days longer. I promise you they will do no further damage. But they must stay there, and you must not interfere, for your sake as well as for the sake of Sharqiya."

Ida was shaken by the earnestness of his tone.

"You don't want me to see Qasim, do you?" she said shrewdly.

He faced her.

"Of all people, you must avoid seeing Qasim."

"And the American Ambassador? If I complain to him...?"

"I'm afraid the American Ambassador has troubles enough of his own. His complaint would not be heard."

She tried to rise to her feet but to her fury had to allow him to help her. "I see I have wasted my time and yours. I'm afraid I'll have to find another way to protect my property from your precious revolution."

He stopped her as she was leaving.

"Again I beg of you, dear Mother. For your own sake, please wait in your home and do nothing."

Giving him a withering glance, she left.

Pascal had taken his newly-printed posters and had dropped them off at key locations in the center of the city. He had noticed a subtle difference in the atmosphere from most Saturday mornings. People were shopping as usual, but there seemed to be more buying food and fewer buying clothing, as if they were stocking up on necessities. Troops and military vehicles were everywhere.

At the Center he began setting up the exhibit. He stood the paintings against the four walls of the auditorium and placed the large-scale map of the island and the glossies he had shot the previous day and matched them with the original paintings. The photos were black-and-white and would not distract from the paintings. As for the photos not taken, he was ready to make the trip to the north coast tomorrow and develop them that evening.

He saw that there were really not enough paintings to

fill the room. He hoped he could borrow Catherine Potter's, but he wondered how many more there might be in private homes. He decided to ask Zerkaoui.

The number rang repeatedly before a voice was heard. No, Mr. Zerkaoui was not in, and he didn't know where he was or when he might be back. Besides, the gallery was closed today.

Pascal hung up, puzzled. Zerkaoui was always there on Saturday mornings. That was when he did his best business. What was keeping him away today?

Instead of driving from the Ministry of Defense to the Ministry of the Interior, Ida went directly to the American Embassy and was surprised to find at least half of the American complement on duty.

"I didn't think the American taxpayer ever got six days of work out of you people in a week," she said to the Marine on duty.

"Oh, yes, ma'am," the Marine answered without a smile. "We're on duty seven days a week, twenty-four hours a day."

"Then maybe the Ambassador won't mind taking ten minutes off to have a conversation with me."

Potter helped her to an easy chair and closed the door.

"Did you hear what they did to my beach house?"

"I was told Pete Pascal found it broken into."

"Saw it broken into and occupied by thugs from their Navy," she said in outrage. She told him of her visit to Karim al-Rashidi. Potter listened intently.

"So they really are getting ready for something. We'll know more when Jack Warnecke gets back tomorrow."

"You still haven't told me what they're getting ready for."

"Ida, all I can say is there are rumors of a mercenary invasion to put a pro-French regime back in power. And from what you say, the rumors are being taken seriously."

"I should think they would be. The people of this country would be overjoyed to see the French back, and so would I."

"I wouldn't go that far, Ida. Besides, a successful invasion would depend on surprise, which obviously has been lost."

"Now tell me what we are doing in all this."

"There isn't much we can do, Ida, except send warnings to all parties and hope the invasion will be called off."

Ida frowned. "You mean you wouldn't try to help them bring this country back to sanity?"

"Ida, this is a sovereign nation. Their internal affairs are none of our business. And furthermore, we don't have the power or the will to control events here."

"That is the most outrageous thing I've ever heard! The United States doesn't have the power to control events! I am shocked at hearing an American Ambassador say such a thing!"

"If I may say so, Ida," he replied gently, "that is because you have not lived in the United States for a long time. Very few Americans have ever heard of Sharqiya, and very few of them would be willing to sacrifice American lives in a conflict between neo-colonialists and fundamentalists."

"Well, I am not a military expert," she sputtered, "but I do know the difference between right and wrong. And I want my country to be on the side of the right."

"Where I hope it will always be. Are you willing to help?"

"Did I say I wasn't?"

"Then please do as I say. Stay home until all this is finished after next Sunday. Your piazza is the best observation post in town. Let Millie visit you again today and take more pictures to compare with the ones she took yesterday. This way we'll keep tabs from day to day on what's happening. But whatever you do, keep away from the ministries. The less conspicuous you make yourself, the more help you can give us."

"In other words, I should just shut up and keep out of the way."

"I wouldn't put it that way. I'd say keep your eyes and ears open and tell Millie what you find out. After all, you are our most valuable source of information."

Ida was somewhat mollified.

"Well, you can't stop me from visiting my orphanage. I

told them I'd be there this morning, and if I'm not there, they'll think something is wrong."

"Go, by all means," Potter said. "And pass on to Millie anything you pick up. But please don't come here to the Embassy again. You understand why."

"You diplomats are too deep for me," Ida muttered, rising. "Sometimes I think we'd be better off just to land Marines and set up a government we can deal with."

Catherine Potter knew that Brahim Zerkaoui did most of his business on Saturdays. It would give her an opportunity to thank him for lending Larbi's paintings to Pete Pascal for the exhibit, and note his reaction.

She was driving her own car as she had with Hanifa the day before. She maneuvered the vehicle into an empty spot a block from the gallery, locked the doors and walked up the avenue toward the shops. After several minutes she realized that she had passed the gallery and, retracing her steps, saw that the gray corrugated iron shutter had been pulled down. The gallery and shop were closed.

She asked at the hairdresser's next door. No, the gallery was not yet open. Would it be open later? They couldn't say. Wasn't it usually open on Saturdays? Perhaps. Perhaps Madame should come back in an hour.

Exasperated and troubled, she walked to the alley on the side street and found the bicycle repair shop open. She asked the proprietor in rapid French about a supposed repair job on her bicycle. Then, satisfied that his French was fluent, she asked him where Mr. Zerkaoui could he found.

The man frowned. "I don't know him."

"But I saw you speaking to him in your shop yesterday afternoon. He was wearing a light brown suit, Western style. You must remember him. He owns the gallery across the street."

Ignoring the ten-dinar note she held up to him, he clicked his tongue against his teeth. "I do not know him. You want your bicycle repaired?"

She thanked him coldly and went to the cobbler's in the

alley. This man also knew nothing. She gave up and returned to her car.

She drove straight to the Embassy, where she was just in time to see Ida's limousine disappear around the corner. She found her husband at his desk writing a cable.

"I've done a little sleuthing for you, dear, and I have some news. I know who used your typewriter."

He listened as she recounted her visits to Zerkaoui's.

"And I suppose you'd also like to know how the memcon got from Zerkaoui to Pascal's desk," she pursued.

"Tell me, and I'll see if we agree."

She handed him the manila envelope. He took out the photos and grimaced. "Lovely," he sighed.

"Charming. Now put them back, dear, like a good boy, and do your duty. I want her out of here on the first available flight."

"You haven't proved the connection with Zerkaoui."

"Isn't it obvious? She planted it for him during her tryst with your Public Affairs Officer. And you might think of asking for his transfer too."

"Not if there's an invasion in the works. I'll need all hands, and I'm thinking of the damage to Lou if he loses Marilyn."

"Think of the damage if she stays. Her behavior is notorious. Would you rather have the Foreign Ministry ask you to remove her?"

"If they're the ones who are using her, they may calculate she does us more harm by being here. "

"That's all the more reason for removing her and depriving them of their weapon against you."

He looked at her with grudging respect.

"I guess you're right, darling. As always."

"Not always, dear. Just when your future and the good of the Service are at stake."

3

Potter sat at his desk, staring at the wall map. The whole chain of events was apparent now. The only question was what else Zerkaoui might know about the inner workings of the Embassy and why he had chosen to give the game away at this point. No doubt it served his purposes to create as much havoc as possible. The entire government wanted the invasion to fail, and the fundamentalists wanted the Americans out while they took over the government.

So score another point for Catherine Brent. She was forcing him to take an action which could destroy the effectiveness of his staff just when he needed them most.

He might as well start with Lou.

Cross looked haggard to him. It was obvious he had not slept; in pity Potter motioned him to an easy chair and took a seat on the couch.

"How is the security situation shaping up, Lou?"

"Pretty good, sir. Everybody knows the procedures. When the alarm goes off, we all head for the vault. We can lock every door on the ground floor and this floor from the Marine desk, and we can see any crowd gathering through the TV monitors. As for individual terrorists, we can box them into whatever room they're in just by throwing a switch."

Potter noted his pride in his meticulous preparations, then asked a tougher question.

"What kind of attack do you expect?"

Cross hedged. He had been taught to prepare for anything, not to estimate probabilities.

"Well, any way it comes we can handle it."

"I'm sure you can, Lou. But I guess you know there's something else on my mind."

"Yes, sir," Cross blundered on. "That security violation. Well, I've got a theory on that. I think it may be someone from the language school. There are a lot of floaters among the teachers--you know what I mean..."

Potter cut him short. "Lou, I think we both realize we need to have a serious talk about Marilyn."

Cross sank back in his chair, relieved it was all coming out. "I know, sir. Her drinking problem hasn't been getting any better."

"That's right, Lou, and I'm afraid if we don't do something about it soon, it's going to cause the Embassy real trouble."

Cross began to squirm. "I'm doing everything I can to find things to keep her occupied, sir, like teaching English and..."

"It's not enough, Lou. We're a permissive society, but overseas what we do gets talked about. Especially in a Muslim country with people just looking for a pretext to close us down."

"Maybe I should send her home on vacation for a month or so," Cross offered.

"Would she go?"

"If I told her about the threat..."

"You can't do that."

"Then if you made it an order and mentioned some vague kind of threat...?"

Potter forced himself to look the man in the eye. "Lou, I don't want to hurt your career. An official request from me for a medevac because of alcoholism would hurt you both. Does she have anyone else in the Washington area?"

"She has a sister in Fairfax County."

"Then let me give it to you straight. That security violation was no fake. There could be a landing on this island a week from tomorrow, and I want Marilyn out of the country by then for her own safety. If you can guarantee she'll be on Monday's flight, I won't have to do it the official way. How does that sound?"

Tears began to fill Cross's eyes. "I do love her, Mr. Ambassador. I've done everything I could to make her happy. But she just doesn't seem to want to try..."

"So you'll have to try that much harder yourself. Will you give me your hand on it?"

Cross wiped his eyes and shook Potter's hand.

"Thank you, Mr. Ambassador. Thank you, sir.".

Potter pressed the hand sympathetically, wondering if he had been a fool. A medevac could have forced a solution. Now Lou would have to convince her. What if she refused and threatened to stay with Pascal?

The phone rang. It was the Ministry of Foreign Affairs. His Excellency the Minister wanted to see him at the Ministry immediately.

"It's Saturday, and I am not properly dressed. I'll have to go home and change."

"That is not necessary. His Excellency is waiting to see you now. The Director of Bilateral Relations will accompany you."

The atmosphere in Suleiman Smaili's outer office was no less frigid than on the previous day. Smaili came out and bowed formally. "Monsieur l'Ambassadeur, I am to accompany you to the office of His Excellency. Please follow me."

Potter knew Abd el Kader Ibn Aziz fairly well. They had attended each other's national day receptions and had chatted on other occasions. Ibn Aziz was a career diplomat, slim and elegant and thoroughly French in training. Potter regarded him as a first-class technician, and the servant of his masters on the Supreme Revolutionary Council.

"I trust you will excuse me, Monsieur le Ministre, for appearing in a sport shirt," said Potter. "It is Saturday, and I just happened to be at the Embassy to complete some work."

Aziz brushed the apology aside. "It is of no importance, Monsieur l'Ambassadeur. What I have to say will only take a moment."

Potter waited for an invitation to be seated. None came.

"Monsieur l'Ambassadeur, yesterday you informed M. Smaili of an alleged invasion plot against the Democratic Republic of Sharqiya. I cannot guess the real purpose behind this crude attempt to trouble the serenity of a peace-loving country. I can only imagine that you had your instructions."

"On the contrary, Monsieur le Ministre," he responded as smoothly as he could, "I had no instructions. I acted as a friend in calling your government's attention to a rumor I had heard. I told Monsieur Smaili I was unable to evaluate the report. Had I withheld it, your criticism might be justified. As it is, I feel I have nothing to reproach myself for."

"Be that as it may, your subsequent actions have been less than friendly. The very next day you sent your Defense Attaché on a mission of espionage along our north coast. He was apprehended thanks to the vigilance of the Sharqiyan People's Security Forces in the very act of photographing Sharqiyan military installations and is now on his way back to Al-Bida."

Potter broke in. "If Monsieur le Ministre will permit me to say so, the American Embassy has received from your government a list of installations which are not to be photographed. Commander Warnecke informed me yesterday of his desire to pass the weekend on the north coast with his family, and I am certain that none of the forbidden sites were on his itinerary."

The Minister did not flinch.

"A new list was issued this morning which includes them," he said coolly.

Potter knew now what to expect. He cursed himself for allowing Warnecke to make his trip. He should have realized the government would seize on any pretext to make trouble.

"But since it has not been received by the Embassy," he put in lamely, "surely Commander Warnecke cannot he held responsible for not observing the new restrictions."

"The list was affixed to all official bulletin boards this morning at seven o'clock. Your Defense Attaché was expected to adhere to its contents."

"Then permit me in the name of my government to apologize for any violation which Commander Warnecke may unwittingly have committed. Surely his ignorance of the new regulation is a mitigating factor. Furthermore, I shall be happy to have him turn over to the appropriate authorities any photographs of military installations which he may have taken."

"That will not be necessary. His film has already been confiscated."

"Then I can only reiterate my government's apologies

and assure Your Excellency that Commander Warnecke will be more careful in the future."

Aziz took from his desk a white envelope, which he handed to Potter.

"Monsieur l'Ambassadeur, the peace-loving people of the Democratic Republic of Sharqiya are not in the habit of being spied upon by the representatives of a supposedly friendly government. In view of the gravity of Commander Warnecke's actions, I must inform you that he has been declared *persona non grata* and that his departure from our territory is desired within forty-eight hours."

Potter took the envelope. "Monsieur le Ministre," he said, "this is a harsh and unjustified measure against a man who, whatever his mistakes, is a sincere friend of the Sharqiyan people."

"Nevertheless, Monsieur l'Ambassadeur, I shall trust you to see that the decision of the Sharqiyan people is carried out without delay. Good day."

Lou Cross sat alone in his office with the door closed, examining the nude photos of his wife through his tears.

He couldn't believe it. How could she do it to him? And with Pascal of all people!

The face looked back at him, the features repeating themselves endlessly, an infinite number of prints to be drawn from the negative of her darker nature and distributed to the entire world, to all except the one guy who had worked and sacrificed to make her life a happy one. And this is what she did to him in thanks, make a laughing stock of him in front of the whole Embassy!

The telephone rang. It was Sgt. Hernandez. Would he like to go upstairs and see what they'd done to make the vault comfortable for you-know-who?

Sure, anything to make life comfortable for you-know-who. Hernandez was a good Marine. He ran his detachment by the book: short haircuts, PT at 5 a.m., TGIF once a week to make money for the Marine Ball and no horsing around. Each Marine had a girl, and that was it. But every outfit has one goof-off, and Hernandez would not be allowed to stand in the way of his plans for Corker.

He climbed the stairs to the top floor and touched the buttons of the combination lock on the door. Now another door: the entrance to the vault. There was still an iron grill between him and the inner rooms. Charlie Agar was visible inside a smaller office. He pushed a button, and the iron grill opened.

"How's the house guest doing?" Cross asked.

"No problem. Just lies there reading Sci Fi. I think he wishes he was on Mars."

"That's where he may find himself. Let's have a look at him."

"Go ahead. I gotta distribute this stuff. Lock up when you're finished."

With Agar gone, Cross walked into the big room. The vault filled the whole end of the building, but one partition hid the communications equipment from sight, and others made a storeroom, an office of sorts and a toilet. It was air-conditioned, and there was a trap door to the flat roof and a small window under the eaves with a locked grill in front of it. There was even a hot plate and a refrigerator. A few people could live here for a while if they had to.

In a far corner a cot had been installed. Corker lay on it reading a paperback. When he saw Lou Cross, he dropped his book and sprang to attention.

"How's our combat Marine?"

"Just fine, sir. I can't complain."

Cross noticed Corker was trembling. His crewcut seemed to stand up out of sheer fright.

"You shouldn't. These aren't bad quarters at all for someone who ought to be in a Sharqiyan jail."

"Yes, sir. I know that, sir."

"Come to think of it, a Sharqiyan jail would be a good place for a wise guy like you."

"Yes, sir. But I couldn't help what I did, Mr. Cross. I was jealous, I guess, and I just went crazy."

"Yeah, sure. Lover boy."

"I do love her, Mr. Cross. That's why I couldn't stand seeing her with another guy."

"Sure. Lover boy just can't stay away from women. Knocks his girl's teeth out and breaks her jaw, and then goes after an officer's wife. Real wise guy."

Corker's eyes widened in terror. "No, sir, I didn't. I swear I didn't."

Cross smiled as he saw the effect of his words on the Marine. "What didn't you do, Corker? Tell me."

"I didn't do anything, Mr. Cross. She wanted me to, but I didn't. I swear it."

"Who, Corker? Who wanted you to do what?"

"Mrs. Cross, sir. I mean, I swear I didn't touch her."

Cross knew he was on the right track. He'd get the truth now. "That's not what my wife told me, Corker."

Corker frowned. "I don't get it, sir."

"What don't you get? You mean you didn't think my wife would tell me when a punk like you tries to rape her?"

"Mr. Cross, I didn't. I swear it. When she took off her clothes, I just turned and ran. That's all I did."

Cross felt his face flush. Now he was getting somewhere.

"Sure, I believe you, Corker. You just happen to be with a beautiful married lady in her bedroom, and she takes her clothes off and stands there all naked in front of you because she just can't resist you, and you don't do anything. Sure, Corker."

Cross didn't care now. He was hearing the truth, at least part of it, and it was like a knife. But that didn't matter; he had ways to get even.

"Honest, Mr. Cross, it's exactly like I said. She had me take a shower and put on clean clothes, and then before I knew what she was doing she took off her robe and dropped it on the floor."

Cross saw it in his mind. He saw his Marilyn offering her naked body like fruit to this Marine. "And what was underneath, Corker?"

"Nothing, sir. She was naked."

Cross's heart was beating faster now. He stepped up to Corker and stuck his finger in his face.

"You're lying, Corker. You tried to rape my wife because she wouldn't take off her robe for you. You never saw her naked. You're a goddamned liar, Corker."

Corker stepped back from Cross but faced him with feet planted apart as if ready to fight. "I'm not lying. She was naked, Mr. Cross. She was all red except where she wore her bathing suit. But I didn't touch her."

Cross laughed. This was proof. It satisfied his need to know everything, to be able to see it all in his mind.

"Sure, I believe you, Corker. You saw all that, and still you didn't touch my wife. You just turned your back on that beautiful naked woman and walked away."

"Sir, I ran away. I didn't want to touch your wife. I never put a hand on her. I just ran back here."

Cross leaned forward, grinning now. "Then how come she had to change the sheet?"

Corker frowned. "What sheet? She didn't change no sheet while I was there."

"Not while you were there, Corker. She changed it after you left because you raped her on it and it showed."

Corker was silent, conflicting emotions visible on his face. His jaw hardened. "Mr. Cross, I don't give a good goddamn what you think. I never touched your wife, even when she said, 'Call me Marilyn, Ron darling, and be real good to me.' Even then I never screwed your wife."

The feeling was less delicious now. There remained a grain of doubt in his mind, and it was spoiling everything. He'd have to act decisively now.

"All right, I've heard your story. Now let me tell you what happens to wise guy Marines. You've got no diplomatic immunity here, and the Sharqiyan police are after you. So on Monday morning the Ambassador is going to turn you over to the Sharqiyan police. They'll put you in one of their jails, and you'll have plenty of time there to think about what a great lover you are."

Corker reacted fast. "But the Ambassador promised me he wouldn't do that, Mr. Cross."

"That was before I told him how you tried to rape my wife. He didn't know you were the kind of Marine that screwed around with officers' wives. But he knows now, and you're going to pay the price."

Cross left the vault feeling much better. He was tired, but he felt truly cleansed and purged. Only that one small doubt bothered him, and Marilyn would clear that up.

The next thing he had to do was to go home and tell her to start packing.

4

Potter returned to his automobile via the long corridors and staircases of the Foreign Ministry, careful to maintain his dignity despite the inappropriateness of his dress.

Inside the car, he fingered the embossed envelope and unfolded the starched white paper. They work fast when they want to, he mused. Forty-eight hours. That means Monday morning's flight, the same flight Marilyn Cross will be taking, the same one Boyle will be coming in on. They want to deprive me of my eyes and ears and set people against one another inside the Embassy. That way they think they can neutralize us and close us down. But then, why hasn't Pascal been expelled too?

"Let's go to the Cultural Center," he told Youssef.

The limousine drew up at the gate in front of the shiny brass plaque inscribed with the words AMERICAN CULTURAL CENTER in English and Arabic. The old mansion set back among the palm trees, once a symbol of colonial domination, was now one of open hospitality. He intended to keep it that way.

He spotted Pascal standing on the porch in torn and paint-spattered blue jeans and open shirt, his long hair and beard unkempt.

"Excuse the mess, Mr. Ambassador," he greeted Potter. "Someone decided to put mylar on all the windows just when we were getting ready for the vernissage. It'll be cleaned up by Tuesday, I guarantee you."

Potter made no comment.

"You know the routine," Pascal went on. "The guests come in the front door here and across the entrance hall to the auditorium where the exhibit is. The bar will be at one end, with soft drinks, and there will be a table at the other end to take orders and hand out extra catalogs."

Potter remained silent while Pascal chattered on oblivious in his enthusiasm. They went into the auditorium, where the seats and the wooden stage had been removed and a cur-

167

tain drawn across the movie screen. The paintings were mostly still on the floor or propped against the walls. The electrician was busy adjusting lights while a handyman cut lengths of wire to hang the paintings. Pascal was still talking.

"And here's the result of a brainstorm I had day before yesterday. These works are so observant, so literal in their naïveté, that I thought it would be a tribute both to the artist and to Sharqiya itself if I showed the sites he used for the backgrounds."

He took two or three large glossies and held them up in front of the paintings. "See this one? That's Ras el-Kebir, the western tip of the island. But look at how he transformed it and brought it to life using the most primitive means imaginable. Remember, he's had no formal instruction whatsoever. I hate to throw superlatives around, but this man has genius."

Potter examined the glossies and spoke for the first time.

"When did you take these pictures?"

"Yesterday. I was up on the mountain all day with Larbi, and then along the coast. The one I couldn't get was of Ras el-Qasr, where Ida Gant has her house. The Navy was in the cove and actually broke into her place. I told her about it this morning, and she said she'd complain to the Ministry."

"She already has," Potter said drily. "And no one stopped you from taking pictures or bothered you in any way?"

"Nope. I admit we stayed away when we saw what they were doing, but otherwise we had no trouble."

"That's interesting. What else do you have to show me?"

"That's it, sir," Pascal said, surprised now at Potter's lack of enthusiasm, "except for the map."

"Map?"

"A large-scale French military map of the island that I'm going to put up with the site of every painting spotted on it. Thirty-five paintings so far, the work of almost half a decade, and photos to go with most of them. I believe this is going to be the outstanding artistic event in Al-Bida this year."

Potter examined the paintings, walked around the room

with his hands in his pockets and returned to stare Pascal in the face for a long minute. Then he spoke quietly.

"I'm sorry to have to tell you this, Pete, but your exhibit is not going to be shown at this Center. I want every one of these paintings, and especially the map, taken out of this room and put away. I'll keep the photos, but your exhibit is off."

Pascal looked at him and laughed as if Potter were joking. "You're kidding, sir."

"I am not kidding. I want it all down and put away. Now."

"But Mr. Ambassador, the posters are up. The ads are in the papers. The catalog is printed. The invitations are out. We've had heavy expenses already."

"I'm sorry about that. If you'd come to me with your plans none of this would have happened. Let it be a lesson to you."

Pascal began to pace the floor with his hands to his head, twirling on the balls of his feet in a sort of mad dance.

"I can't believe it. You wouldn't do this to me. Think of the Center's reputation."

"I am thinking of it, and if you'd spoken to me I would have given you the benefit of my thoughts. Now take back your posters, and start printing apologies. Invent any excuse you want, but this exhibit is cancelled. And if you want to know why, come see me in my office after you've cooled down."

He took the photos and left Pascal standing in the middle of the auditorium amidst the debris of his exhibit, his arms outstretched in a gesture half pleading, half disbelieving.

And that, said Potter to himself, is what happens when an Ambassador fails to pay enough attention to what his staff are up to.

Millie Novak found Ida in a foul mood.

"Go take your pictures," she said sharply. "That's all America can do here—watch while others act. We're nothing but a government of voyeurs."

"Ida, I'm shocked," Millie scolded her jokingly. "I'll bet you don't even know what a voyeur is."

"Oh, don't I, though? The trouble with your generation is you think you invented vice, or sex, or whatever you want to call it."

"Maybe we don't think of some things as vice or sex."

"And that's where you've made your mistake. You've taken all the pleasure out of it. No wonder you've had to move on to drugs to find something new."

"Drugs? Me, Ida?" Millie batted her eyelids demurely.

"Not you, silly. You're no doubt a virgin."

Millie flushed. "You are in a nasty mood today."

Ida realized her mistake. "Forgive me, my dear. It's just that this has been the most frustrating morning of my life. First I learn my beach house has been broken into. Then one of my favorite foster children, who has the power to help me, refuses to do so. Then our own Ambassador tells me America is impotent--yes, that's another word I know--impotent to do anything about it. And now I've come from my orphanage, the orphanage I've nourished for forty years, and they tell me I'm no longer allowed to make gifts."

"What do you mean?"

"I mean the regime has now put its hands on private charities. For years I've brought in clothing, bed linen, toys, medicines for my orphanage, at my own expense. And now they tell me that hereafter I'll need a permit for each shipment and that even if I'm lucky enough to get one everything I bring in will have to be handed over to the government to distribute. And our Ambassador tells me America can do nothing while my gifts go into the homes of government officials or onto the black market!"

Millie lowered her camera from her photo-taking of the port area and turned. "Ida, you can't be serious."

"I am perfectly serious. These governments think they have to control everything. They can't admit their own people are in need because that reflects on them. And look at the possibilities for graft."

"Then why don't you bribe them if you have to?"

Ida's jaw dropped. "I swear your generation has no morality whatsoever, I'll see them in hell first."

"And your orphans will go without."

"I'll find ways. Karim al-Rashidi will help me. I won't let him forget who raised him, or where."

Millie was impressed. "You mean the Minister of Defense?"

"Who else? And he's only the most important one at the moment. I have children all over this country in high positions. Where else can they find educated and competent men but among my children?"

"Most of them are French-educated, and yet they're not pro-French."

"That's different. France was the colonial power. America has never done a thing to these people but help them. You diplomats have all kinds of advantages if you'd only use them. Instead you allow countries with nothing but guns to come in and take over."

"Ida, it isn't our country. It's up to them who they decide to let in."

"Hogwash! What do you think they do, vote on it? There are a handful of extremists in the government who hate everything Western, and they manipulate all the others. I just wish I could get to whoever is supposed to be invading this country next week. I'd tell them how to do it right."

"How would *you* do it?"

"I'd come in before they were ready for me, that's what. I'd have my own people here beforehand, and I'd take that beach house away from them and commandeer their patrol boat before they could use it against me. Then I'd place my observers in this house and direct the invasion by radio from here where I could see everything that's going on."

Millie looked at her in amazement.

"Ida, every time you speak you surprise me. Where did you learn about strategy?"

"Tactics, my dear. Strategy is for the deep thinkers. Well,

I can read. Just because there's no television in this country to speak of doesn't mean I can't learn things. Besides, I do have medals from two World Wars."

They finished eating, and Millie looked at her watch.

"I promised the boss I'd go to the office this afternoon and type some cables. I have to drop this film off too. May I come back tomorrow even though it's Sunday?"

Ida hesitated. "I don't mind about it being Sunday, but at my age tomorrow is a long way off. Why don't you come back this evening for a drink before dinner? I feel lonely."

"Of course. I'd love to. The sunsets are so beautiful."

"And bring someone with you. Pierre Pascal, if you like."

"Frankly, he and I don't get along that well."

"Then the other one, young Finley. I don't like to see you alone all the time."

"Aren't you worried about my virginity, Ida?"

"Oh, stop it. I'm through trying to understand any of your generation."

It was noon and Lou Cross was just leaving the Embassy for home. Pete Pascal drove up in his jeep. There was no way to avoid him.

"Hi!" said Cross as casually as possible. "If you're looking for mail, there wasn't any."

"I wasn't looking for mail. I was looking for you."

"What can I do for you?"

"You can clean up the mess you left at my Center."

"What mess?" Cross was wary. Pascal was the last person he wanted to see today, and a mess at the Center was far from his thoughts.

"The mylar mess, Mr. Cross. You waited until I was gone before you started. Were you afraid to ask my permission?"

Cross didn't want to argue with this guy. "You may be glad some day when they start throwing rocks. And by the way, it's too bad you weren't available. The Ambassador had questions to ask you about security at your place."

Pascal frowned. "Why is everybody taking a sudden interest in my Center? First you try to put mylar on the windows, and then the Ambassador tells me to cancel the best exhibit we've ever had. What's going on, anyhow?"

"I don't know anything about your exhibit. But if you can't see what's going on from that document they found on your desk, then I can't help you."

"I told you I had nothing to do with that. What are you trying to do, close me down completely? Because if you do that, it means no more English courses. And if that happens, it means your wife won't have any place to go three nights a week."

Cross flushed. "Let's leave my wife out of this, all right?"

"That's fine with me. Why don't you tell her to stay home?"

"Because she enjoys teaching, and she does what she wants."

"She sure does. I just wish they enjoyed having her teach."

Cross's eyes shone with moisture. His voice trembled as he spoke. "Why don't you just leave her out of this?"

"Then have her do her drinking away from my Center."

Pascal turned and went into the Embassy. Cross watched him go, his eyes filling with tears. I didn't want to have a fight with him, he told himself.

He got into his car and started driving. The briefcase was beside him on the seat, and inside was the envelope with the photos. Pascal took those pictures, he thought. She probably asked him to, but he didn't have to do it.

He tooted his horn at the gate and drove into the driveway without a glance at the old man or at the gardener. They probably knew all about it and were laughing up their sleeves at him too. Well, in two days it would be all over. She'd be gone. His Marilyn would be gone. Then at least he'd have some peace and get the respect he deserved.

She was playing the piano when he came in--something she worked on all the time that drove him crazy. That's one thing he wouldn't have to hear any more.

"Hi, honey. I'm home."

The piano continued to play.

"Whatcha been doing all morning?"

"What's it sound like?"

"Why don't you stop for a minute and let me tell you something?"

"Because I want to get this right."

He went to the sideboard and poured himself a whisky. The table was set, and the maid was ready to serve luncheon. Suddenly the right notes emerged from the piano, and the music resumed and continued to the end of the piece.

"All finished?" he asked.

"What is it?"

He'd hoped she would turn, but maybe it was better to talk to her back, after all.

"How would you like to go back to the States for a while?"

Now she did turn. Her eyes narrowed. "What's that mean, a while?"

"I'll tell you. The situation here is getting dangerous. There's actually the possibility of real trouble next week, and the Ambassador thinks we should get some of the dependents out. Nothing that might attract attention, just sort of casual."

"Sounds fishy to me."

"That's the way it is. Even Pascal's exhibit at the Center has been cancelled. I can't explain why."

"And when does this evacuation take place?"

"Monday."

"You mean the day after tomorrow?"

"That's right. You'll have just time to pack a few things. I can send you some air freight later."

"What if I say no?"

"Honey, the Ambassador wants you out, and he's the boss. I suppose if he wanted to he could order you out."

"Meaning?"

"Well, you know. He's got the authority. He can put it on any basis he wants."

"You mean like having a drunk among the ladies of the diplomatic corps to embarrass Her Highness? He'd call that notorious conduct bringing discredit on the Service, or something like that. Then he wouldn't have to go into detail."

"Please, honey, let's not talk about those things."

"Why not? You always do. At our last post I had a love affair, as you reminded me last night. So here I've spread out a little to spare your feelings. Safety in numbers."

"Honey, don't..."

"Shall we count them? Get a pencil and paper. We'll do the names first, and then I'll try to remember how many times with each."

"I said cut it out, Marilyn. Now I mean it."

"Sorry. I didn't mean to bruise your inferiority complex. I guess if they were high-ranking, you wouldn't mind so much. If I'd gone to bed with the Ambassador, for instance, it might have helped your career. I can just see the rating he'd give you: loyal, discreet, tactful, self-sacrificing..."

He'd sworn he wouldn't let her taunt him into a fury. He'd promised himself he wouldn't say or do anything he might regret. But she just wouldn't stop.

"You know about Pete, of course. Your detective friend no doubt will find our secret passageway when he comes. Remind me to send him a photo of us, will you?"

He felt the tears again. "I've seen the photos of you, Marilyn."

She was startled. She didn't think her lover boy would be spreading them around. She came back at him.

"Is that so? Well, I suppose they were intended for lonely men."

"Marilyn," he pleaded, "I know what it's like for you, and I can't stop you. All I ask is discretion. Do it with someone who keeps his mouth shut, not with some jerk of a Marine."

"Oh, so that's it! You mean that nice boy Corker. Poor kid, I guess I scared him off. Next time I'll be more mysterious and hard to get. I'll tease him till he takes me."

"You mean he didn't... ? "

"He ran away, poor kid. So you know what I did? I found a substitute. Now wouldn't you like to know who? An ambassador, maybe? Or just a stranger? Or maybe it was someone you see every day—the driver, or maybe the cook or the gardener... ?"

He slapped her. He'd never done that before.

"God damn you! I tried to be good to you, and you've made me the laughing stock of the Embassy. Well, after Monday it's finished. So you'd better start packing."

She was still laughing, but he wasn't listening to her any more. He was outside getting into the car. He'd eat downtown and then go back to the Embassy for the rest of the day. There were plenty of things he could do there.

It occurred to him he could apologize to Corker. But he wouldn't; he'd be damned if he would. Let the bastard sweat it out; it would teach him a lesson.

As he pulled out of the driveway the old man at the gate smiled all-knowingly, and the gardener, clutching tightly at the upright rake handle in front of his chest, watched him go.

5

Potter cleaned up his desk. A wrap-up of the situation was on its way to Washington. It told of the break-in at Ida's and her visit to the Defense Ministry. It told of his own summons to the Foreign Ministry, and it speculated on the real reasons for ignoring Pascal's expedition and declaring Warnecke *persona non grata* for doing the same thing. It also told of Marilyn's coming departure without going into detail as to the reasons. Finally, it mentioned the cancellation of the vernissage and exhibit at the Cultural Center.

Ridgeway would go up the wall. He had clearly gone beyond his instructions, and the departure of a family of four, plus Marilyn, hardly constituted business as usual. Furthermore, by canceling a scheduled cultural program he had ignored Ridgeway's recommendation, to say nothing of his offer to assist in the event of an invasion.

Well, so be it. The instructions had been unrealistic. Sharqiya figured in no one's calculations, and U. S. policy there was being formulated by Clayton Ridgeway, a disgruntled country director recently passed over again for promotion. Nevertheless, a defeat for U.S. interests in Sharqiya would not be laid at Ridgeway's doorstep. If anyone's head rolled, it would be Potter's.

The intercom rang. "Are you free to see Mr. Pascal?" asked Millie.

"Send him up." He might as well have one more showdown to make the day complete.

Pascal had made an attempt to groom himself. His beard was trimmed, his hair was combed and he wore a clean, pressed safari suit. Did he still hope to salvage his project?

"Pete, I want to know the history of this exhibit. Who gave you the idea? How did you hear about this painter Larbi?"

"Mr. Ambassador," Pascal began, "Zerkaoui was one of the first contacts I made on the local cultural scene. Then when Mrs. Potter bought a painting at his gallery, I went there and liked what I saw. I felt it would be a feather in our cap to be first to recognize an authentic Sharqiyan talent and bring him before the public. I still think so."

"You won't when I've finished. Now whose idea was it to take pictures of the sites and display them with a map?"

"Zerkaoui's, I guess. That's right; I said I'd like to know where each one was painted, and he suggested taking the pictures. But I planned the trip and took Larbi along. I'm the one who got the photos."

"But you didn't tell me what you planned to do, did you?"

"No, sir, I'm afraid I didn't. I guess I should've."

"More than that, you should have asked my opinion, because I would have told you to call the whole thing off right then. Do you realize that you went on a photo-reconnaissance mission along a coast where an invasion force is rumored to be landing next Sunday, and that you planned to display the photos to the public along with a military map spotting the sites?"

Pascal's face registered shock. "But sir, I went out of my way to make sure there wouldn't be anything military in the shots I took. I even let a couple of patrol boats go by so that they wouldn't appear in the photos."

"Wrong again, Mr. Pascal. Shots of the patrol boats would have been useful to Jack Warnecke. If you'd come in for a briefing, I might have let you reconnoiter the coast on the theory that Zerkaoui was using you as a patsy, which he was. As it was, I let Jack Warnecke do the same thing this morning, and they confiscated his film and declared him persona non grata. Which proves they wanted you to have your exhibit in order to compromise the whole Embassy. Do you know where Zerkaoui is right now?"

Pascal was shaken and resentful at the role forced on him. "That's just it, sir. He wasn't at his shop this morning, and he wasn't at home either. I can't figure it out."

"Did it ever occur to you that he might be one of the master minds behind all this?"

"I'm sorry, sir, but I don't get it."

Do you remember what was in that forged document?"

"No, Sir. I just glanced at it. Rumors of landings. But it was forged. It wasn't for real."

"How do you know I didn't write a real one with the same information?"

"You mean there will be an invasion?"

"There may well be, a week from tomorrow. And you were about to signal to the world that we were expecting them. We would have been seen to be allied with the neo-colonialists and ripe for expulsion if the extremists come out on top. Another thing, the painter Larbi. Where is he?"

" He's ready to go back with me tomorrow if I need him. I can reach him through his family in the medina."

"Well, you won't be needing him for awhile. Did it ever occur to you that Muslims are not supposed to paint any of God's creatures? For painting what he did and displaying it in an American facility, your friend Larbi would be considered a blasphemer by the fundamentalists. So think of that next time you go off on your own."

Pascal was aghast. "I can't believe it, sir. I know these people. I've got many friends here."

"And a few enemies too. Now I want you to stay close to the Embassy from now on. And be ready to come in on a moment's notice."

"Anything you say, sir." Pascal shook his head, still not totally convinced.

As he was leaving, Potter held up a manila envelope. "By the way, I believe these are your photos."

Pascal was caught off guard. He grasped the back of a chair to steady himself as he took the envelope.

"Not that it matters any longer," Potter went on, looking him steadily in the eye. "She'll be leaving Monday morning for the States. For health reasons and to be out of the way if anything happens."

Potter turned away and walked deliberately back to his desk, thinking the shock treatment might work even with Pascal.

When he looked up from his chair, Pascal was gone.

Marilyn had been considering her new situation as she waited for Gaston Girardot's visit. Two more days, and she'd be out of this Third World backwater. She'd felt a pang of regret in spite of everything. It had happened just as she was making new friends; so what was the point of even seeing Girardot?

He arrived punctually at three, carrying a bouquet of roses. Marilyn's regrets were momentarily forgotten. He kissed her hand.

"Monsieur Cross is not here?"

"He's at the Embassy. He's duty officer this weekend."

"How embarrassing. I chose Saturday expecting he would be here, for even a harmless old fool like myself should not pay a call on a married lady in her husband's absence."

"Don't worry about it," she said airily. "Let people think what they want, I always say."

Through the glass doors she saw Ali the gardener hard at work in another flower bed. The old man was seated behind the gate as usual, asleep or awake it mattered little to her now.

"The bar is over there," she said. "Make your own drink. I'll have a gin-and-tonic."

Girardot navigated his bulk across the living room and returned with her drink.

"Thank you. Where's yours?"

"My dear lady, I have unfortunately reached the age when the remaining pleasures of life are few. Despite temptation, I am forced to discipline myself, even when the inclination is strong."

"What a shame. You look well to me."

"I manage to maintain myself. Fortunately, I can still enjoy painting and music."

"I'm afraid I'm just an amateur, Maître," she said carefully.

"Don't be modest. You promised to show me your work. Let me see. Do I recognize anything on the walls as yours?"

He walked around the room, his bifocals perched on the end of his nose. "Aha! This one!" he exclaimed before a pale watercolor of a flower arrangement.

She smiled shyly. "How did you guess? I never signed it."

"My dear, I knew it was yours. It has something of you in it."

"It wasn't done here. I did it at our last post."

"And it reflects a happy period in your life."

The pleasure in her eyes was tinged with regret. "It's true. I was happy there."

"Now show me more. I must see more of your work."

She led him into the dining room, where two more watercolors hung side by side.

"These are more timid," he said. "You had not yet found yourself. You were seeking a style."

"Maître, you frighten me. You can tell everything about me from these paintings."

"Yes, but now I want to see what you've done here in Sharqiya. I want to see the you of today."

She made a helpless gesture. "There isn't much."

She went to a closet and brought out a half dozen canvases, which they placed side by side on the couch and on the chairs.

"The colors here are much stronger," Girardot said. "But the forms are less rigid, more obscure. I would say you have entered a new period. You are freeing yourself from old restraints, allowing your true nature to emerge. You have not yet found the form you need to express this new nature. But you are on the right track. You will find it."

Marilyn caught her breath. She felt tears coming, but she didn't care. "I've tried, but it's been so discouraging."

"You mustn't let yourself be discouraged. Now listen to me. What you need is a retrospective of your work. Yes, why not? I detect three periods just in the few works you have shown me. There is talent in all of them, real talent. But you need encouragement to bring it out. You have an American Cultural Center here. Why don't you have your retrospective there? It would do you good, really."

The tears were visible now. "Maître, I can't have an exhibit here. It's too late. I'm leaving on Monday."

Girardot's surprise was visible in his raised eyebrows and open mouth. "What? That's not possible. You've been here such a short time."

"I didn't know it myself until this noon. The Ambassador wants some of us to leave, for security reasons. I suppose I shouldn't say it, but he's expecting an invasion or something next week. He's even cancelled the art exhibit at the Center. It was to have opened Tuesday evening, and now it's all off."

Girardot had listened without interrupting. "But who is leaving? Not all of you, I hope."

Marilyn, like the others, had been warned not to discuss Embassy business with outsiders. But it didn't occur to her that Girardot was in that category. "Myself and maybe some others," she said. "That's all I know."

"But that is very strange indeed. I wonder if something I said may have had anything to do with it."

"Something you said?"

"My dear, there are so many rumors all the time, especially in a country where the press is controlled. One hears the most fantastic things. One should never act on them without confirmation."

Marilyn was in the dark. "All I know is what my husband told me. I'm taking the Monday morning flight to Paris."

Girardot brightened. "But you'll be back in a week or two."

"I'm not so sure."

"I promise you will. And then you'll have your retrospective. You'll see. Now I want to hear you play the piano."

"Marilyn became more self-confident. "I've been practicing hard for the past two days. But I don't promise much."

She sat down at the Yamaha upright she had shipped from post to post halfway around the world and began to play a

Schubert Impromptu. This time she managed the broken chords of the allegretto without a mistake. But it was in the trio that her fingers found themselves. With the introductory lacework behind her, she gave herself over, in this apparently simpler and easier middle section, to the yearnings of her heart. Girardot heard it, and his eyes closed as he sat back to listen. Then when the section ended and the light gambols of the allegretto returned, each note carefully placed as by a conscientious student, he relaxed and smiled.

"My dear," he said when she had finished, "in the opening and closing passages I see the same applied skill of a good pupil that I saw in your earlier paintings. But it was in the middle section that the true Marilyn Cross expressed herself—may I say it?—a bit clumsily but with deep feeling, the same feeling I see in your latest paintings. My dear lady, you are a true romantic."

Like a child, Marilyn could hardly contain her joy. "I can play Bach too, and Mozart."

And she did, inventions of the one and a sonata of the other, playing as if sound were coming out of the instrument for the first time.

When it was all over, he repeated his praise, thanked her and rose. "Now I must say au revoir, my dear lady. Not adieu, because you will be returning to Sharqiya. You must return."

"I'll write to you, Maître. I'll keep in touch."

She saw him to the door, watched him drive away, watched the old man close the gate again and saw the gardener puttering in the flower bed. Then she returned to the empty living room, with its one painting of hers on the wall, and the music that was gone, and threw herself down on the couch and wept.

The Warnecke ranch wagon, caked with dust, pulled up in front of the Embassy just as Harold Potter was leaving to go home and dress for dinner at the Greek Embassy Residence. The Defense Attaché and the Ambassador met at the front door.

"They stopped me cold," Warnecke said. "Turned us around at the Hôtel de la Plage and sent us home. Took our film too."

"They did more than that. They called me in and PNG'd you. You and your family are to be out of here on Monday morning's flight."

Warnecke whistled. "Sorry about that, sir. I tried to be discreet."

"You were doing what I asked you to do. My guess is they want you out of here before the shooting starts to deprive me of my eyes and ears. I'd like to know if the same thing is happening to the French."

"I can ask my counterpart. We get along."

Potter thought for a minute. "Maybe I'll bring it up with the Chargé at dinner. We're innocent. We're on the sidelines in this affair. So I see no reason to keep it secret. Go ahead with your man." He clapped Warnecke on the shoulder. "Tough luck, fellow."

Warnecke smiled. "Guess I'd better break the news to Gladys and the kids. Oh, by the way, they didn't get all the film. I've still got a couple of shots of Ida's cove."

"Good man. And believe it or not, I've got over a dozen beautiful ones taken by Pascal all up and down the coast."

"I wonder why they didn't stop him," mused Warnecke. "Even without military subjects his photos can be useful to us."

"They were setting him up to get us all thrown out, that's why. He was going to display paintings and photos of all the landing areas a few days before the actual landings—and with a French military wall map locating the sites, if you please."

Warnecke whistled again. "He needs a little instruction on what to do and what not to do overseas."

"Well, stick close," Potter told him. "I've got to go to a dinner tonight. Keep your radio on, and if anything happens, call in. Otherwise, come in tomorrow morning at eight, and we'll see where we stand."

"Right, sir." Warnecke shook his head and turned to the dust-caked ranch wagon and its dust-caked passengers. "Oh, my poor wife and kids!" he sighed.

Phil Finley didn't mind accompanying Millie Novak to Ida's. As consul be was responsible in a way for the old lady's welfare, and though he had lunched at the Watch Tower, he had never seen the famous sunset. He did have a dinner party to attend, but Millie had promised to have him back in time to change.

"Well, young man, did you bring your camera?" Ida asked.

"I should have, but I forgot. I guess I'll just have to have Millie shoot the sunset for me."

"Millie's not here to shoot sunsets. She has far more important things to do."

"Oh?"

He watched Millie fit the telephoto lens onto the camera and point it at the port area. She noted the time on her steno pad. She took several more pictures and put the camera away. It was still broad daylight, and the clouds in the western-sky were just beginning to turn pink.

"Aren't you going to shoot the sunset?"

"I can't. I don't have color film. This is just black-and-white, to be developed here."

"Then what's the point ... ?"

"My dear Mr. Finley," Ida said, "you obviously have not been brought into the secret of our deep, dark plot. Millie is photographing the port area at least once a day to help the Ambassador keep track of military movements."

"But what on earth for?"

"You mean you don't know about the invasion?"

Finley gave a superior smile. "You don't really believe there's going to be anything like an invasion, do you?'

"Harold Potter believes it. Doesn't he, Millie?"

"Well, he isn't taking any chances," Millie said, displeased that Finley had been let in on the secret.

"But I've been hearing rumors for months," Finley said. "If I believed all of them, I wouldn't be able to sleep."

"The Sharqiyans apparently believe them too," Ida said. "I saw a convoy of trucks moving out this morning."

"What are we doing about it?"

"We're trying to learn what's going on and report it to the Department," Millie said in exasperation.

"That's it," Ida chimed in. "Watch and report and do nothing. I'm almost ashamed to be an American."

"Then why don't we do something?" asked Finley, a puzzled look on his face.

"Do what? Tell us," Millie snapped at him.

"I don't know. At least take Mrs. Richard down to the Embassy where she'll be safe."

Ida reacted quickly. "I'll stay right where I am, thank you. You have a copy of my will, don't you?'

"I suppose so."

"Then that's the only part of me you'll get. Your boss doesn't want me there, and I don't want to go. This has been my home for over sixty years. You people can come up and take your pictures every day, but you can't take me back with you."

The sunset was at its most splendid now. They stopped and gazed as the brass turned to copper and then to bronze.

"I always watch it," Ida said. "And because I'm an early riser I watch the sunrise too. Each day the world is born and dies. I see the beginning and the end over and over again."

They left her standing at the top of the steps, looking down at them and leaning on her cane. She had nudged Millie an instant before and squeezed her arm. "What's wrong with this one?" she whispered. "Take him." But Millie made a face.

She wanted no part of Phil Finley. Ida shrugged. "I just don't understand this generation."

"See you tomorrow," Millie said.

"Yes. There's always tomorrow."

The Greek Ambassador's buffet dinner had been planned two weeks earlier. It was to be outside, with tables on the lawn and a view through the trees to the coast.

Harold and Catherine Potter were one of more than two dozen couples. They noted with relief that the setting was informal. This would give Potter a chance to make a few more soundings. He saw to his regret that the French Chargé was absent and decided to try the British consul first.

"I do hear rumors," David Clark told Potter, "and I've noticed the troop movements too. But as for assessing their meaning, I was just about to ask your opinion."

"You didn't hear a date mentioned, such as May 13th?"

"Sorry, not even that."

"What about some of the members of the old French community? Have any of them approached you?"

"None. You see, there's very little we could do to help even our friends."

"Well, if you should hear anything in the next few days, I do wish you'd let me know."

He moved away to engage the Counselor of the Chinese Embassy.

"The people of China are extremely happy that such friendly ties exist between our two countries," said Mr. Li, smiling from ear to ear.

"The American people too are very happy. And we hope that as a result we shall be able to keep each other's embassies informed of coming events."

After a few more such fruitless exchanges, Potter spotted Bensalem, the Algerian Ambassador, who as the representative of an Arab state and a former French possession was particularly welcome in Sharqiya and who as a business partner of the United States was on good terms with Potter.

"Whatever happened to our friend Zerkaoui the art dealer?" Potter plunged in. "His customers have been looking for him all day."

"I cannot say. I am not an art lover, and I do not think he has many clients outside the European community."

"He's one of yours though, isn't he?" Potter pursued.

"Zerkaoui? No, he must have a French passport."

"You may be right," Potter admitted. "In any event, he doesn't seem to be bothered by religious restrictions. He deals in portraits, landscapes, everything."

"Like so many corrupted by the French."

Oh oh, thought Potter. So this one may have ties to the local radicals. He decided to confront the man. "The rumor mill has been grinding all week. Coups d'état, invasions, anything you want to listen to. Have you noticed?"

"Coup rumors," the Algerian answered, shrugging his shoulders, "are the work of agents provocateurs. The government is vigilant. There will be no coup and no invasion."

Bensalem was stonewalling him. After a few pleasantries, they separated. Potter looked around. In all this sea of smiling tennis and golf partners there wasn't a single face which he could count on as being both friendly and able to help.

The guests lined up at the buffet and were regaled with delicacies from Greece and the Near East. Potter, preoccupied with his unsuccessful questionings of his colleagues, found himself seated unwillingly next to Nadia Busheira. He was trapped. He braced himself to hear more questions about Nadia's son's scholarship to an American university.

Instead, she managed to do worse.

"Monsieur l'Ambassadeur, I've just received your invitation, and I'm so thrilled."

He smiled expectantly, flipping through his mental file cards but finding nothing. Nevertheless, he continued to look at her with encouragement, waiting to be enlightened.

"We'll certainly be there, won't we, Hamid?"

In the social world, Hamid Busheira's assent went automatically to any and all suggestions made by his wife.

"You know," she went on, "we are both great art lovers...."

My God, she's talking about the vernissage! thought Potter.

"...and the thought that a simple goatherd, uninstructed and illiterate, could be touched with genius and capable of producing works of art, is a source of pride to all of us. And all Sharqiyans must he doubly proud to think that it was an American--and such a nice one as Mr. Pascal--who will be the first to exhibit his works to the public."

"Well, unfortunately," Potter said carefully," we've had to put off the vernissage for technical reasons. I spoke to Pete about it this morning, and apparently there are some paintings which have been promised and haven't been delivered."

His voice trailed off. He smiled helplessly.

"But that's terrible!" Nadia exclaimed. "The whole city is talking about nothing else. If you put it off, people will not only be disappointed; they'll be confused. Half of them will come anyway."

"And find the Center closed, I'm afraid. You'd be doing us a favor if you would inform your friends."

"Can't something be done? My husband and I have two of Larbi's paintings which we would be glad to lend."

"That's very kind of you, but it's more than that..."

"I'll tell you what. Let me call Brahim and have him round up all the paintings he's sold so far; I'm sure he could bring together enough to make an exhibit."

"Have you seen him today?" Potter asked.

"Brahim Zerkaoui? No, not today. Why?"

"No one else has either. His shop was closed this morning."

"That's strange. He's always open on Saturday mornings. But don't worry, I know where he lives. I'll give him a call, and I promise you your exhibit will be on again."

"As a matter of fact, he's not at home either. We've tried to reach him there."

She frowned. "That's very strange. Nevertheless..."

Potter smiled. "Well, it's too late now. we've canceled the ads and put a notice in the newspaper. But don't worry. Pete has promised to reschedule it as soon as possible."

"It's such a disappointment," she said, biting her lip.

Then, after a moment of reflection, she batted her eyelashes. "I don't suppose you remembered to ask M. Pascal about my son's scholarship...?"

"You mean he hasn't contacted you yet?"

She pouted. "No, he hasn't."

"Well, darn him! You know, He's been working so hard on this exhibit that it must have slipped his mind. I promise you, I'll mention it to him again first thing Monday morning."

She beamed. "I knew you would."

The dinner progressed from dolmas through pilaf to baklava. They were drinking their Turkish coffee, and Potter was beginning to feel better. Then, from another table, they heard loud voices.

"Oh, Magda is reading fortunes!" Sophie exclaimed.

Magda Szekely was the wife of the Hungarian Chargé, and her renown as a fortune teller was widespread in Sharqiya. She had asked her table companions to turn their coffee cups over on their saucers and was reading their fortunes in the fine powder left in the bottom of the cups. She had just told the lady opposite her, who was pregnant, that the baby would be a boy; and now she was telling the gentleman beside her that he would be named an ambassador at his next post. People were gathering around from the other tables and begging to be next. Catherine, watched for a moment and then walked across the lawn to her husband.

"Come, darling, it's time to have your fortune told."

Potter winced. "Cat, don't be silly."

"I insist. I want to know what our next post will be." Then, sotto voce, "It had better be an important one."

He allowed himself to be dragged across the lawn with an empty coffee cup in his hand. He sat down with Magda Szekely, who studied him with green Hungarian eyes, then stared into his cup.

"I'll bet it's something extraordinary," said a woman who had admired him from afar.

"With Ambassador Potter," proclaimed Nadia Busheira, "it can only be good luck."

"I see great turmoil," said Magda without looking up. "There are difficult decisions for you, one in particular. You are in the midst of great events, and not everyone will be helpful, even among your most well-meaning friends."

"That's not very encouraging," said Catherine. "At least tell us everything is going to turn out well and what our next post will be."

Magda continued to look down into the cup. She squinted, frowned, turned the cup around and then back again. Then with a brusque movement she pushed it away from her.

"I can't see any more. You didn't empty the grounds properly. It's too confused."

"Oh, Magda, don't disappoint us," Catherine begged.

"That's right, Magda," the others chimed in. "Tell us."

"I am sorry. That is all I can see. Give me another cup."

She looked up into Potter's face, her green eyes searching his. Then she shrugged and spread her hands. "What can I say? You did it wrong." And she turned to the next guest.

"Wasn't that maddening?" Catherine asked on the way home. "I did so want to hear where we'll be going next. But then, it's all just a game, isn't it? Our guess is as good as hers."

Potter stared ahead as the headlights sought to penetrate the darkness. "Yes, here everything seems to be a guessing game."

7

Pete Pascal felt suddenly dizzy as he left the Ambassador's office. He'd wanted to sit down, but Millie was watching him, and so he continued through the outer office, lurching against the door. Now the Marine guard was staring at him, and so he plunged on to the exit.

"You OK, Mr. Pascal?" the Marine asked.

"Sure, great," he answered bravely. Once outside, however, he fumbled with his car keys, missing the lock and dropping the key ring. He leaned against the jeep and rested his head on his forearm.

He sat in his jeep with his face in his hands, waiting for the blood to return to his head. Christ, the photos! He'd been set up. That bitch had swiped them and sent them to the Ambassador. He should have refused to take pictures of Marilyn in the first place, but she always managed to wheedle things out of him or she'd throw a fit. Poor Marilyn! he moaned. She's dumb, but she didn't deserve that. And she doesn't deserve to be sent home for it.

He shook his head and turned the ignition. Now he had to find Larbi and somehow explain things to him. He'd gone once into the medina that afternoon to remove posters. The goatherd wasn't to be found, nor was there anyone who could tell him where he might have gone. And now, with Zerkaoui missing too, he was at a loss.

He drove home, certain a couple of drinks would fix him up. He went through a stop sign and narrowly missed a taxi, but he managed to right the jeep and reached his garage safely. Upstairs in his sanctuary, he locked and bolted the door, took out an ice tray and a glass and poured himself a good shot of Scotch. It went down too fast to enjoy; so he poured himself another, this time concentrating his gaze on the amber liquid slipping around the ice cubes.

After another drink he filled the tub and sank into a hot bath. His thoughts wandered; he couldn't plan his next step. Should he try to see Marilyn and apologize? Maybe she prefers it this way. She'll never make *Penthouse*, but a lot of Sharqiyans will enjoy looking at her. She may get a charge out of that.

No, he wouldn't look her up. It would only make it worse for her jerk of a husband. But Larbi! Man, he had to find him!

He pulled the plug and climbed out of the tub. He was relaxed now, and he had to think of a way out. He lay on the bed in his bathrobe with a drink beside him. Before he knew it he was asleep.

He woke suddenly at eight o'clock, cold sober and famished. Should he go out to eat? No, he had a steak in the freezer this time. He'd fry it and open a bottle of wine.

It was just what he'd needed. As he finished the meal, he felt a surge of strength. Marilyn, you stupid bitch! Why did you let me take those pictures? If only he could hear her say it didn't matter. He could phone. If she was alone, maybe she'd let him try to explain.

The phone rang several times before the receiver was lifted. "Marilyn, it's Pete. Are you alone?"

"What's it to you?"

"Where's Lou?"

"Out."

He could tell she'd been drinking. "Marilyn, I wanted to tell you how sorry I am to hear you're leaving. I really feel bad."

"Who told you?"

"The Ambassador, I guess."

"Well, he oughta be sorrier than you. You got your rations."

"If in any way it was my fault, baby... You know I wouldn't do anything to hurt you."

"You can spare me that crap. I know your heart is full of compassion."

"Why don't I come out and get you? We could go somewhere, and I'll bring you back afterward. It'll be our last time."

A peal of laughter issued from the receiver.

"God's gift to women making me an offer I can't refuse! Well, let me give you some advice, creep. Get lost!"

"Marilyn, honey, you don't mean that. Let me explain."

"No explanation needed. You got what you wanted, and I've had my fill of you. Goodbye."

He held the dead receiver in his hand. Drunken bitch! So she thinks she was doing me a favor. His anger turned to grief. He wished he'd never made the call. He downed another shot of scotch and felt immediately better. Instead of fooling with her, he should be out looking for Larbi.

The air was balmy. There were people in the street. He passed the place where he'd eaten the night before. He passed through the massive arched gate to the medina, where any man was a fool to go with more money than he could afford to have taken away from him. He found the place where Larbi stayed and tried out his Arabic on a man standing nearby. "Larbi? You know the painter? The goatherd named Larbi?"

The man clicked his tongue in the negative.

He wandered through the streets in black despair, carrying the burden of a double guilt. He came to a street where veiled women in jellabas stood at doorways and sat on the steps of ancient houses. One spoke to him in French: "Monsieur, you come with me?" "No," he answered. "You come with me."

He took her home and watched her climb out of her awkward garments. Afterward, he paid her well and threw her out. Somehow he felt it was a way of making it up to Marilyn. It helped him understand her. You see, baby, he was saying, I'm just like you.

Day Four
Sunday, May 6

1

It was well before first light when the call on the emergency radio came. Potter pried the receiver out of its cradle and grasped it to pinch the lever which activated the transmitter.

"Three-zero-zero, this is three-zero-one. Over."

"Three-zero-one," came the crackling reply, "Sir, I think you oughta know there's trouble downtown. I hear rifle and machine gun fire and it sounds like it's coming from all over. Also the city lights are out. Power must be cut. Over."

Potter was fully awake now. He looked at his watch. It was 4:25.

"What about the Embassy? Is the emergency generator working? Over."

"Yes, sir. We're OK. I think I hear artillery too, but I can't tell where it's coming from. Over."

"OK, three-zero-zero. The CRO should be monitoring this channel. See if you can get him. Over."

As he switched off, Agar's voice came on the line. "Three-zero-zero, three-zero-one, this is three-zero-nine. I get you both. How me? Over."

"Hear you loud and clear, three-zero-nine. Charlie, turn off your set and listen for gunfire outside. Check your phone

195

too, and call us back in exactly one minute. This could be the real thing. Over."

Charlie Agar acknowledged and went off the line. Potter did the same, listening in silence for sounds outside.

"What is it?" asked Catherine, wide awake now in the darkness. "Why don't you turn the lights on?"

"Sh-h-h. Hear that?"

"It sounds like explosions."

"It's artillery. Try the telephone."

"The line's dead," she reported.

"Somebody must have cut the switch at the central power station."

The radio crackled again. It was Agar reporting back.

"Power's out here. No lights either. Phone is dead. I hear rifle fire in the direction of downtown. Snipers maybe. And one machine gun burst. Over."

"Listen, Charlie, we've got to send a FLASH to Washington. But we can't go tearing through the streets in the dark with shooting going on. We'll have to wait until daylight. That means at least an hour from now. I want you to keep your head down, stay close to your radio and start a time log of the shooting you hear. Same goes for the Marines. Who's on duty? Over."

"This is Drew, sir. Over."

"OK, Drew. Round up the rest of the Marines, but stay under cover. And keep a log of all the shooting you hear—type of weapon, direction, distance, time. I'll be in at daylight if I can. At least you'll hear from me. Got it? Over."

"Yes, sir. Will do. Over and out."

Potter fitted the receiver back into its cradle. "So if it's a landing they're coming in a week early," he said.

Catherine had put on her dressing gown and was seated on the edge of her bed.

"You mean that story of an invasion was true?"

"Quite possibly. If so, they may figure they're taking the government by surprise at its weakest moment."

"Then that's why the minister was called away from dinner last night."

"What minister?"

"Didn't you see? While we were eating. I think it was the Minister of Communications."

Potter cursed Nadia Busheira.

"So that's it. Well, then they may have had a few hours warning. But they didn't know about it yesterday morning when they expelled Jack Warnecke as of Monday."

"That changes things, doesn't it?"

"It changes lots of things," Potter mused. "It means I've still got a Defense Attaché instead of flying blind. It also means I'm stuck with Marilyn Cross after telling her husband she had to go. I've wrecked Lou's morale and alienated his wife without solving the problem." He thought for a minute. "On the other hand, I've got one more Marine than I'd counted on, that is, if Corker is a Marine you can count on."

"You will be careful, won't you?"

"I'll have to be if we're going to get through this weekend."

Ida woke to the sound of shooting. It was pitch black outside and in, and she didn't dare try to walk in the dark, even with her cane. She rang, and a houseboy brought a candle.

She made her way on his arm from her bedroom to her piazza for a look at the city. There wasn't a light to be seen except for boats in the harbor, the hospital complex and intermittent flashes from the fighting.

"Good!" she said aloud. "They've taken the power station and cut off the electricity. Now let this government of half-wits try to fight back!"

The pounding continued in the distance. It seemed to be coming from behind her, across the ridge. That was good. They were landing. Once they had a foothold, they could come down through the passes into the city.

She asked the houseboy for the time, sending him scurrying for a clock. It was 4:45. It would be light in an hour.

The telephone! She tried it. Good! The line was out.

She hobbled onto the piazza again and strained to see what

was happening. The bombardment over the ridge continued, punctuated by intermittent small-arms fire. There was no way to observe the fighting. Even the runway lights at the airport were out.

There was nothing for her to do but go back to bed and wait for daylight. She wouldn't be able to sleep, but at least she could lie there. She'd need her strength during the day ahead.

Potter had showered and shaved by the light of a flash-light, and Catherine had gone to the kitchen to prepare a break-fast by candlelight. She woke the live-in servant and barked orders at him like a drill sergeant.

The radio crackled again. It was Agar. "Sir, I'm down at the Embassy. Over."

"How the hell did you get there?"

"I drove, sir, in my own car with headlights on high beam. Didn't see a soul in the streets. Didn't hear a shot either--that is, none pointed at me."

Potter exploded. "I thought I told you to wait until day-light. Who would have operated the equipment if they'd stopped you?"

"Millie, sir," said Agar calmly. " She's backup."

"I've got other work for Millie. Now stay where you are, and don't take any more risks, you hear? That's an order."

"Yes, sir. Are you ready to give me the FLASH, or do you want to wait until you get here?"

Potter heaved a sigh of exasperation. Agar had just saved him at least forty-five minutes in getting word of the fighting to Washington. A FLASH message, he knew, was reserved for imminent or actual hostilities and would reach the President within minutes of transmission from anywhere on earth.

"You know my answer to that. Take this down and send it immediately: 'Small-arms fire heard in Al-Bida at 0425, with sounds of artillery in distance. City lights and telephones out. We believe coup attempt and/or landings in progress. Sounds of artillery from north coast suggest landings. Will report fur-ther details after daylight. POTTER.' Got that, Charlie?"

"Got it, sir. You might want to add what kind of weapons they are."

"Well, what are they?"

"Drew says he hears M-16s on one side and AK-47s on the other. And I've heard mortars and 105s."

Are you sure?"

"Yes, sir. I know the sounds."

"OK, put it in, and give me Drew." Charlie knew the sounds, all right. He lived life to the full--vicariously.

Drew's voice came on the line.

"Drew, I want you to call every number on the net. Tell Commander Warnecke and the other officers to come in, and tell the rest to stay home and report what they hear. I'll call you again before I leave the house. Have you got that?"

"Yes, sir. Over and out."

Lou Cross was hauled from his first real sleep by the insistent squawk of the radio. With a groan, he found the receiver.

"The Ambassador told me to alert you, sir. There's gunfire in the city and artillery outside. He wants you to come in after daybreak and report any shooting you've heard."

Wearily, he registered the message. He had finally sunk into sleep only an hour before. As duty officer he had to expect it. And as Security officer and Chief of Admin there were actions he would have to take.

He tried the light, found it didn't work and peered across the king-size bed to where Marilyn lay with her back to him. He could make out the mound of her hip rising softly from her knee and then dropping off precipitously to her waist. One of the photos had reminded him of the size of her hip protruding hugely at the camera with the blond head smiling back over her shoulder at the viewer—any viewer, not just Pascal—any Marine or Sharqiyan who happened to come across a print. Pascal could be selling them, for all he knew.

Abruptly he stopped. He was trembling again with impotent rage, but he couldn't afford to think about it now. Maybe it would be better after she left. People would forget. He had fourteen months left on his tour, and by that time a lot of these people would be gone. Almost nobody would be left who knew about her, unless they saw the pictures, and even then they might not know who it was. She'd be just another big blond showing her skin, not Mrs. Lou Cross.

That gave him hope. When he got to the office, he'd look up everybody's end of tour date. Who knows? Maybe some of them would even have their tours curtailed.

She began to move. The mountain of her hip, outlined more clearly now in the growing daylight, shuddered and disappeared as she rolled onto her belly.

"Will you make up your mind? Get up or go back to bed. I need my sleep."

"I've got to go, Marilyn. Something's come up."

"Then go. Don't just sit there."

"But you stay here. Stay in the house. There's supposed to be shooting in town."

"What do you think I'm planning to do, go jogging at six a.m.? Get out, and take your radio with you."

"I can't. The regs say I've got to leave it here so you can be contacted."

"You leave it and I'll turn it off. You can call me on the telephone."

"The phones are out, and you're supposed to leave the radio on at all times. That's why we've got it."

"If you think I'm the only one who keeps it off, you're crazy."

She stopped talking and remained on her belly. He might as well have breakfast and go to the Embassy. It was better than arguing with Marilyn, and he could look up those end of tour dates.

What was that Marine saying about gunfire? He didn't hear any gunfire.

By the time Harold Potter reached the Embassy it was broad daylight and Jack Warnecke was already there. Warnecke had driven the ranch wagon himself, and Potter had allowed

Youssef to be sent out for him in the armored ambassadorial limousine at Sgt. Hernandez' insistence. There was no use taking unnecessary chances.

Warnecke and Potter lived on opposite sides of the city; Comparing notes, they were able to pinpoint some of the shooting. The port area was under particularly heavy attack, and Warnecke felt this was to knock out the Naval Command Center, which coordinated operations by the patrol boats and shore stations around the island. "If it's an invader attacking the Command Center," he said, "he can prevent any coordinated action by Rashidi's forces."

Potter was thankful for Warnecke. His own infantry training was decades out of date and had never included amphibious operations. Without Warnecke he would have had to guess at the significance of the sounds.

"Let's get all our photos together and some maps," he said. "We'll set up a war room to follow the action."

"I've got maps on the wall in my office," Warnecke said. "But I'll have to bring them up to the vault. Not everybody is authorized in my office."

"You're right, Jack," said Potter. "And in the vault we'll have everything we'll need if we have to hole up."

He called the Marine desk. "Has Mr. Cross come in yet?"

"No sign of him, sir."

"Call him on the radio then."

"I just did, sir. There's no answer."

Potter cursed under his breath. Either Cross and Marilyn were both on their way in or else she'd stayed home and turned the radio off. He preferred to have the dependents stay home, but he wanted them to keep their radios on.

"Try every ten minutes until you get an answer. And send Sgt. Hernandez up to my office, will you?"

Hernandez seemed ready and eager for action.

"Take a couple of your men, Top," he told him, "and help the Commander set up a situation room in the vault. I want a city map and a map of the island; the largest scale you can find. Look in the storeroom for acetate and pins and grease pencils."

This is Cross's job, he thought. Where is he?

As if in answer, the intercom buzzed. "Mr. Cross is on his way up," the Marine said.

"Is Mrs. Cross with him?"

"No, sir. He's alone."

"Good. But keep trying to get her on the radio."

Cross's face was pasty white. Dark circles ringed his eyes. His jowls sagged.

"What's the matter with your radio, Lou? We're not getting any answer."

"I guess Marilyn turned it off. I told her not to."

"Did you tell her to stay home?"

"Yes, sir. But there was no shooting where we live. I didn't hear any until I got into town."

"Well, keep in mind where you heard it. It's all going on the situation map. Hernandez is putting it up now. Take charge of it, will you?"

Cross scurried out, his features assuming a determined air as he received his new mission. Potter buzzed the Marine desk again.

"Any luck getting Mr. Pascal or Mr. Finley?"

"Mr. Finley's coming in, sir. But Mr. Pascal's radio doesn't answer."

"So Pascal turns his set off too. Or else he's sleeping out. What about Millie?"

"She called in about twenty minutes ago, sir. She heard the shooting. I told her to stay home and keep calling in."

"Good boy," he said. But he wished she were up at Ida's nevertheless. What an observation post!

He gathered Pascal's photos of the north coast and went upstairs to the vault. The massive door was open, and two Marines were tacking a map and a sheet of acetate to the wall.

"That looks good. We can hole up here for days if we have to. As long as we have radio contact with the people at home we'll be able to do some reporting even if the phones are out. By the way, isn't Corker supposed to be up here?"

Sgt. Hernandez' face was frozen. "He must be around somewhere, sir," he mumbled.

"Well, don't let him out of your sight unless this vault is locked. Invasion or no invasion, the Sharqiyans will grab him if they can. Tell Drew not to let him out of the building."

"Drew's gone off duty, sir. I'll call Jensen," said Hernandez. He spoke into the intercom, and when he finished his face was grim. "He went out past Jensen about ten minutes ago, sir. He told him you sent him over to the Marine House."

"I what? That means he's skipped again. Now what possessed that stupid kid to do that? Doesn't he realize he's infinitely better off with us than outside?"

Hernandez' gaze dropped. "Sir, he left a note for you. One of the Marines is bringing it up now."

It was a sealed envelope, with the Ambassador's name written in a painful scrawl. Potter tore the envelope open, unfolded the sheet of yellow lined scratch paper and read. "Mr. Ambassador, you said you would not let them put me in a Sharky jail, and now you're going to do it anyway. Sir, I never touched Mrs. Cross and you promised. Now I got to hide. I don't want to go a.w.o.l. but I can't help it. Sincerely, Ronald Corker, Cpl USMC."

Potter passed the note to Hernandez. "Do you know what this is all about?"

Hernandez read the note, still averting his gaze. "No, sir, unless someone told him you changed your mind."

"Did someone tell him that?"

"That's what he said last night. He said, 'I ain't goin' in no Sharky jail, no matter what.' And I said, 'You stay here, and you won't have to,' and he said, 'Yes, I will. Monday morning they're gonna put me in a Sharky jail.'"

Lou Cross had come in a moment earlier, carrying boxes of grease pencils and colored thumb tacks.

"Who the hell would tell the kid I'd turn him over to the Sharqiyans?" asked Potter. "Do you know, Lou?"

Cross looked up, startled. "No, sir, I haven't the faintest

idea." He shifted the boxes from one hand to the other. A grease pencil dropped to the floor. He picked it up and went to the map. "It must have been one of the Marines."

"It wasn't none of the Marines, Mr. Cross," said Hernandez.

"Then I don't know who it was," said Cross, sticking a pin in the map.

Potter watched him busy at the map. Hernandez had already left the room.

2

The sun was already coming in her window when Ida awakened. Well, wasn't that the limit! She'd been up before five at the sound of the bombardment and had only gone back to bed to wait for dawn so she could follow the action. Now, for the first time in years, she'd missed the sunrise. She was furious with herself.

She rose and put on her dressing gown and slippers. The binoculars were always left on the piazza. If she could just navigate through the house she would be able to tell Harold Potter what was happening down in the city.

The bombardment seemed to have stopped. It must mean they've landed, she concluded. Or else the landing had been repulsed. But why was it so quiet?

She heard the sound of machine gun and rifle fire. She remembered France in 1918. She was just a girl then, and it was her first overseas experience. At Neufchâteau she'd handled cases of bullet wounds. They were cleaner than shrapnel wounds, but occasionally they brought in some boy who'd been hit by a dumdum bullet, and that wasn't pretty.

She reached the piazza, and now, as if a curtain had been drawn aside, the whole panorama was spread out before her. It was all the same, yet somehow different. The traffic sounds were missing, and in their place there was the occasional roar of an engine or a siren. Otherwise, everything was silent.

She saw a puff of smoke near the Caserne Maynardier and then another on the parade ground inside. But there was no cannon fire, only a dull thud. Must be mortars, she thought with satisfaction that the memory was still there after so many years. It meant the caserne was under fire from fairly close --a rooftop or an alleyway probably, with someone directing fire from a point in view of the target. So they were in the city already. That was good.

On the other hand, she hoped Karim al-Rashidi was safe. It bothered her to think of her former pupil under attack when she was rooting for the invaders. She hoped he'd joined them and brought some of the armed forces with him, but she feared he'd remain loyal to the government against an outside invading force. As for Qasim, her only wish for him was that he'd be out of a job.

The scream of jet engines alerted her to the two fighters taking off from the airport far to the right. They were heading west toward Ras el-Kebir. They turned slowly, lazily like the swallows she used to watch at nightfall in the Missouri sky over her lawn. Except that it was not nightfall, and these were not swallows. Now, they headed toward the city. One of them was shooting. The tracers issued visibly from its snout like the tongue of a lizard darting out at its victim. Some distance away from the Caserne, a house was apparently hit, since puffs of dust were rising now from an area in the medina where flat rooftops almost touched over narrow alleys.

The other plane came in and repeated the operation as the first one soared upward. She was unable to tell whether they had hit their target, but she noticed that the puffs of smoke in the caserne had ceased. Had Rashidi called in the planes to put the mortars out of action? If so, at least the observer had had to scramble to safety. But mortars were easy to displace. They could be carried swiftly through the alleyways and the baseplate set again on solid ground. The observer would have to find a place of visibility from which to direct fire, but that shouldn't be too difficult since the caserne dominated the horizon west of the Medina.

Still looking through her binoculars, she had just time to notice that the swallows had turned and were swooping down once more. One was coming in from the sea in a direct line past the medina and toward the Watch Tower. And when it pulled up, it would probably fly right over her house. She abandoned the binoculars, unable to hold them and follow the action taking place almost across her entire field of vision. The first one was diving again, its dragon's breath spitting at the houses below, and now it was climbing in an arc just over her head. She clearly saw that the red spittle had not stopped at the intended target but had dribbled on, with puffs of dirt kicking up from perfectly innocent places along its path. Honestly, couldn't they be more careful? These were their own people they were killing. What was Rashidi thinking of?

The second one was diving straight down with its bursts concentrated on its target and pulling up without bothering to stop shooting. Leaning on her cane, she watched with fascination from the balustrade as the line of dirt puffs rose up toward her. What a senseless thing to do! Why, they were going to hit the front lawn and even her house! These hoodlums were always doing something to spoil and destroy the things people loved. She vowed she'd go to Rashidi again tomorrow and give him a piece of her mind.

Potter and Warnecke were sticking colored pins in a map of Al-Bida on which the principal government buildings had been overprinted in red. They had spotted the American Embassy as well as several other embassies in the general vicinity but not near enough to be called neighbors. The Cultural Center was several blocks away, and in one of the streets between was the apartment house where Pete Pascal lived. Other members of the Embassy were scattered in all directions at greater or lesser distances.

With telephones out, power cut and fighting in the city, Potter had to decide whether to bring the dependents in to the discomfort of the Embassy stronghold or leave them in the relatively exposed comfort of their homes. He knew the Embassy had a fortress-like series of protective devices which the Marines were trained to make full use of. The only thing they were not allowed to do was use their weapons except when under direct personal attack.

"Let's look at the E & E Plan," he said.

Cross handed him a black loose-leaf notebook with typewritten sheets marked Secret inside. Potter and his staff had updated a previous Escape and Evacuation Plan with Boyle, the RSO, trying to imagine all contingencies requiring Amemb Al-Bida to be evacuated or to serve as a safe haven for evacuees from another post.

"It says we all gather here," Cross said.

"Only if we' re to be evacuated. If we're just sitting out a storm, I'm not going to risk bringing in dependents through small arms fire."

"My wife and kids are better off where they are," Warnecke said. "It's out of the way, and she knows how to handle herself."

"I'm glad you feel that way, Jack. I really think that's best for the time being. How about you, Lou?"

Cross roused himself. "Oh, I agree, sir. I just wish Marilyn would turn on her radio."

"Even without it she's better off there," said Potter. "And my wife will stay where she is too. As for Millie, she's in her apartment, but she's pretty far out from the center."

Charlie Agar interrupted. "Mr. Ambassador, I can type messages. If that's all there is, there's no problem."

"Thanks, Charlie, but you'll need a backup. This thing could go on for days. I'll let her stay out there for the time being, but later on I'll call her in if the fighting doesn't get worse."

"What about Pascal?" Warnecke asked.

"Well, he's got his Center to look after. I suppose he could be useful here too. But first you'll have to find him."

Agar offered to go to Pascal's apartment and to the Center, but Potter shook his head. "Let him do his own job. I can't afford to risk you too."

They began to locate probable scenes of action on the map. There was mortar fire from the west, possibly near the army barracks, and small arms fire continued near the port. Other sounds, however, were harder to locate.

"Oh, to be sitting up there on Ida's piazza!" said Warnecke. "What a view she must have!"

Potter thought for a minute. "You know, Millie has been going up there every day to take pictures. If she goes today and takes her radio, she should be able to give us some pretty accurate pinpointing."

The intercom buzzed. "Mr. Ambassador," said Jensen,

"I've got Millie on the radio. She says she has to talk to you. She sounds pretty upset."

Potter picked up Agar's radio. "Go ahead, three-zero-eight. 'This is three-zero-one. Over.'"

"Oh, Mr. Potter," came the distraught voice, "they've killed her! "

"What are you talking about? Killed who? Over."

"Omar came to tell me. They've killed Ida. The planes came over and shot her dead on her piazza!"

It was much later in the morning. Marilyn knew this from the sunlight in her eyes as she lay in bed and from the sounds of activity in the direction of town. She heard gunfire too, and she wondered if this was what had awakened her.

No, it was the doorbell. But on a Sunday morning? Couldn't people leave her alone on Sunday? She'd told the guard not to let strangers in. Her head splitting, she struggled to her feet, put on her bathrobe and went to a window overlooking the driveway. "What is it?" she called.

"It is I, Gaston Girardot. I must talk to you. Please let me in."

"You can't come in. I'm not dressed."

"My dear, it is most urgent. You must let me in."

"Well, just a minute then."

She closed the windows and looked at her puffed features in the mirror. I won't, she thought. But she threw on a dressing gown and carefully descended the staircase.

"Come in," she said, "and wait in the living room. I'll be down in a few minutes."

"My dear, I promise I shall not look at you. Please hurry."

But she made him wait. And when she finally appeared, she was as presentable as anyone breaking in on her without warning on a Sunday morning had a right to expect. Besides, she noticed he hadn't even shaved!

"At last," he said. "Now come sit down." There was sweat on his brow, and he had to make an effort to speak coherently.

"You hear the shooting? The insurgents must have landed a week ahead of time, and they're fighting the government forces now. I wanted to tell your Ambassador, but I do not dare go to your Embassy. So I have come to ask you to get this message to him. Will you do it?"

"You mean I should go to the Embassy myself?"

"If you can. If not, you have your radio. Please use it, since there is no telephone. But you must inform him somehow."

She hesitated. "All right. I'll find a way."

"Good. Now listen to me. This is the counter-revolution for which I have been hoping. The former Prime Minister has been gathering forces for an invasion. He has the backing of certain sheiks in the Gulf and of private interests in Europe. There are Europeans involved. If they succeed, French influence will be restored and the fanatics eliminated. The threat to the oil supplies from the Gulf will be ended. Do you understand me so far?"

"I think so. But what are we supposed to do about it?"

"I told your Ambassador it would be next Sunday, May 13. But they have fooled even me."

"Are you one of them?"

"Dear lady, I have lived here all my life. I have enjoyed privileges, it is true. But I have also helped to make this island prosperous. You cannot blame me for wishing to protect my investments."

"So what am I supposed to do? Tell him all that?"

"He knows that much already. What he may not know is which members of the government are really his friends and which are with the *fanatiques*. This list will tell him."

She scanned the list hurriedly, her mind still clouded. "You mean I have to get all these names to him?"

"Yes, because it is important that he know who are his friends and who have set a trap for him. Also there are those who will wait to see which side is winning and who will make the best of the situation that emerges. I am one of those. That is why I cannot appear to be involved and can only warn cautiously. With this list your Ambassador will be able to offer his support where it will do some good."

Marilyn's head still throbbed, but her thoughts were clearing.

"But Maître, how does he know you're on his side?"

"Perhaps he doesn't. But he should know that when the issue hangs in the balance, I am on the side of a restoration of the former regime. Tomorrow, if the battle is lost, I may have to switch sides."

"I think I better tell him that too."

"I could not ask for more." He rose. "And now, my dear, I have another call to make, on a very old lady who does not like me but who shares my interest in the success of this enterprise. I must find a way, in spite of herself, to insure her safety."

Marilyn watched him haul himself up from his chair. "You should think of your own safety too, Maître."

He waved a flipperlike hand as he made for the door. "Oh, I shall, Madame. I have been at this game for a long time."

Pascal lay dozing in the sunlight. He had slept beautifully and, despite a slight headache from the whisky, was refreshed and ready for a day writing cancellation notes and phoning apologies to the many distinguished names on his invitation list. He would take care to call the Marine guard first, but he expected no problems.

He listened to the sounds outside and thought it sounded like Chinese New Year in San Francisco or Tet in Saigon. Did they shoot off firecrackers in Saigon? He couldn't remember. But he did recall the distant thunder of artillery fire outside the city at night and the flashes in the sky like heat lightning.

But this sounds like artillery too, he thought. And the other, close in, that's got to be an AK-47. It can't be a jackhammer, he decided, because they work a French week here and today is Sunday.

Then he heard the pounding on his door. He rolled out of bed and staggered to the vestibule in his shorts.

"Who is it?"

"It's Marge. Let me in."

"I haven't got any clothes on."

"I don't care. Let me in anyway."

"You asked for it." He unbolted the door and reached for a robe.

Her hair was in disarray. She wore an old, paint-spattered shirt and jeans. Her eyes were wide with fear.

"They're attacking the Center!"

"Who?"

"I don't know. Rioters. There's a mob outside. They're throwing stones, hitting the building. I don't think the gate will hold. They may be inside already."

"How do you know all this?"

"I can see it happening from my window. Hurry up!"

He was fumbling with his shoes and socks. "Did you call the police?"

"Don't you understand what I'm saying? They're fighting in the streets. There's no police. There's no telephone and no power."

"Where's your car?" he asked. His hands were shaking.

"My husband took it. He went to look after his school. I came on foot."

The elevator was stalled. They took the stairs two at a time to the basement. With a heave he rolled up the entrance shutter, started the jeep and careened out of the garage. Marge hung to her seat. The streets were crowded with youths screaming slogans. He made a detour through side streets. Each time they tried to approach the Center they ran headlong into the mob and had to back up. Someone spotted their license plate and began to throw rocks. Others joined in, and it was only by swerving onto a sidewalk that Pascal was able to escape. A stone hit one of his headlights before he could turn.

"Bastards! I've got to get there before they find the paintings."

"Paintings!" she exploded. "What about the library, the

classrooms, the language lab? You haven't even seen the place yet. They may be inside now."

"Let's go up to your apartment and have a look."

The flat occupied by Marge Henry, her husband and their children was in a French-leased apartment house used by French *coopérants,* mostly teachers. It looked out onto the elegant old villa which was the American Cultural Center. The view was partially blocked by palm trees, but the mob pushing against the front gate was plainly visible.

"I wish I had binoculars," Pascal said.

She handed him a pair.

"My God, Marge, they're trying to force the gate. If they get into the garden, they can get into the building any number of ways."

A boy held a bottle with a rag stuffed into its neck, while another lit a match. The first youth stepped back and heaved the bottle over the iron fence toward the villa. It landed on the porch, shattering below one of the French windows. Immediately flames leapt upward, licking at the wooden trim.

"They're trying to burn the place down! "

Suddenly the iron grill of the garden gate sprang inward and the mob, like flowing molasses, spilled into the garden. In a moment the windows were smashed and figures were disappearing inside the building. He handed the glasses back to her.

"I've got to get over there and do something. You stay here till your husband gets back."

"Don't you go near that place! They'll kill you!"

"I'll be careful. I promise."

Five minutes later he was mingling with the mob and trying to make his way to the smashed grill. Thank God I can pass for a Sharqiyan, he thought. For once it's doing me some good. They think I'm one of them!

Smoke began to issue from the windows of the old house. The looters continued to run in and out. What could burn besides books? he wondered as he pushed his way through the crowd. A whole list of items presented itself to his mind. Curtains, furniture, rugs—almost everything but the load-bearing walls and the marble staircase would burn, including the paintings, unless he could get to them first.

He broke free and ran around the building to the back door, hoping to be able to reach the auditorium before the looters did. If he could get the paintings down off the wall, he might be able to carry them up the back stairs and into his own office. He had his set of keys, and he was fairly confident they wouldn't be able to reach the second floor because of the iron grill at the top of the stairs.

Once at the back door he realized the chances of doing anything at all unobserved were almost nil. The villa was exposed on all sides. Crowds surrounded it. Dozens of youths dashed in and out like rats through the broken windows carrying booty out and then returning for more. Flames were visible through the windows, silhouetting the figures in the middle ground. Smoke issued from windows upstairs, and the wing used by the English Language School was on fire. At least the flag wasn't burning, he thought, since this was Sunday.

Suddenly there was a splitting noise. He watched in horror as a wooden partition in the library gave way. He heard the screams and before he could imagine the reason three figures engulfed in flames stumbled out of the building and began to roll on the grass. One of them, only slightly burned, tore off his smoking shirt and disappeared into the crowd. Others used jellabas to beat out the flames covering the remaining two figures. They carried away a moaning body with strips of smoldering skin hanging from his limbs. The last one lay motionless and silent as the flames still licked at his body.

Pascal caught the smell of burning flesh and turned away nauseated. He retreated, dazed, to the garden wall and dumbly sat watching his Center burn.

After a while the mob, its blood lust sated and the looting completed, began to melt away while the building burned. Thick smoke still poured from the upstairs windows, and he knew there was danger the ceiling would collapse. He couldn't tell what time it was; he had forgotten his watch in the rush.

The sun beat down now almost from the zenith, hammering repeatedly on the pain which was splitting his head.

The villa was almost empty now, voided of books, furniture, wall ornaments, clocks, stationery, even ball-point pens—anything that could be carried, just as it had been voided of human life. It lay inert in the heat of day like an empty shell on a glutted diner's plate. If there had been a guard on duty, as there should have been, there was no sign that he had stayed after the mob had begun to form.

Pascal's head was swimming. He rose to his feet to inspect the damage and try to salvage the remains of his Center. He made his way gingerly over smoking debris and into the librarian's office with its file cabinets and card files and notebooks carefully stacked, and now forced open like huge mouths with their contents disgorged onto the floor.

But this was not what he was seeking. He went into the library, unrecognizable now with its bookcases overturned, its checkout desk a smoldering shell and its large relief map of the United States blistered and illegible on the wall. Against one wall a bookcase had miraculously remained upright though charred by the flames. He pried a book at random from the long row of unrecognizable volumes pressed together as if for mutual protection. It was blackened along the edges. When he opened it he found the pages as clean and the text as legible as if it were brand new: *Les Aventures de Tom Sawyer*.

Replacing the book carefully, he continued compulsively toward the room he most wanted but most feared to see. He expected nothing. Either the paintings would have been destroyed by fire or the vandals would have made off with them. In this way he tried to harden himself to the sights which would greet him.

He recognized now that he had not taken into account the attitude of the rabble toward an exhibit of representative paintings by a fellow Sharqiyan Muslim in the precincts of the hated imperialists. Each of the thirty-odd paintings lining the walls of the room had first been sliced twice with a knife in a diagonal cross, then torn from the wall, stabbed and trampled under foot. No advanced scientific techniques could restore these paintings. No meticulous work of love could bring them back to life.

Pascal was about to sit down in despair and resignation, thinking, well, after all, Larbi can do more paintings, when he noticed for the first time, as if the sight had been withheld from his view until the very last, a figure hanging from the wall at the far end of the room. He approached it slowly, noting how skillfully the cord had been thrown over a hook projecting from the wall, as if waiting for this opportunity to support the weight of a man hanging with his feet only inches from the floor. The hands and feet were not even tied. The hands were extended with palms open and the head twisted sideways by the rope almost in shy humility, offering the product of its lonely but loving labors on the bare mountainsides of Sharqiya. A placard, with an inscription in Arabic and French, hung from the neck, as if from the neck of a sandwich man returning from a day of advertising someone else's wares. It said: "BLASPHE-MOUS LACKEY OF THE IMPERIALISTS."

Pierre Pascal sank to his knees and wept before the body of Larbi the goatherd.

3

Potter answered the intercom.

"Sir, it's Mrs. Cross. She says she's got to see you."

Oh, oh, he thought, and I can't ask the Marine whether she's drunk or sober.

"I'll be right down. He looked across the vault at the desk where Lou Cross sat deep in calculations of his own. No use telling him. Let's find out what she wants first.

He left the vault and descended to his office. Marilyn was waiting for him in the anteroom. She was overdressed in a frilly frock which oozed respectability. She wore enough *eau de cologne* not only to make him wish the windows were open but to kill any odor on her breath.

"You shouldn't have come into town, Marilyn. It's not safe."

"I had to. Maître Girardot gave me a note for you. He was afraid to deliver it himself."

Potter read the note. "Did he give you any explanation?"

She recounted Girardot's visits and his warnings.

"It's plausible. At this point we're grasping at straws. He could be trying to help, or else trying to get us in worse trouble. Thank you for bringing this in, Marilyn. It could make a lot of difference."

She forced a polite smile. "Well, I'll be getting back."

He steeled himself. "Marilyn, there's one other way you can help. Tell me who gave you that envelope to put in Pete's in-basket."

She flushed and looked down. "I wondered if you'd ask. It was Brahim Zerkaoui. But honestly, I didn't know what was in the envelope."

He pressed her hand. "Thank you for telling me. Now don't worry about it. Just keep your emergency radio on."

After she had left, he returned to his office and looked again at Girardot's list. It contained the names of several members of the GDRS, of the Supreme Revolutionary Council and of the hidden opposition, together with a few lines on each describing his sympathies. If the landings were successful, there was no doubt the pro-Western elements would be back in. If they failed, the opposite might be true—unless nationalists like Karim al-Rashidi and President Abderrahman could dictate their own terms to the extremists. Even an extremist regime would need men who could make the government function. If Rashidi could maintain control of the armed forces, he might remain as a moderating influence on even the most radically fundamentalist regime.

Potter paced the floor. Girardot's estimates were probably correct. They contained a few surprises, but not many. Why should Girardot go to so much trouble? Why had he told him of the invasion in the first place? Where did his information come from? Was he just another opportunist courting both sides at once? Or was he the French patriot he had told Marilyn he was?

He remembered Ida's praise for Rashidi and Rashidi's warning against dealings with Qasim. As Minister of the Interior, Qasim controlled the police and the Gendarmerie. He was responsible for the Warnecke's expulsion and for allowing Pascal to take incriminating photos for his exhibit. He controlled the Ministry of Education and could bring a mob of students into the streets at a moment's notice. For all Potter knew, mobs might be roaming the streets now.

He sat on the corner of his desk and looked at Girardot's list again. Only Rashidi's forces could protect the Embassy against an attack by a mob. Could he afford to be open with him?

The streets were empty. The perpendicular rays of the sun beat down on the still-smoking American Cultural Center. Pierre Pascal staggered from the ruins of his efforts in Al-Bida and without a backward look drove to his apartment garage and climbed to the top floor. He would have to report to the Ambassador, and the sooner the better. He took three aspirin and reached for the emergency radio next to his bed. When he tried the call signs, there was no answer. He'd have to go to the

Embassy now, even if only the Marine guard was there. If the Ambassador was at the Residence, he could call him on the Marine's radio and make his report.

As usual he parked outside the main entrance to the Embassy, under the observation of the TV camera at the Marine desk. Jensen let him in.

"I've got to talk to the Ambassador."

"He's upstairs in his office, sir. Most everybody's here but the dependents."

Good God! Then the Ambassador was right, he thought, and it's not just my Center!

Upstairs, Millie was not at her desk, but he could see Potter through the open door. He knocked and entered.

"Sir, they've burned the Center and killed Larbi."

Potter stared back at him. "Now do you believe me?"

"Yes, sir, and I want to apologize."

"Why didn't you radio us or answer our call?"

"My radio isn't working. I guess I forgot to charge the battery."

"Then sit down outside and write me a complete report while I finish this cable."

Potter was in no mood for levity. Pascal sat at Millie's desk and sketched out on a yellow pad, in chronological order, the events of the morning. Then he listed the presumed losses and took the report into the Ambassador's office.

"How do you feel?" Potter asked as he scanned it. "Are you ready to rejoin the Embassy and do some work?"

"Yes, sir. Anything at all."

"Don't worry. We'll find something useful for you to do."

Millie made her decision. She would go to Ida's. There had to be a reason why they had been thrown together in such intimacy in the last days of Ida's life. Maybe she could learn what the old lady's last wishes were.

She was still crying, but her mind was clear and made up. She took the radio, her steno pad and the camera and followed Omar to the ancient limousine. She knew it was a car no one would shoot at. Like its mistress, it stared down its enemies, shamed them. Later they might sneak up and shoot her in the back, but while she was clothed in the authority of her limousine, never.

They drove smoothly up the mountain road hairpin turns until the Watch Tower gate loomed before them. Omar tapped the horn, and the gate swung open, as if Madame Richard were merely returning from a morning drive into the city.

"Where is...the body?" Millie forced a casual tone.

"In the bedroom, Mademoiselle."

She climbed the outside staircase to Ida's piazza, the aerie from which the old lady from Missouri had looked out for six decades of her life onto the world which she had known and loved from colonialism to independence to socialist revolution, maybe even back again.

Millie could see the brutal line of jagged holes tearing upward through the floor of the piazza where Ida's long watch over the city had come to an end. She made her way into the living room, violated by the impact of a bullet which had torn through one wall and lodged behind a picture on the wall opposite. She walked down a corridor to another room at the back of the house where Ida lay on the bed, wrapped mummylike in Muslim style.

Millie sat on a chair in the dark room. She remembered the Ambassador's notes she had typed the evening before. Ida knew two cabinet ministers. One of them was Rashidi the Defense Minister, and the other was Qasim the Interior Minister. She had liked Rashidi. He was one of her orphans. He had warned her against Qasim, whom she didn't like anyway. But if Rashidi was Defense Minister, it was one of his planes which had killed his foster mother. Should Millie tell him what he had done, or had it been deliberate? What would Ida want her to do now? If only she would give her a sign.

In the meantime she could take more pictures and report by radio to the Ambassador. She knew what he would say: stay where you are and keep reporting what you see. But she wanted to do more than that, even if there was risk.

She took up her position on the piazza and scanned the city below. There were puffs of smoke around the port. Far off to the right, near the airport, there seemed to be fighting. No planes were taking off or landing, but there were vehicles moving on the runways, and what looked like more puffs of smoke. There! A vehicle was hit and was burning. She noted the time.

She heard the booming of cannon but couldn't tell where it came from. Either down the coast to the left or back over the mountain to the north. She made more notes.

She wished she could drive into the countryside to see what was going on. In any case, it wouldn't be enough to call in her report by radio; she'd have to deliver the film.

She returned to the living room and removed the film from the camera, inserting a new roll. She looked over her notes and radioed her report to the Ambassador.

"Good girl! Stay where you are and keep taking pictures. I'll try to think of a way to get your film."

Suddenly she heard a horn and the creaking of the gate. She dashed to the piazza in time to see a Citroën pull into the driveway and position itself to pull out again. She watched with fascination. Who in the world...? Then, as the vehicle settled on its hydraulic suspension like a setting hen, the door opened and a balloonlike bulk bulged into view. It was Girardot.

She watched as he closed the door and began to waddle toward her. This was Ida's former lover, the man who during the war had stayed behind and used Ida's husband's connections to enrich himself, the man whom Ida scorned and to whom for thirty years she had refused to speak. And here he was, paying a call on Ida now, in the midst of fighting in the city.

Afterward, she remembered clearly the sight of him walking across the parking lot below and toward where she stood. It was a sight she had already seen in her mind and was somehow expecting. His walk reminded her of a beach ball bouncing on the grass. Now she would see the surprise on his face as he recognized her. From somewhere above them on the mountainside came the chatter of an automatic weapon. Girardot stopped, raised his arm and ran toward her. She was almost able to see the words forming on his lips as he tried to call. He tripped and pitched forward on his face, rolled over and lay still, his arms outspread.

She screamed. Omar, who had been polishing the limousine out of sheer habit, ran up and knelt beside the body. "Get back! Get back!" she heard herself cry. "They're shooting!"

But they were not shooting any longer. She raised the binoculars towards the rocky mountainside. The glasses focused on the figure of a single young man in shirtsleeves, bearded but really a boy, bounding among the rocks with his weapon slung over his head and shoulder.

She crouched over the mountainous body. The face looked up at her, frozen in the same expression of expectancy, still attempting to impart to her the news he had brought.

She wanted to shake the news out of him. Instead she rifled his pockets. From the left hand inside pocket of his jacket she withdrew an envelope with a two-inch hole in the middle where a bullet exiting from his body had passed through it and soaked the edges in blood.

She held the envelope by its corner. The words: "Mad ... ...chard," showed across the gap. She wiped it on the grass and ripped it open. Inside was a single sheet of French writing paper, folded twice into a square and pierced by the same bullet. Like a paper doll, the hole multiplied itself by four as she unfolded it. The message in French, though interrupted repeatedly, was clearly legible. It was composed in the formal style and flowing script of a family solicitor: "Madame, For.....safety.....you must imm.....ely go.....office of Karim.....di. Your devot.....G.G."

Girardot had come to warn Ida of the danger of staying at the Watch Tower, advising her instead to seek safety in Rashidi's office at the Defense Ministry. In the absence of telephone service, he had been Rashidi's messenger to Ida.

Calling to Omar to ready the limousine, she ran back up onto the piazza, reported what had just happened to base control, gathered the radio and all her things and climbed into the back seat of the ancient vehicle as Omar, in uniform, held open the door. Drawing the curtains carefully across the windows, she sat back in solitary dignity as the stately carriage passed through the open gate, left the violated villa and began its slow descent into the city.

She heard the gate creak slowly closed behind her as she left the Watch Tower to the two ex-lovers, separated by past duplicity and by death. The message had been left undelivered, undeliverable, robbed of meaning by the intervention of fate for everyone but herself.

For Rashidi's message to Ida had become Ida's sign to Millie.

4

Catherine Potter had not remained idle. She had learned of Ida's death by monitoring her radio. Now she knew of Girardot's and kept abreast of information exchanged by others.

She was unable to speak directly with Gladys Warnecke. The distance between their homes was beyond the radio's range, but she learned from base control that Gladys and the boys were safe. She made no attempt to contact Marilyn Cross though she knew she had a responsibility to all members of the mission, not just to those she liked. But each time she went to the radio to call Marilyn, she put the instrument down again.

To prove her good will she put the servants to work making sandwiches for the Embassy, which she would deliver herself with hot coffee. So instead of making the first call to Marilyn, she asked base control if everything was all right at the Crosses'.

Before base control could answer, however, she heard Marilyn's voice on the line.

"Base control, please inform Mrs. Potter that everything at the Crosses' is just perfect. Hubby is at the office, and wifey is at home with her piano and her bottle of gin. Unfortunately the ice cubes have melted and there's no one to keep wifey company. Old Ibrahim is guarding the gate, and Sunday is the gardener's day off. But that's all right. Wifey is getting ready for her great big trip tomorrow, back to the good old U.S.A. And who knows? Maybe Maître Girardot will drop in again to say goodbye."

Catherine spoke automatically. She swore later she had spoken not out of malice but out of concern.

"Base control, doesn't Mrs. Cross know that Maître Girardot was killed this morning by a sniper's bullet at Ida's?"

There was a long wailing sound at the other end of the line. "Oh, no..," the voice was saying again and again. And then there was silence. Marilyn apparently had dropped the receiver. If she was speaking, no one heard.

* * *

Ida Gant Richard's limousine made its way through the deserted streets to the old Caserne Maynardier, where Millie expected to find the armed forces of the Democratic Republic of Sharqiya being deployed against a challenge from without.

The limousine provided its own protection. Unaware that Ida was dead, the guards at the gates snapped to attention as the familiar sedan entered. But when a small figure in blue jeans, with odd pieces of electronic gear over her shoulder and around her neck, emerged before the grand staircase like an overloaded tourist, one of the startled guards reacted.

"I am here to see the Minister," Millie told the man imperiously, "on behalf of Madame Richard."

"Does the Minister expect you, Mademoiselle?"

"Of course," she said, looking him straight in the eye. "I wouldn't be here if he didn't. He sent Maître Girardot to me with a message."

The official snapped his fingers, and another guard appeared. They spoke a few words in Arabic, and the second man ran off toward the Minister's office. Climbing the stairs two at a time, Millie left the first man behind, knowing that at least she was walking in the right direction. At the end of the corridor a door opened, and she found herself in the Minister's outer office. Two secretaries were busy typing on manual typewriters, since neither a computer nor a word processor would be of any use today. She forced herself not to assume the deferential air of a secretary. Like Ida, she would stare them down instead.

She succeeded. The Minister would see her. The door opened, and she entered the ornate office.

From behind a huge French desk a heavy man in combat fatigues approached her. "Who are you, Mademoiselle?" he asked warily in English. "I do not think we have met. And may I ask what you are doing with Madame Richard's automobile?"

"My name is Mildred Novak," she answered in English. "I am Ambassador Potter's secretary and a friend of Madame Richard. Madame Richard was killed this morning by one of your airplanes."

The Minister staggered back and steadied himself on the

edge of his desk. He motioned her to sit and fell into a chair, covering his face with his hands. "You must excuse me," he said. "Madame Richard was like a mother to me. I learned English from her. Tell me how it happened." He waved the guard away.

Millie showed him Girardot's letter and told him what she knew, withholding nothing. When she had finished, he rose and looked out the window.

"So old Girardot is gone. He must have been a victim of the plot too. You did the right thing to leave while you could."

"But sir, I intend to go back there right away," she told him, filled with self-confidence in her new role. "Ambassador Potter wants me to report to him on what I see from Mrs. Richard's piazza."

"You'd better not try. Qasim has probably occupied the house by now, and I expect I'll lose a platoon of men taking it back."

"I don't understand. Why is that house so important?"

"Why were you using it? To observe, naturally. It dominates the city and the coast today just as it did in the days of the pirates. As an observation point for artillery or air strikes or naval activity it is unequaled. But it is vulnerable and must be retaken. Otherwise they can use it to call in fire on the city."

He stopped pacing and looked at her. "Does your Ambassador know you are here?"

"No, I said he told me to stay at Ida's."

"Then it's a good thing for you that you are disobedient. And your radio? Does it work?"

"It worked from Ida's house and from my apartment."

"Then perhaps we can reach Mr. Potter from here."

She pried loose the receiver and tried the call sign. There was no answer. She tried again. This time there was a crackling sound and a voice. "This is base control, three zero-eight. Hear you fairly well. Speak slowly. Over."

"Give me the Ambassador. Over."

She waited again. Then she heard a familiar voice..

"Mr. Ambassador, this is Millie. I'm at the Ministry of Defense. The Minister wants to speak to you. Over."

She passed the receiver to him.

"Monsieur l'Ambassadeur," he boomed. "Ici Rashidi. Comment ça va?"

At the Embassy, Potter snapped his fingers at Agar.

"Get everything we say on tape. It may be in French."

He pressed the lever again and answered jovially. "Ça va bien, M. le Ministre. How are things with you?"

"Comme ci, comme ça," answered Rachidi, then broke into English. "We came under mortar attack this morning, but we drove them off. If we can regain control of the city and get the power going again, we may be able to prevent a takeover by Qasim."

"Haven't the mercenaries landed?"

Rashidi paused, cleared his throat and resumed. "Monsieur l'Ambassadeur, there have been no landings, and no mercenaries. The shooting you've heard is between my forces and Qasim's extremists. The whole mercenary threat was an invention of his to make me scatter my forces, and it succeeded. I swallowed it whole, as you say. I deployed my best units to the north coast to deal with a threat which didn't exist, while Qasim moved to take control here."

Potter listened intently but did not break in. The Minister's words were being taped as he continued.

"Now he has taken advantage of their absence to seize the power station, the armory and the university. With the police and the Gendarmerie under his orders and the Education Ministry on his side, he has been arming the students. Even some of my own forces have gone over to him. He has sunk one of my patrol boats on the north coast, but the other got away and is bringing some men here by sea to support us. One of my pilots shot up the Watch Tower and killed my dear Mother, Madame Richard. Now he can use the place to call in artillery. It's going to cost me a lot of good men to take it back."

"So we were both fooled," Potter said when Rachidi finally stopped. "Frankly, I'd taken your actions as an indication there would be an invasion."

"Then Qasim was too smart for both of us," Rashidi answered. "He waited until the French ambassador was gone, and then he loosed the mob on the city and burned your Cultural Center. It was a classic coup de Jarnac, if you know the expression."

Potter's mind flipped rapidly through his file of French terms for the definition. "Sure, it's what we call hitting below the belt, or a stab in the back." He told himself never to underestimate the ability of the native elite to absorb more French culture than even most of the French have!

"Brilliant, Monsieur l'Ambassadeur. But do you know where the term 'coup de Jarnac' comes from?"

Potter was caught by surprise. "No. Tell me."

"All right, I will. Jarnac defeated his opponent in a sixteenth century duel by slashing the tendons behind his knee in a surprise thrust. But that's not the point. The point is the opponent's name."

"Which was?"

"His name was la Châtaigneraie!" said Rashidi. "An ancestor, no doubt, of the French Ambassador!"

"Ça alors!" said Potter. "You're saying the name inspired the coup."

"Or vice versa. In any case they waited for the Ambassador to leave the country before trying it."

Potter marveled in his chagrin. "He also waited until my Deputy, Mr. Levin, had gone on a month-long trip to the States, leaving me crippled too," he added. "Now how can we help you?"

"Stay out of the streets. There will be more fighting. If your families are at home, they will be safer there."

"What about Miss Novak?"

"I can have her escorted to your Embassy if you wish. But without your radio we cannot communicate. She is safe here if you wish her to stay."

"Let me talk to her, please."

Millie's voice was heard on the line.

"Millie, it's up to you."

"Then I'll stay here, sir. That way you and the Minister can keep talking. Unless you want me to leave the radio here and come in."

"No, I want you to keep that radio and not let anyone but the Minister touch it. If you change your mind and want to come in, call."

Rashidi's voice came back on the line. "Your secretary will be perfectly safe and comfortable here, M. l'Ambassadeur. I give you my word."

"Good. Let's keep in touch through her then. Please give my respects to M. le President and assure him the United States stands ready to help in any way possible."

Again, there was silence at the other end. After a pause, Rashidi was heard speaking in somber tones. "Monsieur l'Ambassadeur, I regret to inform you that the Presidential Palace was assaulted last night and President Abderrahman was assassinated. The so-called Supreme Revolutionary Council has named a provisional government."

It was Potter's turn to remain silent. So the center hadn't held, after all. "Monsieur le Ministre," he finally said, "in the name of my government I offer my deepest condolences on the death of President Abderrahman. The United States hopes for continued and improved relations with the new government of the Democratic Republic of Sharqiya."

Warnecke had joined him. They went up to their makeshift War Room to review the situation.

"So the invasion threat is out," Potter began, "and with it the possibility of a counter-revolution. That's not good news for Girardot's fellow colonials."

"It's not good news for Rashidi either, sir," said Warnecke, indicating the pins he had placed along the northern edge of the Sharqiyan crescent. "I'm showing the bulk of his artillery and infantry up along the coast. He'll have to scramble to get them back here before Qasim can take over."

"So we're looking at the prospect of a civil war," Potter concluded, his face grim.

"Unless he uses what he's still got to good advantage. So

far, Qasim has only AK-47's and a few mortars. But if he appears to be winning, there may be a danger of more defections to his side from Rashidi's forces."

"Well," Potter sighed, "that puts us in a worse position than with an invasion on. Now we're up against Qasim and his radical fundamentalists face to face."

He leaned back against a desk and thought for a minute. Then he gave a laugh and shook his head. "Poor old Girardot!" he said. "They fooled him too. He was their patsy. They were sure he'd tell me what they'd said—which he did, but a day after the forged memcon was discovered. To him it was good news, of course. A mercenary invasion would have allowed him to repatriate his investments to France."

He thought for a minute, then laughed again. "If the forgery hadn't come to me a day early, would I have had the time or the presence of mind to warn Châtaigneraie before he left? He was right, you know. He pooh-poohed the idea of an invasion, and I wasn't convinced. But he wasn't expecting a coup de Jarnac."

"What about Ida?" Warnecke asked. "Was she looking forward to an invasion too?"

"No doubt she was. But all she really knew was what she saw from her front piazza--the troop movements ordered by Rashidi, who just admitted he'd been fooled too. But by jumping to conclusions about it I played into their hands! Oh, they were clever, all right. But they haven't pulled it off yet. We've still got a chance with Rashidi."

Marilyn stared at the radio on the floor. Sounds continued to issue from it, but she no longer tried to make sense of them. She never listened regularly and when she did it had to be the old bitch asking about "things at the Crosses'." Marilyn had given it back to her, but how could she have known the old hag had a knife ready to drive into her heart?

Distraught, her mind clouded by gin, she paced back and forth in the huge empty living room as the radio squawked on.

Abruptly, she stopped and wiped her eyes with a handkerchief. That's it. She'd go to Ida's to see him, as a gesture of respect and farewell. What for? He was dead, wasn't he? No matter, it was a gesture. She was an artist, not a goddamned Foreign Service wife. If she'd been true to herself, she'd be playing before an audience or exhibiting her paintings instead of hiding out on a Third World island in the middle of an invasion. If only there'd been someone like Maître Girardot to encourage her when she was young! Well, she wasn't dead yet. This would be an act of defiance as well as one of tribute to him and faith in herself and her future.

She applied lipstick and powder to her ravaged face. There. Now something respectable to wear at a funeral. She went out into the garden and cut a single rose. Why? They'd think he'd been her lover. Then let them. She didn't have to explain that he'd done more for her in an hour than her husband had done in five years of marriage.

Perfect. Now into the car and off. But first she had to lock the house. She wasn't crazy. And when she saw it, she remembered the radio. Potter had told her to keep it on. You never could tell when she might need it.

The radio was under the front seat of her car, and the single rose on the seat beside her. Marilyn was in the driver's seat, head high as old Ibrahim opened the gate and gave her that flat-handed French army salute.

She knew Ida's place from a garden party there the year before on the Fourth of July. Ida liked to show everyone she was an American, but she didn't live like any American woman Marilyn had ever known. You wouldn't catch Marilyn staying here any longer than she had to.

Her head was a little clearer as she drove out the main highway toward the mountain. "I've got to be crazy," she said aloud with a defiant laugh, "or why would I be going out in the middle of a war to put a rose on the body of an old man? Who do I think I am, Sarah Bernhardt? Or Blanche Dubois, maybe?" She reached the end of the straight road. Now began the hairpin turns.

She came to a halt and blew her horn, gently, out of respect. She even found herself putting on a solemn expression, although what she really ought to do was tear her hair like a widow in a Greek tragedy. She hadn't even thought to bring a rose for Ida, but then, she didn't really know her. Besides, it would have diluted the gesture for Gaston Girardot, who even now might be smiling down on her like a guardian angel. The thought gave her comfort.

The gate hadn't opened. She tooted again, more insistently this time. She heard the bolt being thrown back, and the white metal barrier began to swing inward. She shifted into low gear and drove into the open parking area. To her left the garden wall followed the precipice above the city and the sea, and to her right it traced the contours of the mountainside like a miniature Wall of China. In front of her, to the left of the house, was the long outside staircase leading to the porch, with its gorgeous view of the coast and the city.

A figure appeared at the top of the stairs, and she heard the gate close behind her. It was a man, but she couldn't make out who it was, though there was something familiar about him. Someone opened the door of her car and began to pull her by the arm. It was a thin, bearded young man, with a gun slung over his shoulder. Another man appeared from the car port. Like the first, he was bearded and wore an open shirt and carried the same kind of gun. She heard the voice of the man on the outside staircase.

"Madame Cross! How nice of you to pay us a visit."

Now she saw who it was. Slim, elegant, as neatly dressed as ever, greeting her like a host, like the new master of the Watch Tower—Brahim Zerkaoui.

5

Pascal had been put to work in the vault plotting reported scenes of fighting on the 1:10,000 city map affixed to the wall. Where the Cultural Center was located he placed a red thumbtack with a string extending to the edge of the map. On a three-by-five card he wrote: "Burned and looted—1100, May 6. At least one looter dead on grass, another burnt badly but taken away. Body of painter Larbi found hanging from hook on auditorium wall, apparently after death."

It was a laconic statement to describe events he had witnessed just that morning. So was the statement on the card extending from Ida Gant's Watch Tower: "Am. cit. Ida Gant Richard, age 89, shot dead by aircraft during strafing run, 0845, May 6; Gaston Girardot, French cit., killed by sniper's bullets, 1120, May 6."

The heroine was Millie Novak. Her name was on a card extending from the Ministry of Defense. Pins of another color spotted each of the radios, from base control at the Embassy to 301 at the Residence through Millie's 308 at the Ministry. His own 307 was beside him being charged, and all the others, including Finley's, were here at the Embassy. Finley himself had appeared without warning at 1020 and was busy drafting messages with the Ambassador. Only Corker's whereabouts were unknown.

It was dull work for Pascal, but it took his mind off the sights of the morning. Millie was radioing in reports from Rashidi on Qasim's police and Gendarmerie units as they were identified. The Ambassador needed to know this in the event any of them moved on the Embassy. Pascal, for once, was fully aware of its importance.

He wondered how Marilyn was doing at home. Her house appeared out of the line of fire. He imagined her drinking herself into a stupor after hearing of Girardot's death. Funny. What could that old man mean to her?

Cross came in and went to his desk. There was no conversation between them. Cross opened the manuals he had brought and was busy writing on a yellow pad. Out of pure curiosity Pascal passed behind him and peered over his shoulder, but Cross quickly covered the pad. "What's the Amby got you doing?" Pascal asked offhandedly. But Cross looked up coldly and said, "Sorry; classified." His expression had said it all.

Actually, he'd seen enough to know that Cross was calculating his pension. He'd also drawn up a list of all the Americans at the Embassy, including the Marines, with a departure date after each name. Pascal shook his head but concluded it occupied his mind in the midst of his domestic troubles just as Pascal's own work sticking pins in a map kept his mind off the destruction of his Cultural Center and the life and paintings of the goatherd Larbi.

A loud whisper over Cross's radio interrupted Pascal's train of thought. The sound was turned up. It was Marilyn. Before he could reach the set the voice abruptly stopped. He called the Marine. "Jensen, did you hear that?"

"Yes, sir. It was Mrs. Cross."

"What did she say? She sounded strange."

"I didn't get it, sir, but we tape every call that comes in. I'll have it for you right away."

"I'll be right down."

Jensen was rewinding the tape when he reached the Marine desk.

"It's kinda hard to understand, sir. Let's try again."

He set the player in forward motion. The whisper was already going on when the tape began to pick it up. "...at Ida Gant's," it began. "Zerkaoui's here with a gang of thugs ... They're armed ... I need help ... Come and get..."

The whispering stopped.

"That's it, man," said Pascal. "Give me a pistol."

Sgt. Hernandez answered. "Sorry, sir. Not unless the Ambassador says so."

"Somebody must have a weapon I can use. We can't just leave her up there with Zerkaoui."

Lou Cross appeared. "That was my wife. We've got to do something to get her out. Send some of the Marines...."

Pascal looked at him. "Have you got a gun, Mr. Cross?"

"Of course not. Civilians don't carry weapons here. This isn't Viet-Nam, you know."

"Too bad it isn't."

Pascal dashed back to the vault.

"What are you looking for, Mr. Pascal?" Agar asked.

"A weapon of some kind. Any kind. I'm going to Ida's to get Marilyn."

Agar looked at him strangely, then pulled up his pants leg. "Would this do, maybe?"

Pascal stared at the sheathed knife strapped to Agar's calf. "Why not? Can I borrow it?"

Agar's eyes gleamed. "Brand new. Never been used. Wished I could go too, but I can't leave here." He unstrapped it and gave it to Pascal, who strapped it onto his own leg.

"Thanks. I'll try to get it back to you."

"No sweat. Like I say, I wished it was me goin'. Let me know if you do use it. I'll put a notch in the handle."

Pascal went to the kitchenette but found the knives too big, too fragile and all unsheathed. He saw a carpet-cutter. It fit easily in his grip, and he put it in his pocket. His eyes fell on a pistol lying as if for him on a desk. He checked the magazine, slipped it into his other pocket and left. He needed both of them more than their owners did.

"Does the Ambassador know I'm going out?" he asked Jenson.

"I don't think so, sir. I didn't tell him."

"Then don't. But if he asks, tell him I said I went to put my jeep in the garage. I'll call in from the Watch Tower."

Pascal had hardly left the Embassy when Catherine Potter drove up with one of her servants in a car loaded with food. She parked in the garage underneath, and together they carried the thermos and the cardboard boxes of sandwiches and fruit upstairs.

"Here comes Santa Claus!" she called gaily, bringing cheer like a USO worker to men holed up in a bunker.

"Cat, that's very thoughtful," said Potter. "But don't you realize we've got enough food for several days, and you just risked your life to bring us more?"

"I didn't see a thing on the way. The streets were empty," she replied. "Didn't even hear shooting nearby."

"Nevertheless, you'd better get back home right away. I don't want you out after dark."

"We may all have to stay here a while," she replied, contradicting herself now. "There seemed to be a crowd gathering in front as I drove up to the garage."

She wants to be in on the action, thought Potter. Well, so be it if there's no other way.

At that moment Jensen called from the Marine desk. "Mr. Ambassador, there's a bunch of Sharqiyans coming up the street, and they don't look too friendly."

Hernandez dashed down the stairs. "You're right," he said. "Turn your camera around and see what's coming the other way."

The image on the screen panned to the opposite angle and settled on a second group approaching from the other direction. Some were carrying placards in Arabic, and two or three carried crowbars and long, slender metal bars.

"Looks like rebar." Hernandez cried. "They could do a lot of damage with that stuff. Get out the tear gas and call the Ambassador."

A figure on the screen was making faces at the camera. Another was trying to dislodge a paving stone with a crowbar. Others joined in, arming themselves with stones when the first was out and hurling them at the camera.

"Bastards!" Hernandez grunted. "Gimme one of them tear gas bombs."

The stones had done no damage, but before Hernandez could arm the grenade a man with a long, hooked piece of rebar ran up to the door and began poking at the camera. It was placed high, but the bar reached it, the metal striking the lens and the hook pulling on its support. Hernandez and Jensen watched helplessly as the screen registered each blow and then suddenly went blank.

"That's it. They're blinding us," Jensen said.

"They're getting the tear gas anyway," Hernandez cried. He ran upstairs to the barred window behind Millie's desk and looked out. There were at least thirty of them now, and more were arriving. He opened the window and tossed the grenade out. Within seconds a cloud of smoke formed, and the crowd began to disperse.

"That's enough for now. Don't waste your ammo."

Potter was standing behind him, perfectly calm.

"There's another camera over the garage entrance, sir. But it doesn't cover the front."

"Well, you can count on their knocking it out too," Potter said. "'But they won't get into the building for a while, and we're not exactly helpless. Pass me that radio."

He placed the radio on the coffee table and took the receiver. "Three-zero-eight, three-zero-eight, this is three-zero-one. Can you hear me? Over."

Millie's voice answered immediately. "Loud and clear, sir. Over."

"I need to talk to the Minister. Over."

"He's out, but I'll try to find him for you. Over."

"Tell him there's a mob outside the Embassy. We need troops to break it up. Over."

"I hope I can find him. He said something about taking back Ida's house. Over."

"Tell him to be careful. They've got Marilyn Cross up there, and they can probably hear us on her radio. Tell him we need his help here urgently. Over."

"I'll call back in a few minutes. Over and out."

Potter replaced the receiver, his face grim.

"Sgt. Hernandez, get the section chiefs, all of them, in here right away."

Hernandez started out, then stopped. "Mr. Pascal isn't here, sir. He left half an hour ago."

"Left?! To go where?"

Hernandez's voice came haltingly and with embarrassment. "I think he said something about getting Mrs. Cross out of Mrs. Richard's house. But I can't say for sure, sir."

Potter sat back in exasperation. "Some embassy! Now they'll have two hostages if Pete doesn't get himself killed. Well, get the others in anyway. And I want you here too, Sergeant."

We may be able to hold out for a day or two, he thought as Hernandez dashed out. He wondered if Zerkaoui would be smart enough to use Marilyn to make him give up the Embassy.

Pascal knew he had no way of approaching the Watch Tower in his jeep without being detected. Anyone could see the vehicle come straight up the highway from the city. It was only in the final three or four turns that the edge of the precipice would prevent his jeep from being tracked. By that time they would have a good idea of who it was.

There was one item in his favor. There was an unpaved trail up the mountainside. The city map at the Embassy showed it leading up to the very base of the rock on which the Watch Tower perched. From there a goat path continued upward and around the Watch Tower to the mountainside above. If he could drive the jeep to the end of that road and then make his way up the path, he might be able to climb to the spot where Ida had shown him the hole in the garden wall. There he might have a chance of getting into the property unseen.

It was already late afternoon. He could hear the pounding of artillery from the direction of the north coast, with occasional bursts of small arms fire from the city below. But without binoculars he was unable to make much of the situation. In a couple of hours it would be dark—pitch dark in the absence of power. He knew the Embassy had its own generator, but he wondered how the fighting in the city would go without lights.

There were shanties on the side of the mountain above the last village. A hundred meters beyond was a single farmhouse, in ruins. He parked the jeep under a lean-to, satisfied that the vehicle would be out of sight from above and below. He was locking it when a barefoot urchin in rags appeared.

"Garder voiture, M'sieu?"

Every kid on the island seemed to know enough to watch a parked car for pennies. He dug into his pocket, found a coin representing twice the usual amount and with a conspiratorial wink gave it to the boy.

"Voilà. Tu gardes bien."

The boy smiled broadly as Pascal put his finger to his lips and patted the boy's head. Waving back at him, he started up the path.

It took much longer than he had thought to reach the rock. As he planned each foothold up to the garden wall, he wondered whether night might fall before he reached it. Already the clouds gathering in the west were beginning to take on a late afternoon glow. He did make it, however, to a ledge from which he could see the break in the wall. He could make his way there without difficulty. But for now, he would make himself as comfortable as possible on the ledge and wait for darkness.

As he reached for a handkerchief to wipe his brow, the pistol fell out of his pocket.

"Shit!" he said, watching his best weapon bounce down the cliff and out of sight below. He glanced at the Western sky. It would be dark before he could retrieve the pistol and climb back, even if he knew where to look. He would have to make do with the knife and the carpet-cutter.

Warnecke was briefing Potter and what remained of his Country Team in the vault. The city map and the country map were covered with colored pins.

"So the only contact we have outside the building is with your family at home and Millie at the Defense Ministry," said Potter. "We can assume Marilyn's captors are monitoring everything we say on the net."

"I'm afraid so, sir. Pascal took his radio with him. But it was being recharged and may not be working yet."

"Let's wish him luck anyway. And let there be no mention on our radios of where he is or what he's doing."

"As for the GDRS," Warnecke went on, "Qasim's people at the Interior Ministry control the Presidential Palace, the Revolutionary Council buildings and the Ministries of Labor, Education and Social Welfare. They also control the police barracks, the Youth Movement, the Labor Union and the paramilitary militia."

"'But we don't know whether all of them are loyal to Qasim," said Potter.

"No, sir. But he has a network of fundamentalists in key slots. So most of the ministries are at least infiltrated, though we don't know to what extent."

The Defense Ministry had come under mortar attack early, but fighter aircraft from the air base had riposted, and one of them had killed Ida Gant. There had been no more shelling of the caserne. The only planes taking off from the airport had been flying to the north coast, presumably giving close support to Rashidi's forces there.

At the port there was fighting, but who was winning they couldn't tell. With the lights out at night, they would know even less, and roving bands of hoodlums would have the freedom of the city.

"What about the French?"

"Sir, outside their Embassy compound all they have now is their aid mission and their cultural center. There are lots of French here, official and unofficial, but I doubt they are any better off than we are. If Qasim wins out over Rashidi, they'll be as vulnerable as we are."

"Then how do you rate Rashidi's chances?" Potter asked.

"He's got the loyalty of the field-grade officers and most of his regular troops. But the draftees and the junior officers have been worked over by the fundamentalists. I imagine it will be touch and go for some time."

"Thanks, Jack," Potter said. "Questions?"

They heard Millie's voice on the radio, giving her call sign. Potter picked up the receiver and acknowledged.

"Mr. Potter, I've looked everywhere. The Minister is out somewhere with his troops, and no one will do anything without his orders. I'm afraid you'll have to stay inside the Embassy until he gets back. Over."

Potter glanced at the others. "Keep trying, Millie. We'll be waiting for that cavalry charge. Over and out."

Cold sober now, Marilyn Cross stalked the living room of Ida Gant's Watch Tower, cursing herself for walking into a trap. She'd been able to reach the radio and whisper for help before they took it away. Zerkaoui had chided her, saying, "Very unwise, my dear. If you hadn't taken your radio out from under the seat, we might not have found it and been able to monitor their conversations."

"That's all right," she'd answered defiantly. "They'll know better than to give you any information you can use."

She flipped through the books and magazines in Ida's living room, bemused at the old lady's Victorian tastes and wondering how she had managed to stay as closely in touch with the world as she had.

Zerkaoui entered from somewhere in the back of the house. He did not make a sound. He was just there.

"You will be happy to know, Mrs. Cross, that Madame Richard has been moved from the bedroom to the garage next to Maître Girardot. The bedroom is now yours to sleep in."

"Gee, thanks. What other good news have you got for me?"

"Only that since you will be spending the night here, we shall try to make you as comfortable as possible."

"Into the old girl's bed tonight, and down into the garage with her and Girardot tomorrow. Well, for that news the least you could do is offer me a drink."

"Of course. In fact, I can offer you as many as you'd like, from Madame Richard's liquor cabinet."

"Now you're talking. Make it gin and tonic."

A houseboy was placing candles around the room. They would be needed in a very few minutes as the sun set and night fell. The drinks would be served without ice cubes.

"You know," Zerkaoui said as he made the drinks, "what happened today at the Cultural Center was absolutely beyond my control. I don't mean the burning of the Center. That was the normal reaction of a people too long under foreign cultural influence. But the death of Larbi and the destruction of his paintings could and should have been avoided. I sincerely regret the loss of an irreplaceable talent and his works."

"Sure, especially when you stood to make a fortune out of them," she shot back, taking the glass he offered her.

"I don't deny I had a commercial interest," he replied, raising his glass to hers. "But religious fanaticism has no place in a socialist society. I myself am not averse to taking a drink. I regard fanaticism as useful in hastening the revolution, but it does not justify the destruction of art, which on the contrary has a valid role to play in the revolution. In short, I regard the loss as an unfortunate sacrifice in the cause of socialism."

"So you're not one of the fanatics then," she laughed. "I thought socialism had been discredited around the world."

"Not in Sharqiya, my dear. Here the two can co-exist, and I am for any regime which will damage the capitalist West."

"I'm sure Larbi the goatherd will feel better knowing that." She drained her glass and handed it back for a refill. "Say, as long as you're not selling paintings today, why don't you take off that necktie and be comfortable? You give me the creeps."

"Thank you, I am perfectly comfortable. I was just thinking of what will happen to your friends at the Embassy when it gets dark."

"Don't worry about them. They've got their own generator."

"I didn't mean that. I meant with an aroused Sharqiyan people beating on their door. We've been listening to their conversations with the Defense Ministry, you see, and we know the students are outside demanding justice. We also know the traitor Rashidi will soon be able to free a unit of the army to disperse the students. Now we realize martyrs are useful to a revolution, but our leader feels it would be foolish to sacrifice those students and much more in our interest to have them capture the Americans and expose them for conspiring with the reactionaries to invade Sharqiya."

Marilyn became wary. She tried to clear her head.

"Let me get this straight. I thought you were the leader."

"Hardly, my dear. Our leader is Mohamed Qasim, until last night Minister of the Interior. During the night the Palace was occupied by students and the President unfortunately lost his life. Dr. Qasim was chosen by the Supreme Revolutionary Council to head a provisional government. Now the turncoat Rashidi is stubbornly refusing to place the armed forces at the disposal of the provisional government. We think that with your help we may be able to convince him he should do so."

"How?" Marilyn tried to focus her thoughts even as she took another swallow of gin and tonic.

"By having you call your embassy and the Defense Ministry and outline our position to them—that the students only want justice, that your ambassador and his staff will simply be expelled after admitting their guilt and that you and the other wives will be free to join them, but that any attempt by Rashidi to disperse the students will result in harm to you. I am sure your ambassador will be anxious to make Rashidi understand."

Marilyn fought for time. "Why do you need me to tell them that? Why don't you tell them yourself?"

"We wish to prove to them that you are alive and well. If they think you are dead, they will have no reason to accede to our wishes. You see, your life is precious to us."

"And what if I decide not to say anything?"

"Then we shall have to twist your arm, as the saying goes —but literally, to make you cry out. You see, we need your voice not for what you may say but only to prove you are alive."

"OK," Marilyn agreed. "Bring in the radio. I'll say anything you want me to."

The radio was brought in. Zerkaoui pressed the lever and spoke. "American Embassy, can you hear me?"

There was an instant of silence and then, "This is base control. Identify yourself. Over."

"What is your call sign, my dear?" Zerkaoui asked.

"Wouldn't you like to know?"

Zerkaoui shrugged. "I'd hoped you wouldn't be difficult." Then, pressing the lever, "This is Mrs. Cross's radio. As you know, she is at Mme. Richard's house under the protection of the Provisional Revolutionary Government. She wants you to allow the students to enter the Embassy and discuss the situation with the Ambassador. She hopes the reactionary Rashidi will not attempt to disperse the students, and she has our assurance that once the students are inside the Embassy and speaking to the Ambassador she will be returned unharmed to her home. Now I shall pass the radio to Mrs. Cross."

Marilyn took the receiver from his hand.

"Base control, this is Marilyn. Is the Ambassador there?"

"This is Hal Potter, Marilyn. Go ahead."

"Mr. Potter, I just want you to know I'm all right here. I don't think this creep Zerkaoui has the guts to kill me. So don't let them in. That's all. Over and out."

Zerkaoui took the receiver from her and smiled.

"Perfect, my dear. That was very courageous of you. Of course, it won't in any way prevent the Ambassador from letting the students in to save your life. Even better, it shows that you are unharmed."

The sun was down, and a red glow shone through the windows. An explosion rocked the house, and a scream was heard in the parking lot. The sound of a loudspeaker came from the mountainside above them. Marilyn understood no Arabic, but she saw the effect the words had on Zerkaoui. Grabbing a battery-operated bull horn, he took her by the arm and dragged her out onto the piazza to the top of the stairs. Holding her in front of him, he called back in Arabic. Then, apparently confident his message had been heard, he pulled her back into the living room with him.

"Those are Rashidi's men, my dear. Unfortunately, they have less regard for your well-being than your ambassador does. So we'll have to call him again, won't we?"

This time the message was short. "Tell Ambassador Potter to have Rashidi call his troops away from this house, or Marilyn Cross will be the first to die. Do you hear me?"

There was no answer.

"They heard me," Zerkaoui said confidently. "You'll see, they won't throw any more grenades. They'll have their orders in a minute. In the meantime, you and I will stay very close to each other, Madame."

The red glow in the western sky had darkened to purple, and deepening shadows fell across the piazza. The shadows were so dark now that she imagined she could make out the silhouette of a man actually climbing up onto the piazza from below. Mingled with the shadow of the arched column next to him, he seemed to appear suddenly in front of the wrought-iron balustrade. Then he leaned forward toward her, and the face of Pete Pascal, his fingers to his lips, appeared out of the darkness.

Marilyn froze.

Zerkaoui was sitting opposite her, his back to the balcony. "What is it, my dear? You are very silent."

"It is that I need another drink, my dear." She spoke and rose at the same time. He rose too.

"Don't bother. I'll get you one."

"And put more gin in it this time, cheapskate."

He passed in front of her and went to the bar while Marilyn, her arms crossed in irritation, strolled casually toward the piazza.

"Don't try to run away, my dear," Zerkaoui said. "There are men at the bottom of the stairs to catch you, and they are surely less gentle than I."

Instead of turning left toward the stairs, she directed her steps toward the right side of the piazza where the deepening sunset was out of sight from the living room.

"Better come back," called Zerkaoui. He finished making the drink and followed after her. On the balcony, with Marilyn past him and out of the way, Pascal waited.

"I said, come back, Mrs. Cross," Zerkaoui called. "Where

do you think you're going?" He started to follow her onto the balcony. But at the doorway he stopped, saw Pascal and tossed the drink into his face, at the same time swinging the glass by its base against the door frame to shatter it and then, with the jagged edges outthrust, advance toward the figure in the shadows.

Pascal side-stepped, taking a cut on the left shoulder, and swung his stiff right arm in a backhand slash. The sharp blade of the carpet cutter caught and dug in. He pulled away, slicing through Zerkaoui's cheek from ear to mouth. Zerkaoui cried out in pain, spun around and lunged once more with the broken glass extending from his grip. Pascal dropped to the floor and kicked upward, catching him in the groin and lifting as Zerkaoui sailed over and past him, struck the edge of the balustrade and dropped into space.

"Let's get out of here fast" said Pascal before Zerkaoui's death cry had ended. "Grab that radio if you can. If you can't carry it, toss it over the wall so they can't use it."

"Your arm's bleeding."

"You can give me a transfusion later. Come on."

They went over the balustrade on the side opposite the stairs and dropped to a flower bed behind a stone column. A figure with an AK-47 appeared against the steps, pointing it into the darkness and advancing slowly. Pascal retrieved the radio from the flower bed and pushed it behind the gunman and to his left. He reached out and with his finger tip flipped on the switch.

He didn't have long to wait. Within seconds the radio began to talk. "Three-zero-eight, this is base control. Come in. Over."

The last words were drowned out by the chatter of the AK47 as the man spun on the ball of his left foot and let go a burst at the sound. Pascal came from behind the other side of the stone column, and Charlie Agar's knife went in with a single thrust under the man's ribs. Pascal pulled the gun from around the man's neck and withdrew the knife. The radio was still talking.

"Get the radio," he whispered to her. "Turn it off, and go along the garden wall until you come to a dip in the lawn. There's a hole in the wall and a narrow shelf on the other side. Be careful or you'll end up at the bottom with Zerkaoui. I'm covering you."

She did as she was told, removing her shoes and wishing she'd worn her pant suit instead of a dress. From the hole in the wall she watched him back toward her and then slip down until both were out of sight of the house.

"I'll go first," he said. "I know where the path is. Give me the radio and back out after me."

In a few minutes they were at the base of the cliff, taking the path toward the hidden jeep. Once there, Pascal turned on the radio.

"Base control, can you hear me?" he asked softly.

The squawk came back immediately. "We hear you. Identify yourself."

"This is Pascal. I've got Marilyn. We're at the bottom of the cliff below Ida's with my jeep, an AK-47 and Marilyn's radio. Tell Rashidi he can start moving in on the Watch Tower now. And tell Charlie Agar he can cut a notch in his knife handle when we get back there."

Marilyn grabbed the receiver. "And tell the army they can clean up the mob in front of the Embassy. I'm safe now."

Pascal took back the receiver. "We're going in. Be ready to open the garage door when you see our headlights."

Potter's voice came on the line.

"Don't try it. You're not to come in. There's a mob outside. You'll never make it. Your best bet is to take Mrs. Cross home and stay there with the car out of sight."

"Sir, I'd rather turn her over to the Embassy," Pascal answered. "She'll be safer there."

"Did you hear me, Mr. Pascal?" came back Potter's voice. "I said you're to take Mrs. Cross home and keep under cover. Now are you going to obey me this time or not?"

Pascal sighed. "Yes, sir. I'll check back with you when I get there. Over and out."

Marilyn smiled. "Good. Now we're going to my place where I can take care of your arm."

Pascal helped her into the jeep. "OK, baby. But that's all you'll take care of. You're under my protection, and the sooner you're back with your husband, the better I'll like it."

He turned on the ignition and worked the pedals. As the engine started, a small figure appeared out of the darkness.

"Bien gardé voiture, M'sieu? Bien gardé?"

"You sure did," said Pascal, emptying his pocket of change.

6

Catherine Potter found her husband at his desk, tilted back in his swivel chair and facing the wall. His feet were up, and his hands were under his chin. He was staring at nothing in particular.

"Bad news?"

Potter waved his hand at a cable lying on his desk. "Just the latest masterpiece from Ridgeway and Company. Read it."

She picked it up:

"SATELLITE PHOTOS PROVIDE NO REPEAT NO IN-DICATION OF AN INVADING FORCE. WE SUSPECT A COUP ATTEMPT MAY BE UNDER WAY..."

"At least the satellite confirms there's no invasion force on the way," Potter said. "Now read the rest."

"...YOU MUST NOW DO EVERYTHING TO CONVINCE LEGALLY CONSTITUTED GDRS LEADERSHIP WE ARE IN NO WAY INVOLVED..."

"He means the late President Abderrahman. Perhaps if we had Zerkaoui's radio we could speak to Qasim. After having tried to frame us, I'm sure he's ready to have a change of heart."

"At least you've just cabled them about the assassination. They'll have to follow with more instructions."

"You haven't finished this cable," he said. "Read on."

"SUGGEST YOU IMPRESS YOUR STAFF WITH NEED TO KEEP STIFF UPPER LIP. WE ARE IN CONTACT WITH FRIENDLY GOVERNMENTS AND ARE HOPING GDRS WILL ACT EXPEDITIOUSLY TO CONVINCE STUDENTS OF UN-REASONABLENESS OF SIEGE."

"Leaves you speechless, doesn't it?"

"The Department is always cautious," Catherine said. You know that, dear. You mustn't take this as their last word."

"I don't. I expect there will be words coming out of the Department for as long as the Republic lasts. The question remains, how many of them will have any more meaning than these?"

"Don't these have meaning? They do contain instructions."

"Which couldn't be carried out by Superman. In other words, I'm left to my own devices, and any failure will be charged to my account for not having followed instructions."

"Then follow them. Or try. They can't fault you for trying."

"Maybe they can't. But any survivors on this Embassy staff can if we allow ourselves to be taken over by Qasim."

"Don't imagine things, dear. They wouldn't dare harm us."

"I wish I had your confidence. I also wish you'd stayed home."

"A wife's place is at her husband's side..."

"I know, but don't overdo it."

"I'm not. I'm just reminding you that we have a date at another embassy after this one, somewhere in the civilized world. Don't forget that either."

He was no longer listening to her. He was listening to the cries of the mob gathering again in the street. "I've heard that song before," he said.

Pascal had reported from Marilyn's house on arrival. Potter heaved a great sigh. "At least we don't have a hostage crisis any longer," he told Catherine. "Now, if Rashidi can mop up Zerkaoui's men at the Watch Tower, he'll control the mountain road and bring down more of his crack troops to clear the streets, including the gang outside."

The mob seemed to be thinning out even before dark, but the demonstrators must have been eating in shifts and returning. As the afternoon turned into evening, there seemed to be a growing sense of purpose, of discipline, as if professional leadership had taken over what heretofore had been a relatively spontaneous gathering. A bullhorn harangued the crowd in Arabic, and placards bearing inscriptions were raised to the rhythm of chanting demonstrators.

"I wish we had an interpreter," said Potter. "But I can guess what they're saying."

"They're bringing in more placards," said Catherine. "I think they're in French."

They were indeed. "WE WANT AMBASSADOR POT-TER," said one; and another, "AMBASSADOR POTTER TO JUSTICE."

It was only then that he realized they were calling for him. Catherine had read them too.

"Darling, ignore them," she cried. Don't even go to the window."

"Why do they want me?" he wondered.

"As a hostage, of course. They've lost Marilyn Cross, and so they want you instead. It's ridiculous. No one but a fool would go out there."

He remembered agreeing with her absently and wondering why she even mentioned it. Obviously no man in his right mind was going to turn himself over to a mob.

A call came in from Millie.

"The Minister is back. I told him about the mob, and he's given orders for troops to break it up. So hang on. Help is coming."

"Thanks, Millie. I knew I could count on you. We'll celebrate when this is over."

The city was dark. The only light was from the Embassy itself, lying in broad stripes across the street below each window. It wasn't much, but it was enough to keep the crowd there. It occurred to Potter that by dousing the lights and moving to the windowless vault the demonstration might break up for lack of an audience. He decided to give the order.

He was not quick enough. A battery-operated bullhorn was heard before he could even turn out his own light.

"Ambassador Potter, please come to the window."

He recognized his name; the voice was speaking excellent French.

"We have a message for you from President Qasim," the voice continued. "Please come to the window."

President Qasim! Then it was official--or so at least they wanted him to believe.

"Sgt. Hernandez," he called into his radio, "fix up the microphone, please, so that I can speak to them."

The voice continued to call for him while Hernandez scrambled for a mike. "This is Ambassador Potter. Go ahead."

"Please come to the window, M. l'Ambassadeur," came the voice, disembodied but by its volume seeming to emanate from the mob collectively, "so that you can be seen."

"Sorry," he answered matter-of-factly. "You'll have to take my word it's me."

There was a long pause. Then, "Very well. Please send someone outside to receive a letter from President Qasim."

"Sorry again. You'd better read the letter to me."

Again there was a pause. The mob seemed to glide and ripple below them like a monster in the depths of the sea.

"You are being very difficult, M. l'Ambassadeur. However, as you wish."

Potter heard the tearing of an envelope over the bullhorn. "I read: 'Excellence, I have the honor to inform you that the Revolution has triumphed. Liberated from the clutches of the neo-colonialists, progressive forces have taken control of the territory in its entirety, with the exception of small pockets on the north coast which are rapidly being reduced. In these circumstances, I request that you come immediately to the Presidential Palace so that we may discuss together the future of relations between our two countries. You are welcome to use your official sedan on condition that it be driven by one of my men and that two others accompany you for your protection.'" The letter ended with the formal assurance of the new President's highest consideration.

Potter's answer came without hesitation. "You may inform M.Qasim that I have no intention of leaving this Embassy until, first, the mob outside has been dispersed, second, the damage to the building has been formally recognized and compensation agreed upon, and third, either the restoration of electric power or daylight makes it safe to go into the streets."

"In other words," said Potter, covering the mike, "if he's President, which he isn't by a long shot, then let him restore order first--while we gain time for Rashidi's troops to get here."

After another pause, the next response was spoken slowly and with pauses indicating it was being read from a prepared statement.

"We regret the decision of the American Ambassador to refuse to cooperate with the Provisional Government of the Democratic Republic of Sharqiya, and we wish to recall his interview of Friday last with the representative of the Ministry of Foreign Affairs, in which the subject of the American criminal Ronald Corker was raised..."

"Oh my God! They haven't got Corker, have they?" he gasped.

"This notorious criminal," the voice went on, "wanted by the Sharqiyan people for attempted murder and provocatory acts against the security of the state, was seen leaving the premises of the American Embassy and was later apprehended thanks to the alertness of the People's Security Police. Under the emergency laws now in effect, he is liable to be tried by a People's Court for his crime, which carries the maximum penalty of death..."

"The dirty bastards," muttered Hernandez, who understood some French.

"However, in view of certain mitigating circumstances, the Sharqiyan people would be willing to discuss the criminal's status with the American Ambassador. As evidence of our good faith in this matter, if the Ambassador will come to the window, he will see that the criminal, Corker, is safe and unharmed."

"Damn them for breaking that TV camera," Potter swore as he stared at a blank screen. "Where's a window?"

He went into Hernandez' office, which adjoined the front entrance to the Embassy.

"Don't get near that window, sir," Hernandez called, "and don't turn on the light. The mylar won't protect you from a bullet."

Potter made his way along the edge of the darkened room and peered out from behind the curtain. There was movement in the crowd below, and a small figure was half-carried, half-dragged to the front ranks facing the Embassy. It was Corker, bound but apparently unharmed.

"Give me the mike," Potter whispered to Hernandez. The sergeant pulled the instrument across the room to him.

"That goddamned jerk," he said. "If he gets back in here alive, I swear I'll have him court-martialed."

Potter took the mike. "Corker, are you all right?"

Corker, his short blond haircut and white skin setting him off from the mob of Sharqiyans, called back: "Yes, sir, Mr. Ambassador. I'm fine."

"Then don't give up. We're going to get you in here." Switching to French, he said: "I recognize this man as a member of the American Embassy, and I demand that you release him into my custody."

The bullhorn answered: "M. l'Ambassadeur, this man is a wanted criminal, and he enjoys no diplomatic immunity. This is why our President has requested that you come to the Palace to discuss the matter with him in private. Your own diplomatic status will be respected, of course."

"I have already given my terms for going to the Palace."

The bullhorn came into view now moving along the sea monster's back like a small fish. It was held by a bearded Sharqiyan in a jellaba, lean of face, with the deep-set ascetic eyes of a fanatic.

"M. l'Ambassadeur, I must warn you that the patience of the Sharqiyan people is not without its limits. The very presence of this criminal among them is a provocation. They wish to conduct the trial here and now, and it is all I can do to dissuade them. I fear only your acceptance of our President's generous offer could induce them to release him into your custody."

So that's it: Corker for Potter.

"I've stated my conditions," he repeated. "Release this man, disperse the demonstrators, give me written assurance of compensation for the damage done, and I'll give you my word that I will call on M. Qasim tomorrow morning or whenever power is restored, whichever is first."

That's a concession, he thought. But at least I've gained time, maybe even until morning.

"But the President is waiting for you now, M. l'Ambassadeur. You cannot ask him to wait all night. Besides, your safety is guaranteed."

Catherine was beside him. "Don't believe it, darling. They don't know the meaning of diplomatic immunity."

He smiled. "I thought you just urged me to follow the Department's instructions and reassure them of our peaceful intentions."

"Yes, but not by offering yourself as a hostage."

"Then what happens to Corker?"

"They wouldn't dare kill him, not here."

"Ah, you don't think so. You think they'd take him away to a quiet place where we wouldn't have to witness the execution."

"But you've done everything you could for him. You gave him sanctuary when you had no legal right to. The Marines are assigned to protect you, not to be protected by you. You don't owe this one anything."

Potter looked into the face of his wife, dimly lit in the dark room. It was a face he'd admired and loved for almost thirty years. He'd watched the lines in it form and harden and the hair turn gray. With each brush stroke in the aging process the face had taken on a heightened distinction. She was an aristocrat and the daughter of an aristocrat. He'd always recognized that, and he was flattered even now that she had chosen him. In a young graduate student with no extraordinary prospects and no social graces she had seen something no one else had noticed. Not his wealth nor his family background, unexceptional both of them, nor his Yale B.A. nor his army commission, nor even his doctorate had justified in themselves her vision of him as not just a diplomat but an ambassador like her father. For without training in the niceties of protocol or ease in rubbing shoulders with those who had been born to it, he'd been totally unprepared to play the role of a diplomat. "I'm just not to the manner born," he'd told her more than once. But that was precisely the challenge she wanted: to sculpt a diplomat out of human flesh as Michelangelo had his David out of marble or Henry Higgins a lady out of Eliza the flower girl.

Whatever it was, she had succeeded. And now he was faced with a choice he never would have hesitated to make as a second lieutenant: whether to sacrifice one of his men—the least of them—rather than allow the façade which Catherine had spent thirty years building put at risk. It seemed to him he was seeing her face for the first time.

"After all," he said, "I am an ambassador. My first duty is to the President and the country I represent. Corker is only a Marine. If they'd wanted the Marines to have diplomatic immunity, they'd have given them dip passports. An ambassador who placed his own life in danger for a Marine would betray his role as an ambassador. Isn't that right, Cat?"

Yes, he thought, but a lieutenant who sacrificed the life of a member of his platoon to save his own life would betray his platoon and his honor too. Lieutenants were shot in the back, fragged by their own men for that— or even for simple incompetence. But he didn't mention that point to the daughter of Alex Brent.

She frowned and squeezed his arm. "Not the way you say it, dear. But in essence you're right. An ambassador is, after all, the personal representative of the President of the United States."

"How should I have said it then? That one Hal Potter is worth more than one Ron Corker?"

Her answer was automatic. "In our country's eyes an ambassador certainly is worth more than a Marine. And to me, darling, you're worth more than the whole Embassy."

"Sure, look at the investment that's been made to get me where I am: the years of schooling, the parental sacrifice, the language training, the careful grooming. Whereas Corker never got anything but public school and boot camp. He'll never be an ambassador, or even an officer. In fact, if he doesn't shape up, he may not even stay in the Marine Corps."

She tried to seize the momentum of his thoughts. "Yes,

and your value to them as a hostage far outweighs Corker's. Think of the words they could put in your mouth in a forced confession."

This was true, of course. He was a symbol to be protected at all costs. That's what the Marines were here for in the first place.

He looked around at his "retinue," as one of the ancient definitions of an embassy referred to them. Jensen was at the desk monitoring incoming calls. Sgt. Hernandez was scurrying up and down between his men on this floor and in the vault, and Warnecke and the two FSO's Cross and Finley were up there at the map keeping track of the movements of the opposing forces. The rest, including the hapless Corker, were scattered throughout the embattled city. While he, the Ambassador Extraordinary and Plenipotentiary of the President, sat surrounded by and in the protection of all of them, their lives pawns in the sacred obligation to protect his. Wasn't that a step up from his long-ago position as a second lieutenant of infantry!

"You're absolutely right, Cat," he said. "That's why the Marines are here—to protect me! I just hope it doesn't go to my head."

Three times in a row, he counted, Catherine had been right. Each time he'd given in to her. Hal Potter, all-American poor boy struggling to make good, was a myth. The only reality was the instrument of foreign policy he had become, bearing a name, a number and the title "A.E.P.". This was what it all came down to in the end.

"But in fact, Cat," he said softly, "we're all hostages, hostages to fortune, from myself down to Corker and all the other dependents at post, including you. We're hostages exchanged between governments in the expectation that each will respect the other's hostages to protect its own. That's the ancient rule, as you well know."

"Of course, darling," she cried, grasping him by the shoulders. "But not in a country like this, in the control of a gang of thugs--and not even recognized by the rest of the world! They don't know what diplomatic immunity means!"

"Maybe not, Cat. But what they do know is that they can't afford not to keep me alive, whereas Corker to them is expendable. They'll sacrifice him if they have to. But not me."

He broke away and pulled her hands down to her sides, squeezing them as he did so and looking into her eyes with comfort and reassurance.

"So don't worry, dear. Just think of how I'd look to Sgt. Hernandez and the other Marines, or to Jack Warnecke for that matter, if I didn't stand up for one of theirs in a pinch. Remember, loyalty starts at the top. It has to be earned."

He'd made up his mind. When he said the words over the microphone, he realized his mind had been made up all along.

"This is my final offer," he said. "You will untie the man's hands and feet and allow him to walk to the entrance of the Embassy. The crowd in front of the Embassy will then disperse, after which my official limousine will leave the Embassy garage, driven by an Embassy chauffeur, and come to the front entrance. At that time, if these conditions have been met, the door of the Embassy will open, the Marine will enter and I will come out and get into my limousine and be driven to the Presidential Palace alone and by my own chauffeur under the guarantee of M. Qasim that my diplomatic status will be respected."

Turning, he saw Catherine stiffen and her eyes flash.

"Harold, I forbid you to go out there."

He shook his head. "Sorry dear. I'm doing what I have to do. Don't worry."

There was silence in the street. The only sounds were the muffled sobs of Catherine as she repeated softly, "No, darling, no. If only for my sake and the children's, no."

He spoke to Hernandez. "I'm going out, Sergeant, and Corker is coming in. Stand ready with the tear gas, and use your weapons if they try to enter the Embassy. Youssef will drive the car around to the front entrance if the mob looks like it's breaking up." To the others he added, "The car is armored, and there's a loaded pistol inside. I won't use it unless I have to." Then he picked up the microphone and spoke into it in

English: "Corker, they will probably untie you now. When they do, you will walk to the front entrance alone and wait for it to open. As soon as it opens, come inside."

Corker, who had understood nothing of what had been said in French, was alerted by the sound of his own name. "Yes, sir," he called. "But don't you take chances, Mr. Ambassador."

"For once, Corker," he shot back, "you are going to do what I tell you to do. Now let them untie you."

"Yes, sir."

Murmuring was heard in the street. Two of the demonstrators began to untie Corker's hands and feet. When he was free, they pushed him toward the door. At the same time, the limousine's engine was heard starting up, and the garage door was raised. Slowly, responding to rough orders in Arabic, the crowd began to draw back, first to clear a passage for the limousine then thinning out and disappearing into the darkness beyond the light from the Embassy windows.

Potter waited until the black form of the limousine had drawn up in front of the building. He turned and gave Catherine a kiss on the cheek and a pat on the shoulder. "Chin up, Cat. They'll respect my immunity. They have to. Their regime will be compromised if they don't." Then he walked down from the Marine desk to the locked front entrance.

"Open the door," he told the Marine.

The heavy metal door clicked and began to swing open, revealing Corker standing on the steps outside.

"All right, Corker. Come on in."

They stepped past each other, the short blond 19-year-old in his tattered uniform and the lanky former professor with the furrowed brow and the air of deep concentration. The Marine abruptly gripped the door handle.

"Wait a minute, Mr. Ambassador. I'm not going inside as long as you're out here alone."

Potter answered with tense fury. "Get back in there, you idiot. What the hell do you think I'm doing, taking a stroll?"

"No, sir," Corker said stubbornly." I didn't say you could risk your life for me. You get inside."

As Potter took the kid by the shoulders, shoved him through the door and walked down the steps toward the car the sound of heavy vehicles was heard. The demonstrators heard it, and a loud murmur went up in their midst. The bullhorn blared forth in Arabic, and they began to run. Before the first of them could reach the next block, an armored personnel carrier drew up at the intersection. Soldiers poured from an open truck. In a panic the crowd turned and began to run back. It was too late. Two more armored personnel carriers moved up the street. Behind them more troops advanced on foot with weapons at the ready. The mob spilled back and forth in the narrow space like water in a tub. Then the weapons began to chatter.

"Get down, sir," screamed Corker from the doorway. "Get into the car."

Potter thought that the whole Embassy had been lifted up and dropped to the pavement with a thud. He obeyed the young Marine instinctively and fell to a crouch as he tried to reach the open door of the limousine. This is what happens, he thought, when you ignore your wife's wishes. You've disobeyed the instructions of Ambassador Alexander Brent, and the Department is going to see that you pay for it dearly.

Then why, he wondered, did Youssef get out and run around to open the rear right hand door for him? He shouldn't do that, damn it. Now they'd have to wait for Corker, since Corker was of lower rank and would have to sit on the left.

But the problem cleared itself up. Corker wasn't going on this trip. Only Youssef and he, the Ambassador, Harold A. Potter, with flag unfurled on the front fender, would ride in dignity to present his country's best wishes to Sharqiya's new President, who, he was confident now, would turn out to be not Qasim at all but Karim al-Rashidi or (who could tell?) someone even more distinguished.

But in that case a crouching stance was hardly called for. Instead, he would walk upright for the last few steps, which he now did, entering the limousine with great dignity and relief, for Youssef had done something to the vehicle's undercarriage so that it now rose, as if on wings, soaring above the heads of the crowd as all looked up with admiration and awe at the American Ambassador.

From the window he looked back with regret at his Embassy growing smaller in the distance below, thinking of all the business he had left uncompleted but at the same time noticing that the dawn was breaking already and the Palace they were heading for somehow didn't look like the one he knew but instead was much larger, brighter, more distant yet drawing closer at a dizzying rate, so that his only worry now was whether his suit was properly pressed and his credentials in order.

While Corker, kneeling beside the two bodies on the ground next to the motionless limousine, kept calling in despair: "Mr. Ambassador! Oh, Mr. Ambassador!"

Epilogue
The following January

It was a big day for Phil Finley. A year after his arrival in Sharqiya he was passing through Washington on his way back to post from R&R, with only a year more to go. And what did he find at the country desk but his name on the January promotion list!

Now his hopes for a more significant job at his new grade and in an important country might be fulfilled. Sy Levin, back in Sharqiya as Chargé d'Affaires after Potter's death, had done his rating, and Clayton Ridgeway's endorsement in the absence of an ambassador at the post had given it added weight.

All in all, things had worked out beautifully for Phil. The coup attempt had failed. There had been no landings and if some at the Embassy had been fooled, Phil Finley was not among them. He'd gone out of his way to make that clear to Sy—and Ridgeway.

After the coup attempt, in fact, Phil had been in direct phone contact with Ridgeway in Washington over funeral arrangements. He'd carried out Ida's wishes by having her cremated, her ashes scattered from the piazza of her Watch Tower. It was too bad she hadn't lived to see her protégé become President. But Rashidi had been at her funeral, and Finley had had an opportunity to meet him and, with Sy Levin and Jack Warnecke, hear him outline his plans for Sharqiya." If only my dear Mother were here." Rashidi had told them. " I owe every-thing to her, and I shall try to be worthy of her teaching."

The Department had gone all out for Harold Potter. Within a day he was on his way back to Andrews in a C-141 out of Ramstein with an honor guard and an escort officer. Catherine Potter had been a model of stoicism, graciously receiving the condolences of the diplomatic community and the members of the new government before accompanying her husband's body home. She had made full use of her connections, even at the White House, to obtain the Department's coveted Medal of Heroism for her husband despite criticism in the corridors of his handling of the crisis. Ridgeway, for instance, had had no difficulty showing that he had not been kept fully informed of events on the island and so could not he held responsible for any lack of support from Washington. His task now would be, with the help of Levin, Cross and Finley, to bring order out of the chaos left at Amemb Al-Bida.

This was a lesson in bureaucratic footwork which Finley would not forget. He had even timed his leave to be on hand, and to be seen, at the ceremony in the diplomatic lobby, with an Honor Guard, when the name of Harold Potter would be added to those of Foreign Service personnel who had lost their lives in the line of duty.

Some of the living had fared less well. Millie Novak had gone to pieces over Potter's death (as well as Ida's and, strangely enough, Girardot's), holding herself responsible for the fact that the troops she had dispatched had arrived just as Potter had stepped into the line of fire. She had requested an immediate transfer to Washington. Findley learned that she'd signed up to be a roving secretary. As a "rover" she would travel almost constantly, filling in for absent secretaries at post after post and never remain more than a few weeks at one embassy.

Pete Pascal was kept busy inventorying what was left of his Cultural Center and planning its rebuilding with architects from his agency. Details of his affair with Marilyn Cross apparently never reached Washington, since no one but Lou Cross could vouch for it, and Lou naturally preferred to keep it quiet. Instead, Marilyn simply left on the next civilian flight, and no more was said. Later she and Lou were divorced, and Phil heard that she had moved to the West Coast and after rehab had gravitated into an artists' colony somewhere. Good riddance, Phil concluded. The Foreign Service didn't need her type.

Lou had recovered well. He received a Meritorious Honor Award for his handling of Embassy operations in the aftermath of the coup attempt and was in line to be Admin Counselor at a small but important post where his career would be followed more closely.

But they'd had a real argument over the Department's responsibility in providing security for Foreign Service people. "They send us out here to these God-forsaken places," he'd complained, "and when there's trouble they tell us to keep a stiff upper lip. I joined the Foreign Service to have a respectable career and see the world, not to seek martyrdom."

But Lou's was the counsel of an old hand who'd seen a lot over the years. "Cool it, kid. Cover your ass, keep your nose clean, make no waves and you'll make it. The Professor wanted to be a hero. He didn't have to do what he did. If he'd waited inside another ten minutes, the Army would have cleaned out the demonstrators without him getting hurt. The Marine? What the hell. That's what Marines are for."

Corker, by the way, had been reassigned to Camp Lejeune and given a general discharge. He was lucky, Cross said. He could have been court-martialed, or ended up in a Sharqiyan jail. Or even killed. Instead, he got his Ambassador killed and was too dumb to see it was his fault. Now he'd find out what kind of career a guy with a general discharge can look forward to.

Finley couldn't argue with that. He'd stayed out of the military and didn't regret it. In the Foreign Service he'd be working mostly among his equals, and even a fellow like Cross, whose career prospects weren't up to his own anyway and had been blighted by an unfortunate marriage to boot, knew a few tricks of the trade which he could use.

Ridgeway had quoted Talleyrand: "Surtout, pas trop de zèle." Phil had certainly witnessed a few cases of excessive eagerness, or zeal, or conscience, and they weren't for him.

So Phil Finley had come through his first crisis with flying colors and was looking forward to his next assignment. It was all part of a Foreign Service career.